# Promise Me Always

## Christine Lynxwiler

**BARBOUR**
PUBLISHING

Cover design by David Uttley/The Design Works Group, Inc.

For more information about Christine Lynxwiler, please access the author's Web site at the following Internet address: www.christinelynxwiler.com

Published by Barbour Publishing, Inc., P.O. Box 719, Uhrichsville, Ohio 44683 www.barbourbooks.com

*Our mission is to publish and distribute inspirational products offering exceptional value and biblical encouragement to the masses.*

 Member of the Evangelical Christian Publishers Association

Printed in the United States of America.
5 4 3 2 1

## Dedication/Acknowledgments:

To the Pinkies—S,T,A,R, & S—Just realized your initials spell STARS.
And you are!

You rock!

To Jan, Vicky, Lynda, & Sandy—Sisters by birth, friends by choice.
God has blessed me with you.

To Mama—good times or bad, I know I can always count on you to be there.
You're not just a wonderful mother, but a true friend.

To Elva and Jana—your friendship is the best wedding gift a girl could get.
I'll treasure both of you for as long as I live.

To my Georgia friends and the other close girlfriends who have been
scattered from my early childhood until now like rare and beautiful jewels—
You know who you are! All together you've taught me the beauty
of Pinky Promise sisterhood. And even though I may have lost touch
with some of you, I've never forgotten any of you!

And last but not least, to the two most important men in my life—My
amazing husband, Kevin and my extraordinary dad, H.B. "Pudge" Pearle.

## SPECIAL THANKS TO:

Susan Downs—I couldn't have done it without you!

Jan Reynolds and Sandy Gaskin—for your constant support and critiques!

Crit partners—Tracey Bateman, Rachel Hauck,
Susie Warren & Candice Speare

*Trust in the Lord with all thine heart;*
*and lean not unto thine own understanding.*
*In all thy ways acknowledge him, and he shall direct thy paths.*

PROVERBS 3:5-6 KJV

---

Even though I suppose there are little towns named Shady Grove in every state, including Arkansas, the particular Shady Grove in *Promise Me Always* is a purely fictional town, plunked down in the middle of North Arkansas.

## one

Today's my thirty-fifth birthday. And for the first time in my life I wish I were a man.

Don't get me wrong. I wouldn't give up my Bath and Body Works lotion or my favorite pair of strappy sandals to be just any old man. But I'm thinking one with stocks, bonds, collateral, and a perfect credit history would be nice.

Then I wouldn't be sitting in the lobby of my bank, worried silly, waiting to talk to a loan officer who has "concerns" about my application. Nor would I be vulnerable to the whims of a faceless financial institution that—despite warm television ads featuring old couples holding hands and little girls with puppies—tallies my worth or worthlessness, whichever the case may be, by the "-ED" words that describe me—unemployED, overextendED, widowED, and a host of others just as bad, I'm sure.

Forget the fact that I had opened my first savings account at Shady Grove's most respected financial establishment when I was barely out of the Little Girl stage myself. Sentiment and nostalgia have nothing to do with the bottom line.

As if to back up my point about males having less to worry about, two chairs down from me, a man reads a book. If he were nervous like me, he'd have definitely paid the barber a visit and borrowed a suit from his uncle. But no. He appears warm and relaxed in his faded Levis, his bent head showing off brown curls that stop right above his shirt collar.

I, on the other hand, squirm on the block of ice that masquerades as a vinyl chair.

Why do places that make a person nervous have to feel like the inside of an igloo? I can understand a doctor's office needing to be extra germ-conscious, but do banks have to follow the same protocol? So not only am I terrified, I get to be a frozen chicken, as well. My friend Rachel has been trying to instill in our Pinky Promise Sisterhood the habit of finding something good about any situation, but right now my brain cells are almost too cold to move.

Up until my boss, Bob, had informed me of the sale of Coble's Plant Nursery to a large conglomerate two weeks ago, I'd been thankful to have a job. Not a job I loved, but one that kept my daughters and me clothed and fed. Who cared that I always scored low on those job satisfaction quizzes in women's magazines?

I don't have to worry about that anymore, because now, after five years as a hotshot, award-winning (if you count Employee of the Month) office manager, I've joined the ranks of the unemployed.

The conglomerate wanted to "start with a fresh slate" (read: "bring in their own managers"). So, I was at the mercy of the tight job market in my hometown. Since I had a little severance package, bless Bob's heart, I decided to follow my dream and start my own landscaping company. My business plan was thorough, but I hadn't counted on the loan officer having "concerns." Nor had I counted on freezing to death in the process.

I glance over at the guy beside me again, while I'm rubbing my arms to get rid of the goose bumps. He looks up from his book to reveal a slightly crooked nose, as if it has been broken sometime in the distant past, and I'm almost positive that's the end of a scar peeking out of the hairline along his forehead. His quizzical gaze meets my appraising one.

His eyes, deep blue and piercing, make everything else fade into the background.

I feel compelled to say something, even if it's just a comment about the temperature, but providence steps in, taking the form of a gray-haired woman who appears in the doorway, and more than likely keeps me from making myself look stupid. She motions me to come.

I jump to my feet and follow her down the carpeted hallway to an open door.

The room—from the crossed swords on the wall to the statue of a toga-clad youth in the corner—gives me the creeps with its overdone grandeur. A short, black-haired man with a mustache turns as I walk in. I paste on a confident smile and try not to take it as a bad sign that he looks just like Hitler.

He nods toward the burgundy leather chair in front of his mahogany desk. "Have a seat, Mrs. Richards."

"You can call me Allie." I sink onto the chair and wait for him to sit across from me.

He doesn't sit, nor does he call me Allie. Instead, he slips on his reading glasses and looks down at my application as if it were something unfortunate the dog left on his lawn. "Mrs. Richards, here at Freedom and Trust Bank, we're very careful with your money."

That *sounds* positive. But I have a bad feeling that the proverbial other shoe is on a collision course with the polished hardwood floor.

"Your work history with Coble's Plant Nursery *was*—"

Naturally he emphasizes the word *was*. I'd recognized him immediately as a person who would kick you while you were down.

"—excellent, but your credit history does contain a few records of slow pay."

I straighten. "Since my husband's death a few years ago, I've had a couple of unexpected expenses. My youngest daughter had appendicitis—"

"I understand. Unfortunately. . ." He lets the word dangle in the air like a guillotine blade.

I press my fingers against the heads of the tarnished brass tacks that adorn the leather chair's arms and concentrate on the nooks and crannies of the hammered heads.

Ever-positive Rachel, who is also my chiropractor, says I relax easier than any patient she's ever had. I can lose myself in little details like that tiny water spot on her office ceiling and totally escape reality. The bad thing is, my technique only works short-term. So I can't zone out long enough to miss the man's next words.

"Since you worked in the office at Coble's and not with the plants themselves, I see no actual landscaping experience listed here, other than a few summers when you were young. . . ."

I choke and turn it into a cough. When I was *young*? Last time I looked, I wasn't ready to move into an assisted living home yet.

"When we consider your lack of expertise in your proposed business, coupled with your uncertain income and questionable credit history..." He pauses again and peers at me over his reading glasses. "It's just not in our depositors' best interest to approve this loan."

My breath whooshes out in a feeble "oh."

"Your business plan was very well thoughtout, though."

He must have just remembered that you're supposed to sprinkle some positive in with the negative. *Too little, too late.* He offers me the most insincere smile I've ever seen.

What traits does a person have to possess to qualify for his job? I can see the want ad now—Do you love to disappoint people? Would you like to crush hopes and dreams, not just as a hobby but as a full-time job with a great salary and benefits?

"Mrs. Richards?"

My hands still grip the arms of the chair. The loan officer is looking at me. I think he's trying to decide whether he'll need to call security to get me out of his office.

I try to rub the nail-head impressions from the tips of my fingers with my thumbs while I consider all my options. Short list. Get a job.

Smoothing down the front of my black slacks, I rise to my feet. "If I could come up with more collateral...?" *Oh, that's good, Allie. Nothing like a little groveling to top off a humiliating experience.*

"No, I'm sorry. The decision is final."

"I see." I know I should say thank you, but I just can't. Not if

I want to get out of here before I disgrace myself completely. Biting the inside of my cheek, I march across the ornately decorated lobby with its vaulted ceilings and skylights, head held high.

*"Careful with our money?"*

I snort, and a brunette in an Ann Taylor suit and black heels looks over at me, a moue of distaste forming on her glistening lips.

I duck my head and hurry out to the parking lot as fast as my trembling legs will take me. Hot tears roll off my face like a tropical waterfall by the time I collapse into the worn driver's seat of my SUV.

Why do I have to cry when I'm angry? When you're rip-roaring furious, the last thing you want to look is weak. But tick me off and instead of blowing up, I'll drown you with my tears. Sickening.

I grab a napkin from the console, swipe my face, and then rest my head on the steering wheel. Clasping the leather-wrapped surface with both hands, I bump my forehead against it gently. *Bump.* Steering wheels are harder than they look, but the mild discomfort seems a small price to pay for punctuating my current misery.

I don't have a job anymore. *Bump.* I don't have a loan for my dream business. *Bump.* I don't know how I'm going to pay the bills. *Bump.* But I'm all that Katie and Miranda have left.

At the thought of my daughters, the appeal of a pity party wanes. Which is kind of sad, because it was going so well. I really had rhythm with the whole *bump, bump, bump* thing. Usually my pity parties are just unorganized messes. Kind of like me.

Oops. I guess the party isn't over yet.

I rub my forehead and look at myself in the rearview mirror. The tears, still trickling, are leaving black mascara trails over my freckles.

Maybe if I'd cried in the bank, the little dictator wannabe would have been more sympathetic. On second thought, the mascara mixed with the red splotches under my runny makeup makes me look like a raccoon with allergies. I rest my head on the steering wheel again and close my eyes. It's probably better I kept my dignity as long as I did.

A tapping noise brings my eyes open. "Are you okay?" Even through the closed window, the voice sounds deep and Southern.

I jerk my head up and groan. Of course. Mr. Faded-Levis-and-Gorgeous-Eyes. Out of ingrained politeness, I try to roll the window down, but the key is still in my purse, so I can't. I open the door a crack. "I'm fine. Thank you."

His eyebrows draw together. "You sure you don't need any help?"

*Not unless you're looking to invest money in a start-up business.* "No, I'm fine. Thanks anyway." I shut my door, softly but firmly, then manually lock it. Can't be too careful. I keep my head down, until the roar of an engine draws my gaze up, just in time to see my would-be hero astride a Harley in front of me.

A genuine smile touches my mouth for the first time since I entered the bank. It figures. No wonder he wasn't afraid to walk up to a crazy, crying, raccoon woman in a parking lot. He apparently likes to live on the edge.

# two

After the man on the Harley roars out of sight, I sniffle a little and glance at the duffel bag on the seat beside me. My original plan had been to go straight from the bank to Tae Bo. Mama gave me a three-month membership for Christmas. Unlike most things I started in January, like the new diet, reading the Bible through in a year, and never raising my voice with the girls, I've stuck with Tae Bo past Valentine's Day.

The girls are getting off the bus at Mama's anyway. Considering the hostility I'm harboring toward the Hitler look-alike, I should probably force myself to go to class and blow off a little steam. Especially since this is the last week that's prepaid.

But I just can't.

I don't even want to call my Pinky Promise Sisterhood friends. Normally Lark, Victoria, Rachel, and I tell each other everything. But the last thing they'd told me was that I'd definitely ace the bank loan. No way I can face them right now.

I ease out of the parking lot and head toward the house. A few minutes later, the sign for the lake road changes my mind. I jerk my blinker on and swing a right at the last minute. Five years ago, buried in grief and fighting like mad to keep my sanity, I'd taken this highway so many times I could drive it with my eyes closed. Like Winnie-the-Pooh, I have my own thoughtful spot. My girls, at ages ten and twelve, have outgrown the Hundred Acre Wood. When will I?

Maybe never. Today I'm in an Eeyore mood, and there'll be no unglooming me. Remember when the blue donkey thought everyone had forgotten his birthday? I wish everyone would forget mine, but I have no doubt that Katie and Miranda, guided by my ever-patient mother, are icing a cake for me right now. When I do finally arrive to pick up the girls, they'll all three sing "Happy Birthday" with big smiles. And the Pinkies won't be far behind with their phone calls and e-mails. Everyone will be anxious to hear my non-existent good news.

As Eeyore would say, "Thanks for noticing."

Not.

The sun glints off the sparkling water as I near the picnic area. The Lake Oriole ducks became my second family when the girls and I moved back home right after Jon's death. I spent enough time out here, asking unanswerable questions, that I considered sitting on a nest and seeing what hatched. Just in time I realized I had two little ducklings of my own at home who needed their mom. Now I just visit occasionally.

Some people won't believe that ducks have good memories, but these particular web-footed quackers have my number as soon as I pull into the parking lot. They advance on me before I even climb all the way out of the SUV. For a brief second, with a flock of eager poultry coming at me, lost jobs and denied loan applications flee from my mind.

I dig around under my seat until my hand closes on a paper bag. Thankfully, there's almost a whole Quarter Pounder inside, courtesy of losing my appetite at lunch the day before yesterday when I remembered it was my last day of gainful employment. Before I open my door again, I remove the bread and break it into small pieces, filling a second McDonald's sack that I find crumpled under the passenger's seat.

Sure, I may have a few bad habits, but at least the ducks love me. I've been voted their favorite junk-food-eating, messy-vehicle-keeping, lakeside visitor five years straight. Who can argue with a record like that?

"Y'all quack me up," I mutter. Ducks are apparently oblivious to sarcastic corniness because they don't slow down. I toss a crumb to each bird, thankful they keep my mind occupied with their insane squawking. I sit at a picnic table near the water and feed them as the spring breeze cools my face, still warm from crying.

*God, what is it about me? Why do I always have to wish I'm someone else? Today? A man with good credit. A few years ago? Any woman I knew with her husband still alive.*

I'd heard all the sermons about how when something bad happens to you, instead of saying "Why me?" you're supposed to say "Why not me?" I figure that's true, but actually saying it is a whole 'nother story.

I stare down at the remaining crumbs in my hand and decide to try it.

I toss out one crumb in classic he-loves-me, he-loves-me-not style. Why not me to end up a widow with two daughters to raise at thirty? Next crumb. Why not me to get fired unfairly? Another crumb. Why not me to get turned down for a bank loan without being given a fighting chance? I throw out the rest of the crumbs in my hand to stave off the hungry ducks for a few minutes so I can examine the flaw in my experiment.

I snort. Besides being structurally stupid questions, my attempts are also inherently asinine, content-wise.

Don't get me wrong. I get the point of the sermons, and it's a good one—but that's just not what our souls cry out at a time like this.

Or at least it's not what *my* soul cries out. Mine wants to know if I've done something awful that I either don't know about or have forgotten. Then immediately, it wants to know if this is going to keep on or if I've almost paid for whatever it is I did.

I'm obviously not spiritually mature enough to say "Why not me?" so I might as well feed the ducks and try to blank out my mind. I grab the bag again. After about ten minutes, the bread is gone, and my fair-weather friends waddle off to pester someone else.

Once they desert, the only sound is the lapping of the water on the shore and the occasional fly buzzing. The events of the last few days play in my mind like an irritating movie. You know the kind, where the plot has so many bad things happen to the hero that you want to leave but hate to be rude.

I stare out at the water, and tears blur my vision again.

*What good can I think of in this situation, Rachel?* My positive scenarios are obviously becoming more of a stretch with each passing minute. Next, will I be thanking God for not letting the fabled Lake Oriole monster come up out of the water and swallow me whole?

The water stirs a little beside me, and in spite of myself, I scoot across the picnic bench away from the shoreline.

Pitiful, I know. Believe it or not, I wasn't always such a basket case. When I was twenty, I married my handsome prince and lived happily ever after. For about five minutes.

I packed away my goals and dreams in storage, along with my high school yearbooks and awards. My prince wanted to become a. . .(dramatic pause). . .*doctor*. His dreams were larger-than-life and certainly larger than mine.

I applied for jobs with landscaping companies and even had a couple of promising interviews, but in the end I took an office job, the position that offered the most money to a college dropout.

When Jon was killed, we had two little girls and I was juggling a million responsibilities. Hardly the time to dust off those goals and reevaluate, right? Or should I have at least tried?

I've rehashed the past so many times, and it never does any good. Did I love Jon? Yes. But when I accepted his proposal, I should have focused more on the marriage and less on the fairytale wedding. Did he love me? Probably. At least as much as a man destined to be a legend can love someone else. Did God take him from me because, even though I loved him, I had times when I didn't feel very happy being married to him? That one's still up for grabs.

I rest my head on my forearms and talk to God for a while. The future looks so bleak to me. I'm hoping against hope that the future He sees for me is considerably brighter. I spill out my dreams, just in case He wants to know what I *think* I want. Then, for good measure, I mention that all the other young widows and widowers in my grief group had remarried by the time they'd been spouseless for five years. How did they know it was time? And that they'd found the right person?

Ah. Now I can say it. *Why not me?* My eyes suddenly feel as heavy as my heart. . . .

*I'm trimming hedges, looking sharp in my royal blue Tender Loving Care Landscaping polo shirt. My employees are hard at work around me. Together, we're transforming the grounds from fine to fantastic.*

*Suddenly, the door to the huge house opens and the owner steps out. Check out his suit and tie, his briefcase, his mansion, his shiny black hair and dark eyes. Besides being unbelievably handsome, he looks so responsible. I'll bet he's got life insurance and a 401(k). He smiles at me, and the sun dims in embarrassment.*

*He might as well be wearing a nametag that says MR. RIGHT. So naturally, when he holds out his arms to me, I run to meet him.*

*Our hands are about to touch, and I think I even hear the faint tinkling of wedding bells. Very faint. But then a huge motorcycle suddenly appears between us. I screech to a halt, my heart pounding with horror, as right before my eyes, his black hair changes to brown curls, the suit to faded jeans.*

*He jumps on the bike and roars the engine to life. "Wanna ride?" he calls, balancing his briefcase over the handlebars. His amazing blue eyes seem to see all of my fears and insecurities.*

*"No, thanks," I say, weakly. "I'm fine."*

*I'm not sure he even hears me, but he* vrooms *down the driveway, without so much as a backward glance.* . . .

The pain of the mesh-wire picnic table on my cheek wakes me. I lift my head and run my hand over the imprint on my skin, my heart pounding in my ears.

What was up with that crazy dream? The part about my own landscaping company is self-explanatory. Until the bank debacle, I'd been dreaming that even when I was awake. And that Harley-riding guy in the parking lot must have lingered in my subconscious. (Not that it gives him the right to hijack my dreams.) But Mr. Right? And me, like some love-struck sap, ready to run into his waiting arms? For Pete's sake, I'm a thirty-five-year-old widow with two kids. Not a dewy-eyed damsel. I've been watching too much Lifetime TV.

And spending way too much time here, snoozing. I squint at the sun sinking in the western sky. It's past time for me to get home.

Fifteen minutes later, I park the SUV in front of the carriage house. Lark, Victoria, and I christened the tiny cottage at the back of Mama and Daddy's property when we were growing up. Who cared that it had never even remotely resembled a real carriage house and had more likely been a mother-in-law's quarters? Even as preteens, we were true romantics.

Where had that gotten us?

Victoria, too much of a romantic to go along with her father's insistence of a pre-nup agreement with her knight-in-shining-armor, is raising her son alone since Sir Likes-a-Lot (of Other Women) left her for his secretary three years ago, taking half of Victoria's money with him.

And Lark? The year before she turned thirty, she'd taken a hiatus from her thriving ad executive career in St. Louis to come home to Shady Grove and help her granny recuperate from a broken hip. When the local plumber swept her off her feet, she happily made the hiatus permanent so she could stay home and raise babies. Only—though we don't talk about it anymore—the nursery is still empty.

Rachel came later in our group, but she was definitely a romantic, too. Romantic enough to believe that some guy who wanted sex really loved her. Her romantic nature was summarily crushed, though, when she turned up pregnant at seventeen and never heard from him again. That's when we met her, the summer before I married. She gave the baby up for adoption to her older sister and brother-in-law out of state and then went on with her life. But I see a haunted look in her eyes sometimes, and I'm not sure she's ever completely healed.

And then there's me—widowed, raising two preteen daughters on a really frayed shoestring, and living in my mother's carriage house. Oh, and of course, recently unemployed. How much more romantic can you get?

I'm thankful for the private driveway. *See, Rach? In spite of it all, I'm still thinking positive.* I can wash off my mascara tracks and possibly even take a quick shower before I tromp up the path through the small clump of trees separating the two residences and allow my mother and daughters to serenade me.

I grab the mail from the box and my gaze falls on the top envelope. Wonderful. Another hospital bill. I rip it open, just to make sure they credited my payment for this month, meager though it may be. After the rest of today, I'm not even surprised by the content of the enclosed note.

> *If we don't have the balance—$4200—within 60 days, we'll have no choice but to turn your account over to an outside collection agency.*

So much for the myth that as long as you're paying on a bill, they won't turn you over to collection.

Fresh tears sting my eyes. Happy birthday to me.

As I fumble with my key, our yellow lab goes berserk in the back yard. "Sorry, Buddy!" I call. He expects me to let him in the house as soon as I get home, and sometimes I do, but today I'm in no mood for a frolicking romp. It won't hurt him to stay outside until I get back from Mama's with the girls.

I finally get the door open with my free hand and dump the duffel bag inside. A rustling noise makes me look up.

"Surprise!" The word echoes around the room.

# three

I blink at the crowd, uncertain smiles frozen on their faces. *Oh, look! My in-laws. Can a widow still have a mother-in-law? If not, I need to know, because I sure do.* Mama, Katie and Miranda, Lark and Craig, Victoria and Dylan, and Rachel are in the forefront. Behind them my three uncles and aunts surround Jon's parents.

An uneasy quiet settles over the small room.

"Hi." I force a smile and try to wrap my mind around the fact that I'm living a scene straight out of a bad movie. My voice sounds as weak as I feel.

Lark spares me an apologetic glance then bursts into a halting, off-key rendition of "Happy Birthday." *Forget it, girlfriend. Not a chance. I'm not forgiving you anytime soon, or Victoria and Rachel, either. Maybe if you hadn't invited Jon's parents, but no way now.* The rest of the group joins in, hesitantly at first, then with spirit.

Ever mindful of my daughters' concerned gazes, I smile until my cheeks ache.

My mother comes forward to hug me before the notes fade away. "Don't worry, honey, I'll handle this," she whispers.

21

Too horrified to speak, I nod slightly, then stand back and watch a master at work.

She steps a few feet away from me, successfully drawing the attention to her. "Allie's going to take a quick shower." She smiles with a nod toward the duffel bag I'd dumped inside the door.

All the eyes in the room obediently flicker to the bag. My mother could lead a cat to water and convince him to jump in for a swim with just a few well-chosen words and nods.

"Tae Bo, you know," Mama says matter-of-factly. "We'll just visit until she gets back out, and then she can cut the cake."

She puts her hand to the small of my back and gently pushes me toward my room.

"Thanks," I whisper.

"Do you need me to come with you?" Her words are so low they're barely perceptible.

I cock an eyebrow. "No, now that I'm thirty-five, I think I can operate the shower without my mommy," I whisper back, but I give her a reassuring squeeze.

She grins. "It's about time."

I glance back at the group who—except for the Pinkies who are huddled together furiously trying to figure this out, I'm sure—are still milling around like a bunch of accident onlookers. "Seriously, you'd better stay here to make excuses for a long shower. I'll be fine." The way Mama has a solution for every problem drives me crazy sometimes, but the same trait makes her a lifesaver in situations like this.

Most everyone apparently accepts her explanation for my appearance. Before I reach my bedroom door, at least five separate conversations are back in full swing. I start to close the door behind me, but a size-nine tennis shoe stops it. I peek out and see guilt etched on Lark's face. Rachel and Victoria are right behind her.

"Sorry," Lark whispers.

"You didn't get the loan?" Rachel asks, her voice thick with sympathy.

"Not a chance." I open my bedroom door all the way and they file in. What had they been thinking? Throwing a surprise party, I can understand. I'd half expected at least some of these people to be at Mama's later when I picked up the girls. But everyone knows that there's an unwritten surprise-party code. You drop just enough inadvertent hints that the surprise-ee doesn't ruin things for the surprise-ers by doing something stupid like appearing on the doorstep looking like a *Survivor* contestant who's just been voted off the island. Nothing brings down a party like the I-threw-myself-on-their-mercy-and-still-lost motif.

I close the door firmly behind the Pinkies and throw myself backward on the bed. Lark perches in my vanity chair and Rachel sits down beside me. While I tell the story of Hitler and the ducks, Victoria paces beside the bed.

When I finish, Rachel says, "What are you going to do?"

"Get a job." I pull the pillow out from under my head and cover my face with it.

Victoria yanks it off and puts her hands on her hips. "That's ridiculous. I'll finance your company, shugah," she drawls. "I know a sure bet when I see one."

"Pinky Promise Sisterhood Rule Number 3—No borrowing or loaning money among Pinkies," I intone.

"Unless they leave their lunch money at home," Victoria finishes. "Those rules should have been defunct when we finished school. Don't be stubborn."

I just look at her and shake my head again. Static from my comforter makes my head tingle. I sit up and look around at my friends. Misery might love company, but the sadness on their faces is more than I can bear. "Guys, I really appreciate y'all doing this for me."

"Humiliating you beyond belief?" Lark asks with a hint of a rueful grin.

"Yep. Only true friends would have done that."

"We aim to please," Victoria drawls. "If we go and let you get a shower, are you going to be okay?"

I nod. Even if the rest of the family bought Mama's inference that I just overexerted in Tae Bo class, my girls are astute enough to know I've been crying. I won't cause them any more worry. *Get a shower, Eeyore, and get back to your party. No gloominess allowed.*

"I'll be fine. Give me a few minutes."

They hug me and go back out to keep the party going or disband it, I'm not sure which, and except for the girls' feelings, I really don't care.

I stand under the hot spray of water longer than necessary, but some things can't be washed away. Like reality. After toweling off, I lean in under the big round bulbs and stare at my face in the bathroom mirror. The shower has at least gotten rid of the remains of my crying jag, including the mesh picnic table imprint on my cheek. I can imagine everyone wondering how I came into such close contact with a waffle iron.

A light touch of mascara and lipstick nicely cover up the fact that my dream has been destroyed and I have no way of making a living for myself and the girls. The red tee I've chosen to wear with my Levis looks almost too jaunty, so I toss on a short black jacket over it. Satisfied that I look perky, but not pathetic, I slip into my matching red Gucci sandals, aka my eBay deal of the century. They always make me feel stylish *and* savvy. Now, I'm ready to face the crowd.

Okay, maybe that's an overstatement. But I'm as ready as I'll ever be.

The bad thing about the Langston family is the noise. All three of my dad's brothers talk so loudly you'd think they were deaf. The truth is they have perfect hearing, they're just competitive talkers.

It takes some getting used to. My aunts, though not as bad, aren't quiet by any stretch of the imagination, nor are my cousins. Even my brother and I have been known to talk a little louder when we get excited in a tense game of Trivial Pursuit. Mama is the only one who seems to stand above the raucous fray.

As I reach for the bedroom doorknob, I realize that, in a time like this, as is the case so often in life, the flip side of the coin is identical—the good thing about my family is the noise. Sure enough, they hardly notice when I enter the room.

A constant clack-clack-clacking reverberates from the small table in front of the big living room window, where my three uncles and Lark's husband, Craig, are playing a game of dominoes.

Years ago, my dad and his three brothers had been out duck hunting and ended up coming back in to the domino table to rest. Tempers were on edge. Mama says that's because they got up before dawn, sat in a cold duck blind all morning with wet feet, and never saw a single bird, but that's another story.

When the game got ugly, Uncle Doyle, always a hothead but a young hothead then, grabbed up his gun and cocked it, aiming it at his own *partner*, no less. My dad jumped up and so did Uncle Troy, and between them they wrestled the gun from Uncle Doyle's hands before any damage was done to Uncle Jeff.

My mother hid the dominoes for two years.

I was little, but I still remember those poor men while they were grounded from their favorite game. Our house had never seemed so small. They tried Rook, Pit, and UNO. They even played a mean game of Chutes and Ladders with me more than once. When I dragged out Candyland, though, my Uncle Doyle formally apologized and begged Mama to give the dominoes back. She conceded, but ever since, the tension has been considerably less around the Langston game table. Since Dad's death, whenever Lark and Craig are over, Craig takes his place—with the understanding that he doesn't have to be Uncle Doyle's partner, of course.

"Hi, guys," I offer in the general direction of the table.

They all four nod without looking up from their ivory rocks.

"Happy Birthday," Craig hollers, and the other three nod again.

"We saved you some pizza," Lark calls from the dining room. She, Rachel, Victoria, and the aunts are playing Cranium.

Aunt Sue is frantically acting out something for Aunt Harriet that could only be "gravity" but, judging by Aunt Harriet's blank look, I know she isn't going to get it. Lark holds the answer card, so I mouth the answer to her behind their backs to see if I'm right. She nods.

The apology is still in Lark's eyes, but the carb overload has muted it some. It's our sisterhood motto—nothing seems like as big a deal after a slice of thick-crusted pizza dripping with cheese.

*I'd better have two slices, at least.*

Since two are all that's left, I grab the box from the foyer and carry it over to an empty spot on the dining room table. I don't see my in-laws, but I'm not looking really hard. They're probably sitting in a corner, still wondering, even five years after his death, what kind of crazy family their son married into.

"Where are Mama and the kids?" I ask Lark under the roar as everyone teases Aunt Harriet for not recognizing Aunt Sue's brilliant rendition of Sir Isaac Newton's whole apple moment.

"In the kitchen, getting the cake and ice cream ready." Lark touches my arm. "Sorry again," she murmurs. I plop down between Victoria and Rachel. Rachel grabs my hand and squeezes gently, and Victoria gives me a one-armed hug, the familiar smell of her Obsession perfume wafting toward me. We've tried to tell her that twelve years with one scent goes beyond preference into. . .well, obsession, but she won't budge. "You look beautiful, Allie. Happy birthday."

Victoria's dark brunette curls, swept up in an elegant French twist, and her flawless face make it hard to take her compliments seriously. Sorta like Einstein telling you you're smart. But she loves me so much I know she means it. "Thanks." I finish my pizza in silence, then stand. "I'm going to go say hi to the girls."

"You can be on our team, Allie," Aunt Sue offers.

"Yeah, she's hoping you can make up for me," Aunt Harriet drawls. "Come on and help us. Who knows? Maybe you can drag us back onto the fast track."

"Thanks. I might play in a few minutes. Y'all go ahead." I

carry the empty pizza box into the kitchen.

"Mom!" Both of my daughters run and throw their arms around me.

"Grandma and Grandpa Richards had to go. They waited *forever*, but tonight is two-for-one steak night at the country club, and that only comes once a week," Katie says.

*No doubt a direct quote from Grandma.* I slide the pizza box into the stainless steel trash can. "That's okay, honey. I understand them not wanting to miss that."

Mama smiles at my attempt at tact.

I hug the girls tight and give Mama a one-arm embrace, as well, over Katie's head. "Thanks for saving me in there."

"No problem." She grins, but the concern in her eyes is apparent. "Want to talk?"

"Later."

The back door flies open. "Hey, sis! Happy birthday." My twenty-eight-year-old brother, Adam, strolls into the kitchen clutching a drippy paper bag. "Hey, how are my favorite munchkins?"

The girls grin. They never get tired of his teasing.

His flip-flops slap the linoleum as he walks over and drops a kiss on Mama's cheek. "Sorry I'm late."

She gives him an exasperated smile. In spite of the fact that he suffers terribly from R.D.D. (Responsibility Deficiency Disorder) and still lives at home, he's her baby and she thinks he hung the moon. "Is the ice cream melted?"

"Just a little soft," he assures her, running his free hand through his shoulder-length hair. "I ran into Matt down at Price Chopper. He just got a new truck and wanted to show me how it ran, so it took longer than I thought. Sorry."

As soon as he's sure she buys his excuse, he scoots out.

Katie tugs on my sleeve. "Why were you crying?" she asks with the intuition of a ten-year-old-going-on-forty and cuts straight to the chase.

"Oh, Katie-baby. . ." I revert to her childhood nickname without realizing it, until I see her grimace. "Things haven't been going exactly my way."

"At work?" I was trying to wait to tell them about losing my job until I could announce the new business at the same time, but twelve-year-old Miranda apparently can see this is more than just a hangnail or a runner in my hose.

I nod, aware of my mother's gaze on my face. "Yeah, sort of." I look down to where Katie still stands with her arm around me and ruffle her hair. "Tell you what. Let's forget it for tonight, enjoy the party, and I promise I'll fill you in tomorrow. Okay?"

"If God is for us, who can be against us, right, Mom?" Katie says, her voice full of confidence.

Those words had gotten me through countless sleepless nights after Jon's death. I've said them so often to the kids, it's no wonder they come to her mind, I guess, but Katie's unexpected recital of the scripture pricks my heart.

I blink back fresh tears and nod, avoiding my mother's eyes. "That's right, honey."

*When did I stop believing that?*

*four*

Y our hometown radio forecast for Shady Grove and all of North Arkansas—Partly cloudy today with highs in the low 70s. Twenty percent chance of rain this afternoon. . . ." I groan and slap at the little box of terror on my nightstand. No way it's morning already.

The perky voice continues to try to convince me I care about the weather at 6:30 a.m. until my flopping hand finally connects with the snooze button. I'll just snuggle under the down comforter and enjoy the luxury of waking up slowly. If I forgo breakfast and grab a cup of coffee at the office. . .

The office.

I squeeze my eyes tighter and roll into a fetal position.

Since my blossoming dream died on the vine at the bank yesterday, today I start looking for a job in earnest.

I pull the covers over my head and surrender to sleep again.

Barry Manilow's mellow voice jars me awake. At least the weather girl is gone.

"Mom!"

I jump and open my eyes.

Twelve-year-old Miranda stands next to the bed, frowning.

"Good morning, honey. Dozed off for a minute."

Apparently unimpressed with my explanation, Miranda is still frowning. "You're going to have to make *her* get up."

No need to ask who "her" is. In our house, it always means the one who isn't doing the talking. Besides, unlike Miranda, who rises at the crack of dawn to prepare for her day, Katie's a sleepyhead. She'd love mornings, *if* they waited until noon to start.

"Okay. I'll deal with her," I say in a froggy but firm voice. Occasionally Miranda likes to pretend she's the mom and sometimes I let her. But not today. "You go on and get ready for school."

She minds me, and when she's gone, I stay in bed for a minute, absently running my hand over the unused pillow beside me. I've been sleeping alone for five years, but in that minute of time between sleep and wakefulness, when peace is the order of the day, I always imagine my husband here, solid as a rock, ready to face life's battles with me.

Reality bites.

But it has to be faced, so I grab my robe and head for Katie's room.

I stand for a minute in the doorway and drink in the sight of my baby. It seems like just yesterday she was a little lump under the covers in the big double bed. But she's ten now, and suddenly she's growing at supersonic speed. She lies on her side, one lanky leg stretched almost to the end of the bed and her other knee bent. Her arm is tossed over her eyes, no doubt trying to block out Miranda's sisterly prodding.

Katie has my fair coloring, but her eyes, along with her sunny smile and eager-to-please disposition, are straight from my dad. Even though he's been dead seven years, some days when I look at Katie, it's as if I'm looking straight into the kind eyes of David Montgomery. Of course, my mother will tell you that, as much as she loved her husband and now loves her granddaughter, Katie also has Daddy's tendency to procrastinate and lack of driving ambition.

I nudge Katie gently and finally resort to toe tickling. When I'm satisfied she won't climb back into bed, I take a quick shower, then spend fifteen minutes studying the Bible. I learned a long time ago that if I buzz through a whole chapter, I can't remember any of it by the time I'm in the vehicle. So I usually concentrate on applying one or two verses to my life.

Most mornings the Word of God covers me like a soft blanket. But occasionally, like today for example, it slaps me in the face like a wet rag. *Philippians 4:6, "Do not be anxious about anything, but in everything, by prayer and petition, with thanksgiving, present your requests to God."*

I have to laugh, albeit weakly. I tossed and turned half the night fretting about our uncertain future, yet my verse of the day begins, "Do not be anxious about anything." Ouch. How can anyone think God doesn't have a sense of humor? Mama would love this. She lives this verse. But I'm not quite there yet.

Forty-five minutes later, Katie and I are finishing breakfast. She's propped on one elbow. Her unruly blonde curls desperately need to be introduced to Mr. Brush. Any minute now I expect her to fall asleep and pitch face-first into her bowl of cereal. But she's dressed for school. That's a major victory.

On the tiny under-the-counter TV, our local morning show host, Blair Winchester, shares a recipe for a peaceful morning. Something about a lavender bath and deep breaths. Lavender bath? Ha!

The idea of Blair giving a recipe for peace rates really high on the irony scale. The single mom blew into sleepy little Shady Grove—apparently determined to take it by storm via the airwaves—right after I moved back five years ago. Don't ask about her first husband. Rumor has it she lured him into her web and ate him.

But I'll stick to the facts.

All I know for sure is Blair was dating my brother, Adam, and when things took a major turn for the worse for him financially, she took a quick walk. . .out of his life. Since that was years ago and Adam doesn't seem to harbor any ill will, I'm civil to her, but I still don't trust her. So I'll forget the peaceful morning and lavender bath and settle for getting the girls to school on time.

Miranda, her straight dark hair pulled neatly into a low ponytail, paces by the door. She looks over at the two of us, blows out an exasperated breath, and launches into a litany of remembers. "Mom, remember you have to go to Wal-Mart today. We're out of toilet paper and dog food." She looks at her sister. "Katie, remember to tell the teacher you have a dentist appointment Thursday."

I'm proud of my oldest daughter. Really. But sometimes her bossy attitude drives me crazy. If Katie is my dad made over, Miranda—the spitting image physically of her own dad—is like my mother, loving and kind, but a driven perfectionist. Which makes it hard sometimes, on all of us. Because I'm an awkward combination of the two. Still, at least for the most part, I understand my kids, and that's something many parents can't say.

"Oh, and Mom?"

I look up from my cereal.

"Don't forget about tonight."

I nod. I have no idea what "tonight" is, but I'm not about to ask. Let me hold onto some semblance of being the adult around here. I can always call the school office later.

Miranda clears her throat and looks at her watch.

I take a slow sip of my coffee and pick up the folded newspaper.

"Mom!"

*Don't be anxious, huh?*

Maybe I can pass this on to my daughter, even if I can't quite apply it yet. I lay the paper back on the table. "Honey, you're going to have to loosen up a little. We're not going to be late."

She turns toward the door.

"Miranda, don't roll your eyes at me."

"Yes, ma'am." Grudging, but respectful. Some days that's the best you can hope for from an almost-teen.

Katie pushes to her feet, so I go ahead and clean off the table while she brushes her hair and wraps a scrunchie around it. I turn off the TV in the middle of Blair's spiel about the upcoming yearlong Shady Grove Centennial Celebration, then double-check to be sure that a yawning Katie has her backpack.

Less than a mile from the house, Katie wakes up and checks out my outfit. "You don't have to go to work today?"

I shake my head.

My going-to-the-bank clothes had been dressy enough to fool them yesterday. How tempting it had been to dress for work today and wait until I had a new job to break the news to the girls.

But since Jon's death, the three of us have clung together in a way that leaves no room for long-term secrets. So my jeans and T-shirt give me away.

"Why?" Miranda asks.

I clear my throat. My girls will pick up on it if there's the least bit of a tremor in my voice. "I'm not working at the plant nursery anymore."

"You quit?" Shock rings in Katie's voice.

*Wouldn't it be easy to just nod?* I force my head to hold completely still. "Actually, Bill sold Coble's to a big company and they have their own managers."

Two sets of blue eyes stare at me in the rearview mirror. I have their full attention. In the tradition of mothers everywhere, I go for the most positive spin. "But Bill did give me some money, so there's really nothing to worry about." The truth is, my severance package might last us a month, *if* we cinch up our already tight belts, but like I said, I'm shooting for positive right now. "I'm going to start looking today for a new job, and soon I'll have something even better."

We ride in silence the last quarter of a mile to school, unless you count the pounding of my heart.

Five minutes later, I pull into the circle drive of Shady Grove Elementary/Junior High. Katie's friends surround the vehicle. "Bye, Mom." She gives me a one-arm hug through the gap between the front seats, jumps out, and runs off to join the throng of girls.

Miranda climbs out slowly and gathers all of her things. When she looks up at me, I recognize the panic in her eyes. "I'm sorry you got fired."

*Fired? Who said the word fired?* "Miranda, you're not to worry." *How do you teach someone not to be anxious about anything? How do you learn it yourself?* "I'll find a new job before you know it."

She nods. I want to ask her to come around for a hug, but we rarely do hugs in public anymore. Before I can find more words of reassurance, she waves and walks away.

As I pull away from the curb, clusters of kids stream in the double doors. Is there such a thing as nostalgic déjà vu? I spent a large chunk of my childhood in that same yellow brick building, trying to be popular and yet not noticed.

Dream world—Yesterday Lark and I were in school with endless possibilities before us.

Real world—Lark and I are thirty-five and our possibilities have definite boundaries.

If I get to choose, I'll take the dream world, because the real world is scary beyond belief.

On my way home, I remember Miranda's dire warning not to forget "tonight." With my free hand, I punch the school's number into my cell phone and leave a message for Betty to call me back.

At the Junior Food Mart, I jump out and buy a local paper from the machine. Across the street and on the corner where Pete's Junk Store used to be, a huge banner jauntily announces the Grand Opening of the new Coffee Central Bookstore.

I know I should just take the want ads home and finish off the pot of chocolate velvet coffee I left on the warmer, but I've been craving a real honest-to-goodness latté ever since news of this place zoomed along our local grapevine.

Ten minutes later, I'm sipping on the most delicious white chocolate latté I've ever had and admiring the design of Coffee

Central. Unlike a lot of chains, the coffee shop is in the middle of the store. At the end of each book section, the tempting aroma of caffeine and sugar draws you in. And from any table in the place, you can see endcaps filled with fascinating books in all shapes and sizes.

I pull my attention back to the want ads in front of me.

"Good morning," a man says as he walks past my table.

"Morning," I mumble, still reading the classifieds. My peripheral vision registers that he stopped, so I look up. Right into those way-too-familiar blue eyes.

# five

My mind races. Is he stalking me? As soon as the thought forms, I realize how crazy it is. Even though Shady Grove has grown considerably since our industrial boom a few years ago, it's still the kind of place where you constantly run into people you know. Or in this case, people you don't know but ran into yesterday. "Hi," I offer.

"Hi. Is that good?" Not counting our meeting at the bank, he looks vaguely familiar, but if I'd ever met him, I'm sure I'd remember.

"The latté?" I ask, like an idiot. *No, Allie, the newspaper. Of course he means the latté.*

"Yeah." He smiles.

I nod and take a big gulp to prove it. "Um." Hot! Hot! Hot! His eyes widen. "You okay?"

*Apparently I'm just a disaster waiting to happen, but that's not your problem, so walk away from the table now and nobody will get hurt.* "Sure." I grab a napkin and wipe my mouth. How long does it take those little bumps on your tongue to grow back anyway?

My cell phone rings—a strident, rather annoying version of "Happy Birthday." I dig around for it in my purse and cast him an apologetic glance. "Yesterday was my birthday and I forgot to change my ring."

I can see he's remembering me from the bank and adding to that the fact that it was my birthday. I turn away before I see the pity I know is coming. Widowed at thirty, I've had enough pity to last me a lifetime. Coming up with my phone, I say, "I'm sorry, please excuse me," and turn my attention to the phone call.

"Allie? It's Betty from the school. You wanted to ask me something?"

"Oh, hi, Betty. I need to know what's going on at the school tonight."

"I don't think there's anything. Let me check the calendar." I can hear her shuffling papers on her desk.

I dare to look up, but the man is gone. A surreptitious glance around shows no sign of him. That funny feeling in my stomach is relief, *not* disappointment.

"Nothing at all for tonight." Betty's voice breaks into my self-reassurances. "A week from tonight there's a PTO meeting, though."

"Ah. Thanks, Betty." I hang up and sigh. Miranda must've been thinking about the PTO meeting *next* Tuesday night. Whew. I'm usually pretty organized, but this morning Miranda's reminders made me feel like a scattered mess. It's nice to know she can be wrong now and then.

By the time I head home and throw together a sandwich for a very late lunch, I've crossed out at least twenty ads. Some for obvious reasons. Transmission Rebuilder. Exotic Dancer. I won't even ask how those ended up in the clerical section. Some I reject for less obvious—but still valid—reasons. Travel Required. Long hours. And I nix one just because I don't like the looks of it. Seeking able-bodied administrative assistant with attractive resume and warm people skills. Talk about a subliminal message.

I'm left with four real possibilities for an office manager/ administrative assistant position. Instead of the vagueness that ads usually emanate, one of the four is specific—to the point of mentioning that the current office manager is retiring. All the details look good. And there's a phone number. I pluck the cordless phone from the table and punch in the numbers before I lose my nerve.

"We're having a wonderful day at Collins and Olson! This is Jeanine. May I help you?"

*Only if you have that perkiness in a bottle.* "Hi, I'm calling about the ad in the paper for an office manager."

"Just a moment."

I draw darker circles around the ad while I wait.

"Susan Kilpatrick here."

"Hello, Susan. I'm Allie Richards. I'm calling about the office manager position."

"You and half the world. I'm going to kill Don when he gets back from vacation."

Okay, not the response I expected, but I've worked with weirder. "Oh?"

"Yes, he thinks he's so funny."

"I see." *Actually, no, I don't.* Is this some kind of a preliminary test?

"I turned thirty yesterday. I came in and the whole office was decorated in black right down to the roses on my desk."

"Black roses for thirty?" I have no idea where this is going or why she's telling me this, but I'm appalled at the idea that anyone could see thirty as over the hill, even as a joke. Don't they know that thirty-one is the new twenty-one?

"Yes, but apparently Don didn't think that was enough. He put an ad in the paper for my job, saying I was retiring."

"You're not?" I try to suck the words back but I can't.

"At thirty?" Her laugh is a combination of disbelief and tired acceptance. "I have at least five good years left."

I'd liked her until that comment. "I'm sorry to have bothered you, Susan. I hope Don gets fired."

"Not likely." She lowers her voice. "He's the boss."

"You're kidding?" I'd pictured a fresh-out-of-college prankster. The boss?

"No, I'm serious. But I'll get him back. He's twenty-five. His turn is coming in a few years."

I can feel the arthritis creeping up my fingers as I push the OFF button on the phone.

Isn't there a theory that you should take a break from something when it gets too frustrating? Or is that just called quitting? Either way, I hobble down the hall to my room to change. I slip out of the feeling of being ancient and into my tattered jeans and stretched-out T-shirt.

Five minutes later, I'm on my knees in the backyard, rejuvenated and ready to take control—at least of the weeds in my flowerbed. As I create order from chaos, my mind mulls over the dream from this morning. Especially the part about owning my own landscaping business. . .

"Allie!"

I jump up, glancing at my watch as I turn. Have I really been weeding over an hour without a break? Time flies when you're dreaming the impossible dream.

Lark waves from the backyard gate.

"Hi," I call and motion her in. Lark and I have been friends since she moved to Shady Grove in third grade. I still remember the day I opened my *Dukes of Hazzard* lunchbox expecting to see my normal ham and cheese sandwich and found Lark's thermos of homemade chicken soup instead.

For two eight-year-olds, having matching lunch boxes is a perfect foundation for a friendship. She sat down beside me and in between slurps of soup explained that her mother needed to "find herself" and Lark was going to live with her grandma for a while. "A while" ended up being the rest of her childhood, but for the next couple of years, I worried that her absentee mother would suddenly show up and snatch Lark out of my life.

Late one night when she was sleeping over, Lark told me her biggest secret—she had never had a daddy. She said I must never tell a soul as long as I lived. Then she taught me how to pinky promise.

It was the first of many.

Through the years that followed, we took two more girls into our Pinky Promise Sisterhood—first Victoria Worthington in fifth grade, and then later Rachel Donovan. The four of us keep each other's secrets, but even more importantly, now that we're adults, Lark, Rachel, Victoria, and I keep each other sane.

I'd e-mailed them last night and shared my terror at starting the job hunt today, so Lark's visit wasn't a total surprise. "Hey, girl. What's up?"

"Not much. Craig didn't need me to run errands today, so I

thought I'd stop by and see how you were doing."

The joys of having a plumber husband. I grin and hold up my trowel. "As you can see, I'm in the middle of therapy."

"I didn't even bother ringing the doorbell. Just had a feeling you'd be out here."

She knows me too well. "I spent the morning sorting through the want ads, but I needed a break." I discreetly wipe my hands on my jeans and give her a hug.

"And your idea of a break has always been getting your hands dirty."

"And yours has always been getting your hair done. I love the new 'do, by the way."

Her black hair is cut short with layers at the bottom that spike out in a style reminiscent of the flip we used to wear in elementary. On her, it looks feminine yet sophisticated. Some people have all the luck.

"I didn't get your e-mail until late last night, and I couldn't sleep because I knew you were upset. This morning I figured maybe I had some residual negativity I needed to get rid of."

"And it collected in your hair? Did Rachel tell you that?" I touch my wavy ponytail. Nothing but tangles. Even though she's strong in most ways, in some areas Lark's a little suggestible. And Rachel is a fantastic chiropractor and a nut about positive thinking.

"No, I read it in *Total Woman's Digest*."

How do I tell her that's just a tabloid dressed up in a shiny cover? Before I can say anything, something moves behind us.

"Hey, guys!" Katie bounds into the yard through the back door.

I didn't even hear the school bus. "Where's your sister?"

"She's in the house, looking for the brownies." Katie plops down in the swing and kicks her feet.

"Brownies?" I nudge Lark. "I'm a stay-at-home mom for one whole day and Miranda expects brownies."

Miranda comes onto the porch and puts her hands on her hips. "Where are the brownies for the soccer meeting?"

The preseason soccer meeting. *Not* at the school. At the community center. I'm supposed to bring brownies. A hundred brownies. My heart plummets to my dirt-covered toes. "I haven't made them yet." I take a frantic mental inventory of my cabinets, but I see no point in mentioning that I have no mixes or even any cocoa.

Miranda checks her watch. "We have to be there in an hour."

How many twelve-year-olds really wear a watch? I'd like a show of hands.

# six

"Allie, how creative of you to bring store-bought brownies instead of those old-fashioned homemade ones we usually have." Blair Winchester (yes, in our small town the TV personalities associate with us normal people) swoops down on me like a beautiful vulture and snags my tray of hastily unwrapped cakes. "Oh, look. You cut them in half on the little indented line. What a neat idea!" She aims a saccharine smile at the man standing next to her. I follow her gaze and my eyes widen.

Maybe he *is* stalking me.

Although if he's with Blair, why would he bother?

He doesn't react to my presence, just nods in agreement, including us both in his answering grin.

Why am I so flustered? No matter how different he seems, no matter how many times I run into him, and especially no matter how blue his eyes are, he's just another clueless man.

Females can be as catty as they want with each other, but as long as they tack on any kind of smile, men assume they mean what they say. Women like Blair always take advantage of that.

"I'll have you know I slaved over these brownies." *Unwrapping all those little packages was beyond tedious.*

I smile back.

Okay, occasionally nice women like me take advantage of the Clueless Man phenomenon, too.

But she started it.

Clueless Man scoops up a brownie from the tray and pops it in his mouth. "Mmm. . .good." He motions to Blair. "Try one."

The repulsed look she gives me is worth all the grief I took from Miranda for not remembering to bake.

Blair plucks a sticky chocolate cake from the fake crystal platter as if it were a worm from the bait bucket. With one long, slender, red-tipped finger she daintily brushes the anemic-looking chopped peanuts off onto her napkin, then raises the brownie to her mouth. "Yum."

When she brings it down, she still has the whole piece of brownie on her napkin cupped discreetly in her hand. The "Yum" was definitely for Clueless Man's benefit.

Seemingly unaware of the trap, he's ladling himself a cup of punch.

*May the wind always be at his back and the terrain downhill as he runs far and fast in the other direction.*

Blair barely manages to slide the brownie into the trash before he turns back to face us.

*Run, Clueless Man, while you still can.*

To my surprise, he hands me a full cup. "I'm sure you don't remember me, but I think we used to go to school together. I'm Daniel Montgomery."

Daniel Montgomery. How could I not remember the bad

boy sophomore I'd had a crush on my freshman year? I'd secretly admired his rebel-without-a-cause air right up to the minute he'd gotten expelled for fighting. The nose was different and the scar added to his tough image, but the eyes were still the same. Hard to believe I hadn't recognized him. "Allie Richards, now. I'm widowed." Why had I said that? Usually I preferred for men to figure it out for themselves or just assume I'm married. I take the offering even though red punch ranks right under prune juice on my list of favorite drinks. "Thanks."

Blair tosses her silky curtain of blonde hair over her shoulder and wraps a possessive hand around Daniel's arm as soon as he releases the cup. She's marking her territory.

*Poor man, you waited too late to run.*

I glance toward the milling crowd of kids, trying to pick out a pint-sized version of Daniel. "The kids seem really excited about soccer."

Daniel nodded. "My sister talked me into bringing my nephew and he couldn't quit talking about it all the way here."

At least he hadn't come as Blair's date. Not that it matters to me one way or the other.

"So, Allie, I heard you got laid off," Blair says, again using her smile to cover for the fact that she's being completely tactless in front of a man who is essentially a total stranger.

"Bob sold the business, so my job ended." Semantics, I know, but I'm in the mood to be contrary tonight.

Her over-painted lips form a little *O.* "I'm so sorry."

"Don't be. I'll find something soon."

Blair clutches Daniel's arm tighter. Is it my imagination or did he wince? "Maybe Daniel has some openings at his bookstore.

Besides working at the station part-time as a cameraman, he owns Coffee Central Bookstore, you know."

Um, no. How could I know since we hadn't been officially reintroduced until thirty seconds ago? "Well, that's really nice of you to offer, Blair. . . ." Not to mention totally inappropriate.

"I'm sure. . . ." Daniel seems to be as much at a loss for words as I am, but his smile gives me hope that he sees through Blair's games more than I realized.

"Mom, come see what team we're on," Katie calls to me from across the room where the team lists are posted. White pages line the south wall, reminiscent of cheerleading tryouts or senior play auditions. Except, thankfully, here everybody gets on a team.

I smile with intense relief and lift my cup in salute to Blair and her luckless prey. "I have several leads on a job, but thanks anyway. Thanks again for the drink, Daniel. Nice to see you again. Y'all enjoy."

Before I even reach my girls, I smell trouble. Miranda leans against the wall and scowls while Katie's doing her best Tigger imitation, bouncing with excitement.

"You said that you'd get us put on different teams," Miranda hisses.

I give her a hard look and she backpedals.

"Didn't you?"

Had I? I remember Miranda protesting when she figured out that she and Katie would be in the same age group this year. But there's no way I said I'd split them up. "I don't think so. If I did, I didn't mean it. I've had a lot on my mind the last couple of weeks." Like how I'm even going to pay for soccer. Or food, for that matter.

"I want to be on the team with Miranda."

*Yes, Katie, I know you do. But unfortunately, your sister has suddenly decided that everything about you is babyish and annoying, even though you've been her best friend your whole life.*

Some things even a mother can't explain.

But that doesn't keep it from hurting.

I give Miranda's glare right back to her, upping the wattage.

She shrugs and pushes off the wall with a huff. I'm guessing she realizes the battle is lost. "C'mon, let's go meet the rest of the losers on our team," she mutters.

We maneuver our way through the crowd to the homemade Hornets banner, where Blair is pointing lost-looking first-timers to metal folding chairs decorated with little construction paper stingers. *Joy be.* Her daughter must be on our team. And look, there's Clueless Man—I mean Daniel—and sure enough, right beside him, a smaller version, only with a straight nose and no scar. Aren't we just one big happy Hornet family now?

Once we're seated, a man in shorts and a Hornets jersey stands up. Even though everyone immediately stops talking and looks at him, he blows his whistle shrilly for at least twenty seconds.

It's going to be a long season.

Just as the whistle-blower, who introduces himself as Coach Smith, starts on the rules, my fellow Pinky, Victoria, with her son in tow, rushes up to our group.

Coach looks at his watch.

She slips into the chair next to me, pulling Dylan down beside her. She pats her hair with a perfectly manicured hand. "Hi, shugah. The orthodontist was running late. I thought we weren't going to make it."

"That's okay. We just started," I whisper and squeeze her arm.

When Coach clears his throat and stares pointedly at us, the events of the last couple of weeks all come crashing down on me. For a second, I imagine myself snatching that silly lanyard off his neck and stomping the whistle into dust. But my stress level has been a little high lately, and I'd probably regret such a hasty action.

Probably.

Daniel catches my eye across the circle and one corner of his mouth tips upward. If I didn't know better, I'd say he just read my mind. Heat creeps up to my cheeks. Maybe he's not as clueless as I thought.

After exhausting the topic of games and schedules, Coach gives us a pep talk and passes out a sheet with our e-mail addresses and phone numbers. As loyal Hornets, we must stay in touch at all costs. It's imperative for the good of the team.

The meeting breaks up and Miranda and Katie quickly scatter to find their friends. I hug Victoria. "If he'd blown that whistle one more time. . ."

"I know. Same here." She motions toward the lists on the wall. "I'm just thankful Dylan is on Katie and Miranda's team this year."

"Me, too." Last year they'd all three been on different teams, and our schedules had been impossible. "Are the Pinkies still getting together tomorrow night?"

"Definitely, birthday girl. Don't think you can get out of it." The four of us meet once a month at the Dairy Bar, and if it's close to a birthday, we each have a hot fudge brownie sundae in the birthday girl's honor.

"We had my birthday last night, remember?"

She grimaces. "How could we forget? But we thought we'd

rewind and do it right this time, the traditional way, with just the Pinkies." She lowers her voice. "Unless you don't want to?"

I'd assured them all that I appreciated the surprise party, but I don't think they believed me. "And miss a hot fudge brownie sundae? I'd go through almost anything for the pleasure of ice cream covered in chocolate."

Victoria shakes her head. "Sorry. The Dairy Bar's closed for remodeling. This month we were going to try out that new coffee place, remember? The one that just opened. What's it called?"

Great. How could I have forgotten? I glance over at Blair wrapped around Daniel like a feather boa. Why was I suddenly seeing this man more than I saw my own mother? "Coffee Central."

Ah, blessed silence. Whoever made up the rule that kids have to go to bed before parents do should be awarded the Nobel Peace Prize. My life revolves around my girls and I wouldn't have it any other way. But these two hours before I go to bed, I'm not Katie and Miranda's mom. I'm just plain old Allie—checking e-mail or playing Spider Solitaire.

I double click on the Internet Explorer icon and smile when the screen appears. INBOX (3). Lark always laughs about what she calls my naïve optimism when it comes to e-mails. Hey, at least I don't believe I have residual negativity in my hair.

To some people, checking e-mail is a drudge. But I get excited every time I get one. Sure, most of the time they're run-of-the-mill, but you never know when you'll open a post to discover that you're the long-lost heiress to a dog food dynasty or that you've been picked to be the grand marshal of the local parade. Yeah, so, it hasn't happened yet, but a girl can hope.

The first one—an offer to get a college degree through the mail—obviously should have gone to my junk folder. I hit DELETE without opening it and move on to a post from Lark.

*Dear Pinkies,*
  *Tomorrow night. Coffee Central. 7:00 p.m.*
                                                            *Lark*

The third e-mail is another one that slipped through my junk mail filter. But the subject line—DO YOU NEED A BUSINESS LOAN?—stops me from deleting. I *never* open spam. Unsolicited e-mails are for losers.

I double-click to open it, then cringe, waiting for the rubber snake to jump out at me.

Guess what? I've been pre-approved for a loan! If only little Hitler down at the bank had known that, we could have saved ourselves a lot of trouble. Of course the fine print reveals a large, non-refundable application fee—Application? What does pre-approved mean anyway?—and an astronomical interest rate. I'm trying to force myself to hit DELETE when a new e-mail pops up. Sender: Coffee Central Bookstore.

Daniel Montgomery must have input the Hornets' e-mail list to send out ads for his new business. I'm surprised by his nerve.

Even though I would never, ever spam my daughters' soccer team, I can't help but wonder how you would go about it. Will it be an ad? A coupon? Or a—*Oh, Allie, you think too much. Just open the e-mail.*

I click on it. *Dear Allie...* He personalized them? Nice touch.

*Dear Allie,*
*I'm sorry if I seemed rude tonight when the subject of a*
*job came up. I don't have any openings at the bookstore right*
*now, but if one becomes available, I'll be happy to let you*
*know. It was nice to see you again after all these years.*
*Daniel Montgomery*

I put my hands against my hot cheeks. What in the world? Did I seem that desperate? I'd convinced myself that both he and I understood that Blair had just been trying to show off the fact that her boyfriend owned the new bookstore. But my first assessment of him had been right on target. I hit REPLY.
*Dear Clueless Man...*
I'm all fired up, shoulders back, fingers poised to tell this man off. Then I sigh. My mama raised me to always be a lady. And I may have dirt under my fingernails sometimes, but polite is my middle name.

~~*Dear Clueless Man*~~
~~*Dear Mr. Montgomery*~~
*Daniel,*
*At this time, I'm not looking for work as a bookstore clerk.*
*If that changes, I'll be happy to let you know.*
*Sincerely,*
*Allie Richards*

53

## seven

A last-minute attack of nerves almost made me cancel, but I couldn't do that to my closest friends, so I slip in the door of Coffee Central a minute before seven. My only hope is that just because Daniel owns the shop doesn't mean he hangs out here all the time.

"Allie!" Lark is early for once and she and Victoria wave frantically at me from a table.

Across the room, Daniel Montgomery leans against the counter staring straight at me. So much for my only hope. I should have canceled. Ever-polite, I nod and he grins, a full-fledged, happy-to-see-you, dimples-flashing grin. He e-mailed me a coupon for a free latté after my polite little diatribe about not looking for a job as a bookstore clerk. No message, just the coupon. I didn't print it out, nor did I reply.

Resenting the heat I feel creeping up my face, I focus on Lark and Victoria and make a beeline for our table.

"Hey, honey." Victoria's one-arm hug envelops me in a cloud of Obsession, naturally. She kisses near my cheek. From anyone else, the Southern charms would drive me crazy, but they're so much a part of Victoria that I can't imagine her without them. Years of summers in Atlanta with her high-society grandmother give her the right to be as much a Southern belle as she wants to be. That and her family money.

Lark raises her hand in greeting. "Hi, girl. Glad to see you made it."

"Me, too." I plop down on the vinyl chair. "I wondered for a little while."

"Job hunting today?" Lark rips open another packet of sugar and dumps it into her cappuccino.

"Yeah." Too depressing to talk about. I nod toward the pile of white paper in front of her. "Think you've got enough sugar?"

Lark shrugs. "I just want to get plenty before Rachel gets here."

Victoria and I grin.

"Rachel can't *make* you quit sugar." Victoria sips her espresso. "She can't even make her receptionist stop playing Spider Solitaire on the computer when she's supposed to be working."

Lark takes a big gulp of her drink. "Yeah, but I promised her I would."

"Promises given under duress don't count," I assure Lark. "And when Rachel starts about the evils of sugar, that's duress."

"Are you girls talking about me behind my back again?" Rachel appears at my shoulder.

Lark fumbles around hurriedly with the empty sugar packets and finally plops her black leather purse on top of them.

I nod. "Yep. You're giving Lark a complex, honey."

Rachel looks over at Lark's big black bag smack in the middle of the table. A lone white wrapper pokes out from under one corner. "Lark, are you drinking sugar tonight?" She sounds like a mother who can't wrap her mind around the fact that her daughter was caught smoking in the girls' room.

Victoria snickers and turns it into a ladylike cough behind her hand.

"Sugar?" Lark picks up her cup and examines it. "No. Um. . . it's a cappuccino," she finishes with a rueful grin.

Rachel slugs Lark gently on the arm and slides into the seat next to her. "Silly goose, it's your body." She smiles. "If you want to poison yourself, that's your business."

"Whew, that's a relief," Lark deadpans and takes a big gulp of her cappuccino.

Rachel's blondish-red ponytail bounces as she looks all around. Her green eyes widen. "This place is fantastic." She nods toward the espresso in front of Victoria. "You like your caffeine compressed into a ZIP file, don't you? If I drank one of those I'd stay awake for a week. Allie, won't they let you have anything?"

I cast a surreptitious glance at Daniel, still manning the counter. "I've only been here a few minutes." I fish in my purse and pull out some ones. "Would you mind ordering me a white chocolate latté when you get your wheat germ cappuccino?"

"Sure, Rachel's the youngest. Let her do it," Rachel mimics in a singsong voice. The freckles dotting her round face make the thirty-two-year-old look about nineteen.

"Someday when we're ninety and you're eighty-seven, that's going to sound even more bizarre," Lark says. We all laugh.

Rachel waves my money away. "My treat. This is your birthday do-over, remember?"

When Rachel's back at the table with our drinks, she leans toward me. "Do you know the guy behind the counter?"

I felt my face grow hot. What had he said? "Sort of. What did he say?"

"He asked if you had a coupon. He knew your *name*."

"You should have seen him last night at the soccer meeting," Victoria inserts. "He couldn't keep those gahgeous blue eyes off her."

"Victoria!" I choke on my latté.

While I'm recovering my breath, she tells Rachel and Lark about the soccer meeting.

Lark slaps her hand over her mouth. "That's Daniel Montgomery?" she whispers. "Didn't he leave town after he was expelled, never to be heard from again?"

"Well, technically not 'never to be heard from again' obviously, since he's here now," Rachel says.

Lark leans forward. "Remember that year you had such a big crush on him?"

I groan. "Don't remind me."

"He'd come to school looking like a thundercloud with a black eye and a big bruise on his cheek." Lark glances toward the counter. "He was always spoiling for a fight."

Even though she's probably right, my hackles rise just a little at her assessment of the boy Daniel had been. "Well, who could blame him with an alcoholic dad?"

"Apparently, a lot of people could blame him. He slugged the superintendent's son. Not the sharpest knife in the drawer."

"I remember him now," Victoria says. "The rest of us were half afraid of him, but you were the classic Miss-Fix-It, Allie. Thought you could make everything okay for him."

Once he'd given poor Lee Flanders a bloody lip, I realized that sometimes bad boys were just bad news. "Thankfully I got over that."

"Maybe. Maybe not." Victoria nudges me. "Tell them about your dream."

"Boy, I should have just taken out an ad in the *Shady Grove Sentinel* instead of telling you." I wrinkle my nose at Miss Mouth of the South, but I know what's coming.

Sure enough, Rachel spouts, "Pinky Promise Rule Number 2— No secrets among Pinkies."

I tell them about the dream. When I finish, Lark glances over her shoulder at Daniel and then back to me. "You know, now that he's all grown up, he does kind of look like your Mr. Right to me."

I try to laugh. "It's the eyes that make you think that." Without turning my head, I cut my gaze to the obvious free spirit behind the counter, his brown hair curling at his shirt collar and his denim sleeves rolled up (to reveal amazingly muscular arms for a cameraman/bookstore owner, I might add. *If* I was paying attention to that kind of thing. Which I'm not). I snort. "But hardly. My Mr. Right isn't a Hell's Angel with a start-up business that he has to take a part-time job to support. That blip was just a matter of recent events messing with a perfectly good dream."

Lark shakes her head. "I don't know. It's not just his eyes. He looks like Aragorn Striker from *The Lord of the Rings* to me. Don't you just want to pour your heart out to him and let him fix everything?"

"Um. . .Lark? Did I miss something? Are you or are you not happily married to the best-looking, sweetest guy in the world?"

"Of course I am." To her credit, she doesn't look the slightest bit flustered. "But you're not. We were talking about *your* dream, silly."

Victoria carefully places her dainty espresso cup on the table. "We have something important to discuss, girls."

My three friends share a look that makes me protest. They obviously have a secret from me. How is that fair? "Hey! What happened to rule number 2?"

"We're getting too old for those rules," Victoria says.

"But a minute ago—"

"Never mind, honey. I've got something you have to see."

She digs around in her purse and pulls out some kind of form, then smoothes it out on the table and pushes it toward me.

I read in silence as all three of them watch me. *"Shady Grove Pre-Centennial Celebration Beautiful Town Landscaping Contest: Help us make Shady Grove the most beautiful little hometown in America."* Farther down on the page, I see the first blank. LANDSCAPING COMPANY NAME. "Y'all, this is for already established companies. I can't do this."

"You remember how Granny said you spell can't," Lark reminds me. "C-A-N-if-I-want-to." Lark's grandmother had died a couple of years ago at the age of ninety-three, but up to the very end, she'd been a fount of wisdom that all four of us depended on. "You can *if* you want to."

My stomach feels like I just stepped off the Tilt-a-Whirl as I read further down. *"All entrants will draw out landscaping plans for the city park, city hall, and the library. Three proposals will be chosen as finalists. Each finalist team will be assigned an area. A small budget will be provided for materials. Entrant will be allowed to contribute* *up to $1000.00 for additional materials and supplies if desired. Payroll will be entrant's responsibility. The grand prize—$7500.00 cash, a new truck with custom company logo, and the city landscaping/ maintenance contract for the next year. Second place—$1000.00. Third place—$500.00."*

A new truck? Cash enough to pay off the hospital and have money left over? With the upcoming celebration, winning would be enough publicity to launch a business. Are these people reading my wish list? "I don't *have* a landscaping company. What about employees? How would I come up with the money to hire them?"

Lark salutes. "Your first full-time employee reporting for duty. And I don't want any money." She winks. "Your eternal gratitude will be enough for me."

"I'll help out on my day off," Rachel offers. "Same pay as Lark."

"I'll do payroll and handle all the tax forms." Sometimes it's easy to forget Victoria's accounting degree, but besides her mother's elegance, she also inherited her father's shrewd head for business. "And for you, dahling, I'll even work outside, as long as I don't have to get dirt in my manicure." Victoria arches an elegant eyebrow at Lark. "Maybe not full-time, exactly. But as much as I can. Eternal gratitude is good enough for me, too. With the three of us working for free, maybe you can hire at least one other person and still come up with the money for extra materials."

Not unless I use almost all of my severance money. But I'm blown away by their loving support. "You guys. . .this is too much."

"It'll be fun," Rachel says.

Victoria grimaces. "We can stand anything for a month."

They laugh, and I latch on to something to distract me from the terror that is welling up inside me. "Look at this small print. By signing below, I agree to cooperate with and be available for publicity appearances for Channel Six to be used as they deem necessary. What do you think that means?"

"Who knows? Maybe they're going to do a TV ad featuring the three winners." Victoria strikes a pose. "Your shot at stardom, dahling."

"We'll go with you to get something new to wear," Lark assures me.

Rachel taps her finger on her lip. "I think that's just standard contractese when you're dealing with the media."

I look up at their hopeful expressions. "So all I have to do is submit a landscaping plan for these three areas?"

Lark hits her fist on the table. "Girls, I think she finally gets it!"

"Do you really think I can do it?" It's been so long since I've truly believed in unlimited possibilities, I hardly know where to begin.

Rachel touches my arm. "You're going to be the best landscaper Shady Grove has ever seen."

Lark holds up her cappuccino. "Hear, hear."

Victoria raises her tiny espresso glass, as well. "TLC Landscaping is born."

My eyes mist over slightly. Good friends are hard to come by, but I've got three of the best. The hopelessness of the last few days falls away from me like a caterpillar's cocoon. A grin spreads across my face. I'm ready to fly. Until I see one more thing. "The deadline is tomorrow!"

"True." Victoria waves one hand dismissively. "You have a

hundred plans already done. Just drive out to the three places in the morning and modify them to fit. We're talking about Shady Grove—you already know the layout of these places."

"Besides. . ." Rachel shoots me an encouraging grin. "You won't have nearly as long to wait this way. In two weeks you'll know if you make it to the finals."

My stomach is churning up the latté. I should forget this nonsense and get a job, but if God gave me this opportunity, do I really want to throw it away?

"Did we do a better job on your birthday this time?" Lark taps the entry form and teases.

"Speaking of Allie's birthday. . ." Rachel raises her hand toward the counter.

I freeze, but the hairs on the back of my neck stand up as all three of my friends stare over my shoulder at the person responding to Rachel's signal. I don't look but I know. Could it be anyone else?

# eight

"I would sing to you, but I'm not doing very well at communicating these days, I'm afraid." The deep baritone voice behind me makes me jump, even though I'm expecting it. Sure enough, Daniel slides a plate onto the table in front of me. A sunshine muffin with a red candle. He produces a tiny box of matches and leans in to light the wick. I catch a whiff of his clean scent, like a crisp breeze off the ocean.

"Shh. . .," he whispers in my ear. "Don't tell the fire chief. I'm not sure this is within code."

I nod, speechless.

The flame jumps to life and he straightens. "Happy birthday, Allie."

"Thank you," I croak. How does he make me feel that way? Security is supposed to be my aphrodisiac these days. And he is far from safe.

My friends launch into a rousing round of "Happy Birthday," and in spite of his earlier protests about singing, Daniel joins in. When they finish, Lark says, "Make a wish," and cuts her gaze at

Daniel in what she probably thinks is a *subtle* hint to me. For a split second I hope he doesn't see her, but by his grin I can tell he does. For the first time I notice a small dimple in his cheek. Did he have that in school? Probably, but he never smiled enough for anyone to know it.

I squeeze my eyes shut.

"You get three and a half wishes. One for each decade," Victoria calls. Three and a half wishes, huh? I blow out the candle, and while they're clapping, I wish that TLC Landscaping will become reality, that I'll meet some nice Christian businessman who brings home a comfortable salary and loves kids, that my own kids will quit fighting, and for the half, that I'll never give another thought to the Harley-driving-bad-boy-turned-respectable-man standing beside me.

Daniel excuses himself to go back to work, and once he's gone, all three of my friends start talking at once. "You still think he's not Mr. Right?" Lark demands.

"Honey, you could almost see the sparks. And I don't mean from the candle," Victoria drawls.

Rachel's smile is wistful. "Did you see how he looked at her?"

"Wait a minute, y'all. Just because I had a crush on him when I was a kid. . . In case you didn't notice, we're both grown up now, and I don't even know him."

Victoria puts her hand on my arm. "Maybe you should remedy that."

I shake my head and lower my voice. "Stop it. If I ever end up with a man again, he has to be stable and settled. Daniel is obviously not those things."

"Hey. He has his own business and works a part-time job to

boot. What more could you ask for?" Lark is obviously staring at him, and I just hope he isn't looking this way.

I can't help it. I glance over at him. He's innocently wiping the counter, hopefully unaware that four women are discussing his finer points. "A nice Christian man settled enough that he won't need life insurance, but smart enough to have it anyway? That about covers it."

"Well, if that's all. Maybe he found the Lord and has life insurance, let's just ask him." Victoria starts to get up, but I grab her sleeve.

"Sit down," I growl. "It's a concept, not a checklist item. He's not my type. The end."

"Like Granny always said, 'Don't close a door until you know for sure you can fit through the window,'" Lark says.

"Uh-huh. Your granny also said, 'Be clear about what you want. And then make it happen.'" I smile to take the sting out of the words. "That's what I'm doing, so let's forget about Daniel, okay? Even if you do think he looks like a movie star."

"You know? I kind of think Lark is right. Especially with that knife scar, he reminds me of Aragorn, too." Victoria gives me a teasing grin.

"Did Aragorn have a scar?" Lark asks.

"Oh, I don't know." Victoria seems to consider it for a minute.

"Either way, he definitely has a reluctant hero air about him." Lark sips her drink. "Do you really think that's a knife scar?"

Victoria nods. "Based on the way he left Shady Grove? Definitely."

"He could have slipped and fallen on a piece of glass after he left here, for all you know," I burst out, unable to hide my exasperation. "End. Of. Subject. Please."

Rachel speaks up. "Allie, do you have an idea for the landscape plan?"

I mouth a "thanks" to her. "As a matter of fact, I do." I snatch a napkin from the shiny rectangular dispenser in the middle of the table and grab a pen from my purse. For the next few minutes, I bore them with a combination of my designs, but at least it effectively changes the subject.

"Don't make it too complicated, dahling," Victoria drawls. "Remember the experience level of your crew."

Lark elbows her. "You've got this contest in the bag, Allie-girl."

"Well, that's a given," Victoria says, throwing a mock-hurt look at Lark. "I thought we all knew that."

"Those judges aren't going to know what hit them when they see your design," Rachel adds.

With the spirit of celebration in the air, for about five minutes I believe them.

# nine

With the contest results about to be posted on the front door of the Channel Six building, the faith I had the night the Pinkies gave me the application is nowhere to be found.

"Nervous?" Rachel asks from the backseat.

I hate to admit that I even think there's a chance I'll win, but I guess if I didn't, my stomach wouldn't be fluttering. "A little." I slouch down in the driver's seat of my SUV and pull my baseball cap lower over my eyes.

Lark snorts. "Only because Victoria keeps calling over and over."

I can't help but laugh. "You'd be the same way if you were at home."

A rueful grin flits across her face. "True."

"I can't believe I let y'all talk me into this," I mutter. "I should have waited to hear the winners on TV." I'm torn between a desire to leave and a morbid need to know who the finalists are.

"And miss this excitement?" Rachel leans up between us and peers at the parking lot, filled with landscaping trucks.

"Look at all those company vehicles. I stand out like a sore thumb." Even if I were to final, all I could do is slap a vinyl sign on the side of my SUV and pull my dad's old trailer behind it loaded with my equipment. What was I thinking?

"Make that a green thumb," Lark says with a grin.

I groan. "That was corny even for you."

"You're going to win," Rachel says for the twentieth time. "I just know it."

"So have you seen Daniel Montgomery lately?" Lark asks.

Even though I recognize the distraction technique, I let her get away with it. What are friends for, if not to distract you when you need it?

Since the night at his coffee shop, I'd actually only seen him once, for sure, at soccer practice on the opposite side of the field. Two different services, I thought I caught a glimpse of him across the church building, but it might not have been him. Could have just been wishful thinking. "Just a few times from a distance, not bad considering I was running into him daily for a while."

"And this is a positive thing. . .how?" Lark asks.

"Oh, hush." If I were being honest with myself, I'd admit that I am a little disappointed that our unexpected meetings have slowed. I don't believe in lying to anyone else, but I figure if I can fool myself, more power to me.

"I think your luck, good or bad, has just turned," Rachel whispers.

Our windows are down, but no one can hear us, so I'm not sure why she's whispering. Maybe my baseball cap and sunglasses are making her get into the undercover frame of mind.

I sit up a little straighter as I recognize Blair Winchester with a sheet of paper in her hand. She waves royally at the small group of people gathered around and smiles at a man traipsing along behind her with a camera on his shoulder. Suddenly I see what Rachel meant. The man behind the camera is none other than Daniel Montgomery.

He pans the crowd, and I pull my baseball cap lower over my sunglasses and slouch down again. "Of all the places I've run into him, this has got to be the worst. Why the camera?"

"Who knows? Don't you ever get the feeling that every second of Blair's existence is filmed for posterity?" Rachel asks as Blair posts the sheet on the glass.

Lark pseudo-shudders. "Just think. Someday they could have enough footage to devote a whole cable station to her. Blair Winchester, 24/7."

"Don't even tease about something like that," I say, barely aware of my words as I watch Daniel steadily taping as the mostly male audience push and shove to see the white paper. Most turn away, shoulders rounded, heads down, but a few high-five each other, and I hear at least one loud *whoop*.

Blair and Daniel break away from the group and start across the parking lot. "What are they doing?" I grab Lark's shoulder.

"They're coming over here," she says, her voice incredulous.

I fumble with the key, but before I can slide it into the ignition, Blair sticks her microphone in my driver's side window. "So, Allie Richards, tell us how it is that in just two weeks you went from unemployed single mom to the owner of a landscaping company?"

I blink at her and at the camera lens behind her. Panic closes off my windpipe, and for a second I see black spots in front of my eyes. She's doing a loser segment and picked me to be the star. And of course I signed that stupid publicity agreement. Doesn't that just figure?

*Deep breaths, Allie. Never let them see you sweat.* Lark's granny always said that, and even though I think she got it off a deodorant commercial, it works. The last thing I want is to give Blair the satisfaction of watching me squirm. I take my sunglasses off and meet her gaze, grateful that I can't see Daniel behind the camera. "I—I used to work in landscaping, and I loved it. Landscape design is fun for me, and I enjoy the physical challenge of doing the actual labor, too. When my friends told me about the contest, I decided to enter." Lame, lame, lame, but true, at least.

"So you don't actually have a crew. . . ."

"I have people who are available to work with me." I keep my shoulders back and my head held high. Time to wallow later. Right now, I need to get rid of Blair and her shadow.

"People available to work with you?" Blair mimics me into the microphone. Then she motions toward Rachel and Lark. "Did your friends here sign on as part of your TLC Landscaping crew?"

Speechless at her nerve, I nod.

Blair turns back to face the camera, her smile splitting her heavy on-camera makeup. "Doesn't this sound like fun? TLC Landscaping will be competing as a finalist in this contest with a rookie crew. And a Channel Six cameraman will be shadowing them and the other teams. Yours truly will bring you a clip of the progress—unrehearsed, unscripted for your viewing pleasure. So be sure and tune in every weekday morning to our new "Get Real, Shady Grove" segment of *Wake Up, Shady Grove*."

Lark grabs my arm and murmurs, "She's saying you're a finalist."

"That's something positive," Rachel whispers weakly from the backseat. In the rearview mirror, I can see her freckles standing out against her white face. But my own reflection is even paler. Maybe I'll pass out and not have to endure further humiliation.

"Congratulations, Allie, to you and the rest of your crew." Blair makes air quotes around the word *crew* and gives the camera another too-good-to-be-true smile. "We'll look forward to seeing you again really soon."

And just like that, Blair is gone, wagging her cameraman behind her and leaving my mind splintered by her revelations— too many, too fast, too unbelievable.

"Want me to drive?" Lark speaks into the unnatural stillness.

I shake my head and start the engine just as my cell phone rings.

Lark doesn't even ask me, she just picks it up and speaks into it in hushed tones. "Yes. No. Not exactly."

In a split second I make a decision. I'm not a victim. I'm a winner. God has given me a huge blessing. And neither Blair nor Daniel is going to take that from me. "Put her on speaker, Lark."

Lark cups her hand around the phone. "She says to put you on speaker."

I take the phone from her with my free hand and hit the speaker button.

"No, I—"

"Hey, Vic. We won."

"Hi, Allie. I saw that. Great job!" Talk about forced.

"What do you mean you saw it?" Rachel asks.

71

My heart pounds as I realize exactly what Victoria is talking about. "It was live, wasn't it?"

"You were great."

"Please don't lie on my account. I know it was awful." I laugh and thump the steering wheel. "But whoo-hoo! We just made our television debut, girls. The worst is definitely over."

"You okay, Allie?" Rachel is straining against her seatbelt. If she could reach me, no doubt she'd put her hand on my forehead.

"No worries, doc. I'm just following your advice and thinking positive." I mean it, but in the mirror, I see the doubt in her eyes.

"Oh, Victoria," I call in the direction of the phone. "One thing you couldn't see. Guess who's going to be following us around with a camera?"

"Tell me it's not Daniel Montgomery."

"None other than our old friend." Attitude is an amazing thing. Of course, I may just be in denial, but it sure is fun. "He sure didn't turn the camera off while Blair was humiliating me in front of the whole Channel Six viewing area, so I'm guessing that innocence in his eyes may be an act."

We pull up to a stoplight, and Lark reaches over and flips up my sunglasses. I obligingly shove them up on my head. "What?"

"Speaking of eyes, I wanted to see yours."

I glance over at her. "I'm really okay. This is something to celebrate."

"Last time you talked to us in this tone you were explaining how glad you were to get the job at Coble's and have a place to live in your mother's carriage house."

I accelerate. "I guess you'll just have to wait and see then. I couldn't be happier."

"Not even if Daniel weren't involved?" Rachel knows me too well.

"Okay, I admit I'd be happier if Daniel weren't involved, but the truth is, it's probably for the best. This just proves what I told y'all at Coffee Central the other night. He's definitely not the man for me."

"Speaking of the man for you," Victoria's voice comes through the speakerphone. "Guess who I ran into at the country club this week?"

"Who?" I'm almost afraid to ask, but surely Daniel doesn't hang out at the country club.

"Trevor Wright."

"Trevor Wright? The president of United Greetings?" Lark asks.

One of Shady Grove's biggest industries is the greeting card factory on the outside of town. A month or so ago, I'd worked closely with the president when he was personally choosing the plants at Coble's for their new landscaping project. He was nice, if overly meticulous.

"The one and only," Victoria drawls through the speaker. "He's way too boring for me, but he's you're Mr. Right with a capital R."

From the corner of my eye, I see Rachel lean forward to talk to the speakerphone. "Or maybe you should say Mr. Wright, with a capital W."

"How cool is that, Allie? After all this talk, Victoria found your Mr. Right at the country club. We just didn't know where to look."

Lark and Rachel high-five and Victoria laughs.

"Very funny, guys. What makes Trevor so perfect for me, Victoria? Is he a nice Christian man with life insurance?"

"He was at the club heading up a fund-raiser for the new hospital wing. And from the look of his suit, he's not doing too shabby in the income department."

"A good Samaritan and successful," Lark muses. "Daniel slash Aragorn might have a run for his money."

"You guys are crazy." While he was stopping by my office all the time, Lark and Victoria had always insisted that Trevor wanted a more personal relationship, but I didn't see it.

"He asked about you," Victoria says, glee evident in her voice.

"Wow, Allie. Look at you. You turn thirty-five, and suddenly you have two men in hot pursuit and a promising new career." Lark flips the passenger side mirror down and examines her face. "When I turned thirty-five back in January, all I got were a few extra wrinkles."

Hot pursuit? My love life must be worse than I thought if this is considered hot pursuit by my closest friends.

"Yeah, right, Lark." Victoria snorts. "Your face is as smooth as it was when you were fifteen. Gotta go, y'all. Dylan's trying to get the mower started, and if I don't help him Mother will send her butler over to do it. Congratulations again, Allie."

"Thanks." Victoria lives in a smaller house next to her parents, too, but where my mother just butts in on her own, the Worthingtons use servants. Since Victoria's trying to teach Dylan responsibility, it's a constant battle.

"Bye," we chorus and Lark hits the END button.

At least with Victoria's call, I'm forewarned about the live broadcast when I go to Mama's to pick up the girls.

"We saw you on TV with Aunt Lark and Aunt Rachel!" Katie screams. Just for the record, we didn't do this on purpose. My girls and Victoria's Dylan calling the Pinkies "aunt" is not some anti-family/pro-friends movement. I think maybe it's a Southern thing. Not to be confused with kids calling their mama's current boyfriend "uncle," of course.

"With that woman," Mama adds, the tightness of her mouth attesting to the fact that she hasn't forgotten Blair's betrayal of Adam, either.

She and Miranda run to me, with Mama right behind them. I grab them all into one tight hug. "Yep, I'm a finalist."

"Way to go," Mama whispers into my hair. "I'm so proud of you."

"Thanks." I release them and smile. "Now the hard work begins."

"Yes, it does," Mama says, "and I've been thinking. . . ."

Uh-oh. I recognize that tone. If I were an *Enterprise* spaceship, I'd be on red alert.

# ten

Sure enough, as soon as the girls go outside to play, Mama pours both of us a cup of coffee. Holding hers, she sinks onto the sofa and pats the cushion beside her.

I slip off my sandals and tuck my feet up under me. When we're both comfy, she raises an eyebrow. "Have you figured out who all you're going to hire?"

I tell her about the Pinkies volunteering to work for free.

"Have you thought about your brother?"

Why wouldn't I think about my brother? I pray for him every night, see him most every day, and he's my only sibling. But that's definitely not what she means. I'm almost afraid to ask. I blow on my coffee to avoid looking at her. "What about him?"

"He might like to be asked to help you."

"Adam?"

"Lands sakes, Allie, how many brothers do you have?"

"You think I should hire Adam." I know I'm stalling, but I also know my brother. He might work a few days in a row *if* he doesn't have to get up too early.

"He's perfect for the job, Allie," Mama says. "I think it might be just what he needs to get him going again."

By "going again" she means back to "shining star" status. Fresh out of college and full of ambition three years ago, Adam and his best friend, Zach, started up a dotcom computer business. Adam was the brains, but once the business was on its feet, Zach managed to dupe my trusting brother out of his share. Adam got a lawyer, but Zach had managed to make it all legal. As soon as it became evident that the money was gone, so was Blair. When we lost our dad to a sudden heart attack six months later, Adam seemed to lose any ambition he'd ever had to get back his company. . .or do much of anything.

Last we heard, Zach was living it up in Las Vegas while Adam is living it down in Shady Grove, playing video games and sleeping in his childhood room. And in spite of my mother's eternal hopefulness, I don't see working for his sister under the constant scrutiny of his ex-girlfriend and all of Shady Grove as a big step up from the odds and ends jobs he does right now. "I couldn't pay a penny over minimum wage. What makes you think he'd even want the job?"

Silence. But the guilt on her face speaks louder than words.

"You already asked him?"

She sighed. "I did mention it."

"And he knows about Blair?"

I watched her consciously smooth out the frown. "I think he realizes he had a lucky escape there. He doesn't hold grudges." She pats my leg. "You and I could learn a lesson from him on that. Might make this whole contest thing a lot easier for you."

"I know, Mama. I'm trying."

"Well, anyway, Adam would love to help you."

I rest my head against the overstuffed cushion and think. I'm staking all of my future on this contest. If I'm going to use my severance to pay an employee, I need to try to find someone with landscaping experience. Or at least someone who'll show up on time every day. I slowly shake my head, bracing myself. "I'd love to help, but I don't see it working." I don't see *him* working is more like it, but I'm trying to use a little tact here.

Apparently Mama has no such reserve. "Do you ever think about what it was like for your brother? Not only was he cheated out of his financial security, he was cheated by his best friend. And humiliated in front of the whole town. Then losing his dad. No wonder he couldn't get motivated again."

Now wait a minute. My life hasn't exactly been a bowl of ice cream. Unless we're talking about Rocky Road. "Everybody has bad things happen, Mama. Sometimes you just have to go on."

She takes a sip of her coffee and seems to consider what she's going to say. "We all know you had a terrible time, Allie. And you pulled yourself up out of it. But you know what? You had the girls to motivate you. After both Jon's death and your dad's. And as far as that goes, maybe it's time you quit thinking that if you work hard enough you can make the perfect life for you and the girls. You're almost as bad as Adam, only in the opposite way. Both of you are going to have to start trusting more in the Lord."

And the new record for bluntness goes to. . .

"I trust God." For the most part. I do. But experience has taught me that the more control I have over things, the better off I am. Is that wrong?

"I know you do, sweetie. To a point. I'm just praying you'll be able to let go of this dream of perfection and actually live the life He gives you." She reaches over and takes my free hand with hers. "About Adam. . .you don't have to hire him." She grins. "But if you do, I'll watch the girls for you every day after school and weekends."

Well, there you go. The girls. My motivation again. Not that I needed an extra push after that speech from Mama. Guilt is a good motivator, too. "Of course I'll hire him, Mama. I just hope he'll show up and work."

"He will." Spoken with the confidence of a mother. "So, tell me about the contest." The excitement sparkling in her eyes ignites my own. In spite of all the hoopla at the station and the dread of being on TV, I *am* excited.

"Each team was assigned a different place in town to landscape. They gave us the Main Street Park."

"Oh, that'll be a walk down memory lane, won't it?"

Will it ever. No telling how many hours we spent playing there when we were little. Adam and I shared a love of swinging. When we were on the swings, both determined to touch the sky, the age difference fell away. "Yeah, that's what I was thinking, too. It'll be fun to see it shape up again, and it's probably the easiest in terms of layout, but it's definitely the biggest job."

"Have you scheduled a planning session?"

A planning session. I love my mother, but I can feel the reins slipping from my hands like they're coated in butter. "Not yet."

"Call the Pinkies and tell them we'll meet here tonight." She jumped up, and I promise she rubbed her hands together. "You just bring the plans, and I'll take care of the refreshments."

I think she takes the shock on my face for uncertainty, because she actually pushes me toward the door. "Run on home and get your stuff together. Call your friends. Adam and I'll see you all at seven."

The whirlwind that is my mother drops a peck on my cheek, and I find myself on the doorstep, exhausted, yet strangely hopeful. At least I have warm bodies to fill the slots and take up space on the video.

How do people make it without friends and family? As I roll my landscaping plan out on my mother's table, Rachel, Victoria, Adam, Mama, Katie, Miranda, Lark, and Craig gather around and give me their full attention. I'm sure not one of them cares much about landscaping. But they all care about me. As far as I'm concerned, that makes them the perfect team.

What they lack in experience, they make up for in enthusiasm, with the possible exception of Adam, who isn't saying much. I motion to the plan. "The first thing we'll work on is the wall on the east side. I'll have the rocks delivered the Monday we start."

"Rocks?" The first emotion Adam has shown since we started the meeting, and it's not necessarily a positive one. He claps one hand on Rachel's shoulder and the other on Victoria's. "Hope you ladies have strong backs."

Rachel laughs. "I only work on Thursdays."

"I'm allergic to working on Mondays. I break out in hives," Victoria jokes.

Adam raises an eyebrow at Lark and Mama. "Well, since Vicky's apparently worried about breaking a nail, it looks like it's up to us. Ready to work on the chain gang?"

Victoria sticks out her tongue at my little brother and the sight is so inconsistent with her elegant demeanor that I bite back a smile. Even though her mother would croak if she knew it, we all shorten Victoria's name to "Vic" now and then, but only Adam calls her "Vicky." He's done it ever since I can remember, especially when he wants to irritate her.

"I think a rock wall sounds lovely," Mama says, her smile growing even broader.

"It's not very big," I put my finger on the plan. "We should be able to do it in a day."

Adam mutters something. I think it's "Dream on," but I ignore it.

"As soon as we get this built, we'll move on to planting. Adam, it'll be your responsibility to pick up the plants we need each day. Without a secure place to store them, we're better off to buy our plants and supplies as we go." I level a look at my brother. "Does that sound okay to you?" Like younger brothers everywhere, he never could stand to take orders from his big sister.

He shrugs, with no evidence of rising hackles. "Since I've got the truck, that makes sense, I guess."

"Miranda and Katie, you'll both be helping on Saturdays, right?"

They nod, their faces shining. Some weeks go by where it seems like I can't make any right parenting decisions, but including my girls tonight was a good move.

"Lark, you sure you're okay with working full-time during the contest?"

She nods. "I'm in."

"I can help on Saturdays if you need me," Craig offers. When Lark got married, I was afraid that it might mess up the dynamics of our Pinky group, but Craig is a true prince.

"Thanks a million, Craig. Adam, you, Lark, and I will be full-time. Victoria, you're going to just come by and help when you can, right?"

Victoria's face reddens. "That's right, but you can count on me for the first day, too. I was teasing about Mondays."

"In that case, I was teasing about you being afraid to break a nail." Adam deadpans and everyone, even Victoria, laughs.

"Have I told y'all lately how much I appreciate this?" Win or lose, I'm already overwhelmed by their support.

"You have, but we never get tired of hearing it," Rachel says, her eyes twinkling.

"Yeah, according to a quiz I took in *Today's Woman* magazine, I thrive on praise," Lark adds.

"Really?" Adam leans against the table and pushes his cap up on his head. "According to a quiz in *Today's Man* magazine, I thrive on Oreos."

Lark yanks off Adam's cap and tries to hit him on the head with it. But he ducks and grabs Victoria to hold in front of him like a human shield. She squeals and wiggles out of his grip.

I hope they can translate this camaraderie into a solid working relationship.

When the laughter dies down, I roll up the design plan. "Okay, we have two weeks to get ready, and then we'll have four weeks to do the job. The judging is six weeks from today."

"Any chance we could start early?" Miranda asks.

Everyone laughs and her face reddens.

"Hey, don't feel bad, kiddo. I asked the same thing," Lark says. "But your mom says the rules are the rules."

I nod. "They're strict about that, but don't worry, we'll have time to get it done. I just need to iron out a few more details, do a little more studying, then we'll be ready."

"Go team," Adam says, waving an imaginary pom-pom.

When we break up, Adam hangs back to walk with me to the door. "Got any books I can borrow?"

Where did this come from? "Books?" I'm mentally scanning my bookshelf for something that might entertain a guy who never reads anything besides computer books and video game magazines.

"You know, something like *Landscaping for Dummies?*"

"Oh, sure." Okay, I'm not the only one making good parenting choices today. I guess Mama was right about me hiring him. Who knows? Now that we're all grown up, maybe we can rediscover the brother/sister bond from our days on the swings.

# eleven

Why do all roads seem to lead to Daniel? No place else in town will have books on landscaping, and mine aren't for beginners. After we leave Mama's, I murmur to the girls something about an errand in town and turn onto the highway instead of heading back to the carriage house. Thankfully, they're too busy discussing their work duties to ask any questions. Only when I cruise the parking lot of Coffee Central and make sure a certain Harley is nowhere to be seen do I ask, "Y'all want to check out the new bookstore?"

I need some down time to explore this want-to-see/don't-want-to-see thing I've got going with Daniel. Maybe after the contest is over. But for now, all I know is he was the one holding that camera steady while Blair humiliated me. Besides, I have to focus on the job at hand.

A few minutes later, the girls are happily ensconced in the kids' section, and I take a shortcut through the coffee area to get to the landscaping books. The rapid clicking of a laptop keyboard draws my attention to a man at a corner table. At the exact second I realize it's Daniel, he looks up, his deep blue eyes slightly unfocused, his hair standing on end.

"Allie," he says slowly.

"I didn't see your motorcycle," I blurt out, then cover my mouth with my hand. Too late. His eyes are focused now and he definitely caught my faux pas.

A half smile twists his lips. "I should have known. You only stopped because you thought I wasn't here?"

I should have just been rude and walked on by in the first place. "I came by to get some landscaping books. You being here is a non-issue as far as I'm concerned."

He waves toward the parking lot. "Then how was it you noticed my motorcycle wasn't here?"

I shift from one foot to the other but can't think of a good answer, so I change the subject. "I just have to know. Do you have hidden cameras here, capturing my book shopping for Shady Grove's viewing enjoyment?"

He has the nerve to look hurt. "Let's get something straight, Allie. Working at Channel Six is just a job. Something I do to support my habit."

"Your habit?"

"Yeah. Eating."

"Very funny. Do you moonlight as a standup comedian?" I start to brush past him, but he touches my sleeve, his eyes full of apology.

"I'm sorry. Look, can we start over? Sit down and let's talk for a minute."

I nod toward the laptop. "I don't want to interrupt you."

He shakes his head. "I needed a break, anyway." He motions toward the empty chair. "Please sit down?"

I fully intend to say no, but curiosity, if nothing else, makes me slide into the chair. "What are you working on?"

"What makes you think I wasn't just playing a game of Free Cell?" He rubs his hand over his hair in a futile attempt to tame it. Not that it needs taming really. The mad scientist look actually isn't a bad one on him.

"Were you?"

"No."

"Fine." I cross my arms in front of me. "Be mysterious." Why did he ask me to sit down if he didn't want to talk?

His laugh is like his voice, not booming but deep, and as bad as I hate to admit it, very pleasant. "Unfortunately there's nothing mysterious about a man in his thirties trying to write the great American novel. It's so cliché, it's embarrassing."

A Harley-driving cameraman who owns a coffee shop/bookstore. Why am I surprised that he writes? "You're an author?"

"An aspiring one."

"And you're writing a novel?"

"Three-fourths of the way done."

"Are you going to try to sell it?"

His face reddens. "I've sent it out to several agents and a few publishers, but so far nothing but rejections."

That figures. But far be it for me not to encourage someone to follow their dream. However impossible it might be. I mean, look at me. "Congratulations on having the guts to send it out."

His smile lights up his eyes. "You're the one who deserves congratulations. For making it to the finals in the contest."

"Thanks. I'm not all that thrilled with the idea of being on TV, but this seemed like a second chance to have my own landscaping company, after. . ." *This man is on Blair's side, Allie. Why are you spilling your guts to him?* I clamp my lips together.

"After the bank didn't know a good thing when they saw it?"

"You might say that. Thanks." I push to my feet. "I'd better run. I need to get those books."

"Can we be friends?" Will I ever get used to his habit of getting right to the point? Probably not, since I intend to limit my exposure to him as much as possible.

"I don't see how that would work while you're following me around with a camera."

"You might be surprised. Think of it this way, if it weren't for Channel Six wanting to do this reality show bit, they probably wouldn't have even had the contest, then you wouldn't get a chance to show everyone how good you are at what you do."

"Very good. Did you memorize that from some of Blair's propaganda? Or did you just make it up as you went along?" Along the same lines as crying when I'm angry, I have some fairly good comebacks, but when I make one, I feel awful. Kind of takes the fun right out it. I bite my tongue to keep from apologizing, but he just grins.

"I made it up. But it's true, and deep down you know it. So why not just try to be friends? If nothing else, it would make this whole thing so much easier for both of us."

I don't want to admit it, but what he says makes sense. And when I look into his eyes, I can't think of any other answer. "I don't see what it would hurt to be friends."

My idea of "friends" and Daniel's are obviously very different. I envisioned us speaking civilly to each other, sharing a laugh now and then. And nodding when we passed each other on the street. But twice this week he's asked me to go out for a "friendly" dinner. Here in Shady Grove we call that a date, and so far I've refused politely. But I'm afraid he's wearing me down.

I've worked so hard preparing for the contest that everything is ready to go with still a week before the start date. Katie and Miranda are in Branson with my in-laws for the weekend, Mama's at a church retreat, Lark and Craig are having some couple time, and Rachel's working a health fair. Even Adam isn't home tonight. Victoria invited me to join her family for a dinner party, but I declined.

When the phone rings, I pray it's not him, but a quick glance at the caller ID says otherwise.

He chats for a minute, then asks me if I've eaten. "I hear the new Mexican place is really good."

"How did you know I love Mexican food?" Are my friends supplying him with secret info to use against me?

"Who doesn't?"

I can think of several people, but I'm overly suspicious where he's concerned, so why argue? Especially since I'm starving. "That sounds great. I'll meet you there. What time?"

"Seven sounds good. Sure you don't want me to pick you up? I'll drive the truck."

I think about it for about five seconds, imagining myself riding next to him in his truck and then him walking me to my front door at the end of the evening. My heart thuds against my ribcage just imagining it. That kind of stress is the last thing I need. We're going out as friends, remember? "I'm sure. See you there."

# twelve

Whenever I'm stressed, Katie always does this thing she calls Day Spa. She spreads towels across the foot of my bed and gets a big bowl of hot water, then insists I lie down with cucumber slices on my eyes. There's even a certain CD she uses with the sound of the lake lapping on the shore intermingled with soothing music and nature sounds.

She wraps my feet in hot cloths, and then massages them with lotion. Finally she washes them with the hot water again. Even though I have to force myself to go along with it when I'm busy, I never regret it.

Last time we were playing Day Spa, she spoke up softly from the foot of the bed. "So, do you think I should work as a massage therapist full-time? Or could I be a dog groomer half the time? You know how much I love dogs."

Under the cucumber slices, tears pricked at my eyes. Where had the years gone? What happened to my baby whose only concern centered around the color of her Popsicle?

Thinking of it now, a week later, with both of my girls miles away, tears threaten again. They're growing up so fast. And I've come to depend on them more than I realize. How will I know what to wear without Miranda to help me pick it out?

I stand in the closet for ten minutes before I finally snort with disgust. "This. Is. Not. A. Date. Therefore, it makes no difference what I wear." To prove my point, I grab the first blouse and pair of jeans I see and throw them on. I start to skip my jewelry box, but then I realize that even if I were going out with the Pinkies, I'd wear earrings, at least, so I stick in the tiny silver hoops my parents got me for college graduation. I pull my hair up in a scrunchie and stick out my tongue at my reflection. Let Daniel Montgomery try to make a date out of dinner with me in a ponytail.

All of my protestations do nothing to make me less nervous. Neither does driving myself. By the time I walk into the adobe-shaped stucco building, my nerves are outjangling the Mexican music blaring over the loudspeaker. Daniel, in jeans and a polo shirt, waits by the fountain inside the foyer.

"Allie. Good to see you." He comes forward and takes my hands in his, then drops a quick kiss on my cheek.

Very cosmopolitan. But I'm just a plain old country girl, and with him that close, my pulse jumps to stroke level. I do notice he still smells like the ocean. Maybe I should ditch the whole "let's be friends" idea and just find out what brand of soap he uses and buy some.

While I'm contemplating that, a dark-haired maitre d' motions us to follow him. Daniel puts his hand at the small of my back, very gentlemanly, and guides me to our table in the corner.

"Friends," I whisper, just a gentle reminder to myself.

He leans forward. "What?"

"Nothing." Riding a loud Harley apparently hasn't affected his hearing.

When we're seated in front of a large basket of golden chips and a generous bowl of white cheese dip, he smiles. "I'm glad you came."

"Did you think I was going to stand you up?" I quip, willing myself to relax.

"Nah. Friends don't stand friends up. That's only for dates."

Touché. "True. Have you been stood up a lot?"

He shrugged. "Not really. You?"

"No, but then again, I haven't really dated much in the last several years." Nor do I intend to start right now. Regardless of his crisp smell and blue eyes and. . .oh, why did I ever start this list? So what if he's loaded with good qualities, I know what kind of man I'm looking for, and Daniel isn't it. I just need reminding now and then.

After the waiter takes our order and brings our drinks, Daniel picks up the conversation again.

"How long have you been a widow?"

"Five years."

"I'm sorry."

After five years, you'd think I'd have a good answer to that, but I don't. "Me, too."

"Was your husband a landscaper?"

I smile. "Hardly. He was an intern. He was walking home from the hospital after a twenty-four-hour shift and got hit by a car. Three weeks before graduation."

Sympathy shines in his eyes. "That must have been tough. I imagine when you're married to a med student, it's your whole life, too. You had to have felt like you lost your future as well as your husband."

No one had ever really understood, but that was exactly how I felt. "Yes."

"How did you handle that?"

"It was hard, but I was blessed. My parents had a house on the back of their property for rent, so I moved back here. I found a job fairly quickly, managing a plant nursery. The girls were little then, and they kept my mind occupied."

"And kept your sense of responsibility keenly honed?"

I smile and pick up a chip. "That, too."

We munch in silence for a minute, then I think of something I want to ask him. "How did you come to be a cameraman?"

"Journalism major. I always wanted to write fiction, but journalism was related and made more sense." He raised an eyebrow at me. "Kind of like you taking a job in the office of a plant nursery when you really wanted to do landscaping."

I'm still recovering from his astute observation, when he goes on. "Filmography was fun, so I took several classes in it. By the time I graduated I was working as a cameraman at a local station in Atlanta."

"You went straight to Atlanta when you left here?"

"Straight?" His grin is rueful. "Not much straight about my life back then. But eventually I did find my way. In more ways than one." He shakes his head. "I spent the first sixteen years of my life counting the days until I could get out of Arkansas." He takes a sip of his water while I digest his words. "And the last twenty wishing I could find my way back."

"Why did you want to come back?"

He shrugged. "It's home. Maybe a better question would be why I wanted to leave, which you probably already know."

"Your dad?"

"Yeah. Alcoholic makes it sound so sterile." He grimaces. "I've gotten used to saying that over the last few years. 'My dad is an alcoholic.' But the truth is, he was a mean drunk."

"Daniel, that must have been awful."

"Well, it was worse for my mom and my sister. But when I was seventeen, three things happened—Mom died, my sister got married, and I got kicked out of school."

"So you left?"

"It wasn't quite as simple as that, but for today, that's enough. I left."

My heart aches as I remember the sullen boy I'd known. Trying to protect the women in his life. "You never married?" *Because if there's a wife and six kids waiting for you down in Atlanta, we probably shouldn't go out, even as friends.*

"Nope, never did." He grins. "But I hope to someday."

What do I say to that? That's nice? Watch out for Blair or it may happen sooner than you think? "When did you move back here?"

"Three months ago."

"Your dad died?" I venture a guess.

"Pretty astute, aren't you?" he says.

"That's what I was thinking about you earlier," I shoot back.

"Maybe we just click."

I open my mouth to protest, but before I can speak, he says, "As friends."

"Of course." I try to sound like I never thought he might mean anything else.

With impeccable timing, the swarthy young waiter slides our entrees off his forearm onto the table.

Daniel clears his throat. "Do you mind if I give thanks for the food?"

Now I'm impressed. Maybe that *was* him across the building at church. "Not at all."

He offers a simple but direct prayer, then he samples his fajitas. "Um. . .this place is good."

I nod. "Should have tried it sooner."

"I've been asking you."

Walked right into that one, didn't I? "I didn't mean that." I hold up my hand. "Never mind."

"How did you get into landscaping?" He changes the subject smoothly, and I'm thankful. Straightforward but can be gracious when it's called for. I like that in a ma— friend.

"When I was young, my grandmother would let me help her in the garden." The tango music stops for a song change, and I lean forward to keep the whole restaurant from hearing. "I love the feel of dirt between my fingers."

His dimple flashes. "I promise not to tell a soul."

"I know it sounds strange, but it's true. After my sophomore year in high school, I got a summer job working for a landscaping company. I mowed a lot of grass, installed some shrubs, planted a few flowers, and developed a forever fascination for all things pertaining to landscaping." I take a sip of iced tea to stop the flow of words. Daniel is unbelievably easy to talk to, but I'm still not sure I can trust him.

"How did you get into the design part?"

"I followed the designer around, taking notes and watching

what she did for three years. I planned to get a degree in landscape design. Got an M.R.S. degree instead." The old joke falls glibly off my tongue. How many times had I told people that when Jon was in school? I glance up at Daniel and smile.

He isn't smiling. But the understanding in his eyes hits me in the gut. He's done it again. Read between the lines and picked up on all I didn't say.

I quickly look back down and stab my chimichanga with my knife and cut off a corner. I should have stayed with my first instinct and said no to his invitation. He tears away my defenses, and without them, I'm not at all certain I can survive.

"You okay?"

*Okay? I'm not sure I've been okay since the minute Daniel tapped on my car window in the bank parking lot.* "Fine." I stuff a bite of food in my mouth.

I manage to keep the talk to a minimum the rest of the meal. When the check comes, Daniel deftly slips it from the waiter's fingers.

"I thought we came as friends."

"And I'm the friend who asked you. So it's my treat."

I give in as graciously as I can manage. I couldn't really imagine Daniel Montgomery splitting the tab with me, but I had to try.

We walk out to the parking lot together, and he keeps up an easy chatter. I'm tongue-tied. Why do I feel sixteen again? I thought I'd avoid the whole "Will he try to kiss me?" scenario by meeting him here, but now that we're in the dark alone, it's playing out in my overactive imagination.

"I enjoyed this. Thanks for coming," he says softly when we reach my SUV.

"Thanks for inviting me." My back against the driver's door, I avoid his eyes and fumble with the key fob. The horn blares repeatedly and we both jump. Great. I hit the panic button instead of UNLOCK. I quickly turn it off with a nervous laugh. "I guess I panicked."

"I noticed." He leans toward me.

I hear ocean waves. Does his soap come with sound effects? Oh no, wait. That's the blood pounding in my ears. "What are you doing?"

"Saying good night to a friend." He tucks a loose strand of hair behind my ear. "Nice ponytail."

I open my mouth to say thanks. Before I can speak, his lips touch mine. Just for the barest of a second but long enough for me to know that my heart is not paying any attention to all my Mr. Right mumbo-jumbo. Instead, it's responding way too much to Mr. Daniel Montgomery. "Thanks."

"Anytime."

Heat floods my face. "I meant—"

He grins. "Good night, my friend."

I choke out a "Good night."

As he walks away, I scramble into my SUV, one question resounding through my brain.

*What was I thinking?*

# thirteen

I temporarily solved my problem with Daniel. Maybe it was a coward's way out (Lark's opinion), maybe it was even childish (Victoria's), or maybe it was the only sensible thing to do (good ol' Rachel), but it worked. I've simply avoided him ever since our non-date. Until today.

The day that will go down in history as either the day TLC Landscaping officially began or simply the day Allie Richards tried to build a rock wall with a totally inexperienced crew.

Look at Daniel holding the camera steady in spite of the fact that our wall is falling down. Did I mention that this would also be forever known as the day I got over my ridiculous crush on a man who rides a Harley? As Miranda would say, "He's so yesterday." Just to make sure he gets the point, I shoot him a glare. Too late it hits me that my dirty look has been captured on film for Shady Grove's "viewing pleasure"—a catch phrase that makes my eggs and bacon roil in my stomach.

"Okay, sis," Adam squares off with his back to the camera and speaks in a low tone. "What do you want to do?" He casts a

97

discreet glance at the latest crumbled section of wall. "I'm guessing the mortar mixture was too. . .something."

I nod. Obviously.

Adam and I started early this morning and dug the foundation. While we laid the landscaping fabric and crushed rock for drainage, Victoria and Lark were supposed to follow the instructions on the mortar bag and mix it. I don't know what happened, and I'm not about to ask with the all-seeing eye trained on us.

I glare at Daniel and his camera again. Surely his two hours with us are almost up. Wouldn't want the other teams to feel left out. "We'll deal with that later. Let's just do general cleanup for the next little while." Even *we* can't mess that up.

"Gotcha." Adam trots off to tell Lark and Victoria the new plan. As soon as I'm alone, Daniel turns off the camera and sets it down.

"Couldn't you have cut us some slack?" I sink down on the rock pile. Sweat makes me cranky. And being humiliated on television doesn't help.

He looks miserable, I'll give him that. "I'm sorry, Allie. This is hard, but I have to do the job I'm paid to do."

"I know." I do know, but that doesn't make me like it.

He sits down beside me and pinches the crease in his jeans with his thumb and forefinger. "I even asked the station manager if I could help you during my time off."

I swipe my forehead with the back of my hand and look at him sideways. "You did?"

"He said no way. Since I'm a station employee, it's against the contest rules."

"I figured. But why would you want to do that anyway?

You need to be writing."

"This is just short-term."

"And we need all the help we can get?"

He coughs, but I'm pretty sure it started out as a laugh. "I wanted to help. Let's just leave it at that."

"Okay. Thanks anyway." I motion toward Lark valiantly fighting an overgrown shrub. "Duty calls."

He stands and scoops up the camera. "Yeah, me, too. See you tomorrow." When he's halfway to the station van, he turns back. "Allie."

Since I'm still standing there staring at him, I blush. Hopefully he's too far away to notice. "Yeah?"

"I can't help you, but I can hope you win." He smiles. "And I definitely do."

"Thanks." I'm not sure how he manages to pull it off every time, but he's an expert at changing my mind about him.

I take a few minutes to regain my composure after he's gone, then call everyone over.

"Sorry about the mortar," Lark says.

"It's my fault." Victoria motions to the bag. "I dumped in too much sand by accident."

"I said it would probably be fine." Lark's hair is lank with sweat. "Sorry."

"It's okay, guys." How can I possibly be upset when they're doing this for me out of the goodness of their hearts? "Let's start over."

Two hours later we have a good start on the wall. And it doesn't look like it's going to fall down. My crew is another story.

Victoria blows at a curl that's fallen over her eyes. Finally she gives up and pushes it back with her dirty hand as she sinks to the ground. "Tell me it's time to quit."

Lark plops down beside her. "It's time to quit."

I glance at the cell phone clipped on my belt. Where had the time gone? "I can't believe it."

"Believe it," Adam says, fanning Lark and Victoria with my design plan.

I snatch it away from him. "Okay, thanks again. See you all at eight in the morning?"

Silence.

Finally, Victoria says, "I'll be here."

"Me, too." Lark grunts as she pushes to her feet. "Unless I'm too sore to get out of bed."

"C'mon, don't be an old fuddy-duddy. I'll bring donuts." Adam loves to tease us about our age since we're six years older than he is, but he looks like he could use a hot shower and a good night's rest himself.

"In that case, we'll be here with bells on, right, Lark?" Victoria says.

"Um-hum." Lark leans against Victoria and they hobble toward the vehicles.

"You all right, sis?"

I stop gathering things and look up at my brother. "Me? Sure. Why shouldn't I be?"

"Pretty tough to think about seeing that on TV tomorrow."

"Yeah, well, to quote the quintessential Southern belle, 'Tomorrow is another day.' "

"Good point, Missy Scarlett." He picked up a level and the rest of the tools, and together we loaded them in my SUV. "One thing about you, Al. You're determined, but you still care about other people."

"Shh. . .don't mess up my hard-as-nails image."

"Your secret is safe with me."

At seven the next morning, I drag my aching body out of bed and find out the real truth—my secrets are safe with no one. After watching brief clips of the other two landscaping teams smoothly beginning their projects, I stare at the screen, horror-stricken, as Blair shows an obviously edited clip of our rock wall disaster. The wall falls, and falls, and falls again, within three or four seconds. Then pan to my hard glare at Daniel. And there's a nice shot of Adam and me desperately whispering. Bring in the clowns, folks. The circus has come to town.

Back to Blair in the studio. "It looks like Allie Richards's Tender Loving Care Landscaping is off to a 'rocky' start, folks."

I quit three times before breakfast. I rehearse how I'll tell the station and Blair that there isn't enough money in the world to make this kind of humiliation worth it. Then I start working on finding the words to let Daniel know exactly what I think of his camera skills. I skim over my Bible verse for the day and am screaming at Katie to get out of bed when it hits me. I haven't even prayed this morning. And the truth is I'm in no mood to start now. Which I know is a surefire indication that I should go back into my room and shut the door.

After a few false starts, I croak out the words to my favorite praise song, assuring my Lord that He is more beautiful than diamonds, more precious than gold. By the time I finish the chorus, I'm able to pray. The tears I've held in check since I saw "Get Real, Shady Grove" break loose and pour down my face. "I can't do this without You, Lord. My family needs this, so please help me put my pride away and meet the challenge."

I think about that for a while after I say "Amen." Meeting the challenge. That was the motto for our college yearbook. Until this contest, I've never really given it another thought. But that's what life is all about. What my life has been all about since Jon died. I pray again that I'm up to it.

# fourteen

We're all moving like the tin man after a rainstorm. If my "crew's" muscles ache like mine do, it's no wonder. "Okay, our goal is to get as much done as we can before the TV camera gets here." I refuse to acknowledge Daniel by name. "If he comes about the same time as yesterday, we have less than an hour."

An older woman strides by me in hot pink spandex, her teased hair an odd magenta color, bouncing as she walks.

What is she doing here? The park is roped off. "Excuse me, ma'am?"

She stops and sticks out her hand. "Call me Tansy. Tansy Michaels."

I shake her hand. "Allie Richards." *What part of PARK CLOSED: NO TRESPASSING did you not understand?* Be nice, be nice. Maybe she can't read. Or more likely, she's too vain to wear her glasses. "I'm sorry. The park is closed right now for renovation."

She smiles, flashing perfectly white straight dentures. "I know that, sweetie. I watch TV. But the mayor is my next-door neighbor, and seeing as how I've walked here almost every day for the last five years, he gave me permission to keep on. Morning and afternoon."

Only in Shady Grove. "You're kidding?" I've never met her before and while I don't claim to know everyone in town, I'm at least familiar with most of the natives.

She raises a brown-pencil eyebrow, her smile fixed. "Do I look like I'm kidding?"

"No."

"Alrighty then." She waves her hand toward us. "Don't let me keep you, Allie. I know you're busy. I promise not to be in the way."

"Yes, ma'am." Dismissed.

"Wouldn't that kill corn hip high?" Lark mutters, falling back on her granny's favorite saying when things went wrong.

"We'll forget all about her." Kind of hard to do since she's weaving in and out of our work area, but somehow we'll manage. "I've got my hands full outsmarting Blair. I'm not up for fighting city hall."

"Today is going to be much better, Al." Adam amazes me with his words of encouragement.

"Thanks, bro."

He flips my ponytail. "It pretty much has to be."

That's the Adam I know and love.

Hopefully he's right, though, because after just thirty minutes of work, the rock wall is taking shape. I call a quick break for Victoria, Lark, and me to "freshen up" a little before our second TV installment. No need for Shady Grove to know we're over here sweating like pigs.

Daniel's late. By the time he ambles up with his camera, sweat has already washed off what little bit of makeup I put on, and several strands of hair have worked themselves loose from my ponytail. "Keep working," I say under my breath to the others. "Pretend you don't see him."

"You trying to give me a complex?" Daniel drawls for my ears only. "I might start worrying that I'm invisible."

I forgot about his excellent hearing. "I just assumed you wanted it to seem natural, not stilted. For the good of the show, right?"

"Nice save. Just pretend I'm not here," Daniel says, loud enough for everyone to hear. He raises the camera and starts to shoot.

We go back to our wall and do our best to ignore him. Lark and Victoria spread the mortar, and Adam and I lift the rocks. I've designed this wall to be ten feet long, two feet tall, and two feet wide. This will be a nice place for people like Tansy to take a break in the shade. Assuming it stands.

"What are the extra rocks for?" Lark asks, nodding toward a pile of untouched rocks.

Mindful of the camera, I think fast. "*Because I overestimated how many we needed*" would be an answer Blair would love. "I thought some rock-lined perennial gardens would tie it all together."

She smiles, obviously realizing too late the trap she accidentally set for me. "Perfect."

"Ow!" Victoria screams.

We spin around to see her holding her thumb.

"I'm sorry." Adam looks at us. "The rock slipped at the last second." He reaches toward her. "Let me see it."

"No." She squeezes it and shakes her head. I'm sure she's unaware that her bottom lip is sticking out.

To my surprise, Daniel has the camera down by his side. "You okay?"

Lark runs up with the first-aid kit from my SUV. "Here, babe. What do you need?"

"We'll never know if she won't let us see it," Adam says, exasperation evident in his voice. "I didn't do it on purpose, Vicky."

"I know that, goofy."

I'm thankful to see that even though Victoria is still holding her thumb, she isn't crying. I feel awful that she got hurt doing a good deed for me.

"Then let me see it." This time when Adam reaches for it, she lets him look.

"Ouch. Looks like your nail broke off into the quick."

Lark pulls out a Band-Aid and wraps it around Victoria's thumb.

"If your granny were here, she'd say it's too far from my heart to kill me," Victoria jokes, and I breathe a sigh of relief. A disaster averted, and Daniel didn't even get it on film. A double blessing.

By the time Tansy finishes her walk and calls a cheery good-bye, we've managed to forget not only about her, but also about the ever-present camera. Not much later, the rock wall is officially done. I wet it down to help the mortar set.

Adam walks toward me, and I instinctively tighten my grip on the water hose. My brother the prankster. But he surprises me.

"Want me to go pick up some lunch?"

I look over at my Pinky friends. They're attacking the next project, our biggest undertaking. I want a border to define the park and give it a cozy, secluded feel. We can use some of the existing shrubs, but many will have to be dug up or transplanted. The girls are marking off the outline of the border with fluorescent orange chalk. I told them to imagine graceful, sloping curves, but it looks a little more like the path of a drunken sailor.

"Sure. See if Lark and Victoria want to ride along, okay? They look like they can use some air conditioning."

"Why don't we just all go?"

"I'd rather stay here and tie ribbons on the shrubs that have to be removed so we'll be ready to tackle that this afternoon, but thanks." Not to mention, I'm itching to get my hands on the chalk and lay out the border the way I want it.

"Hoping for some time alone with the roving reporter?"

"Hardly."

Daniel is packing up his camera. With any luck, he'll go, and I'll get a lot done before the others get back.

Adam grins. "He sure seems to be interested."

I snort. "That's his job, bro." I swat at him, but he's too fast for me.

A few seconds later, Lark and Victoria wave at me. "Ham and cheese with mayo, lettuce, and tomato?" Lark calls.

"Perfect." My regular since elementary school. "I'm so predictable," I mutter.

"Or maybe you're just a person who knows what you like."

I jump and spin around to face Daniel. "You scared me!"

"I'm sorry." He sits in one of two chairs Lark brought for breaks. "I seem to do that without meaning to."

"Not your fault. I should be more aware of what's going on around me."

"I don't know. Maybe you should just relax a little."

We can't all be free spirits, ride Harleys, and write books.

Some of us have to be practical. "Yeah."

He pats the chair beside him. "Sit down for a few minutes."

"I really need to be working."

"Please."

I admit I'm flattered. There's something very attractive about being pursued. Don't get me wrong. In the five years I've been single, I've had men flirt with me, and one or two have even "pursued" me. Men like James Hixson, the postage-meter man at the office. Every time he looked down at me, his glasses would slide down his nose. He'd push them up and say, "So Allie, baby? When are you and me going to get together?"

Ugh.

Daniel may be totally inappropriate for me, but James Hixson he's not.

I sit.

And wait for him to say something. Instead all I hear is the wind blowing through the big oak tree above us and in the distance, a mockingbird. I relax my head against the chair and let the slight breeze cool my face.

"Wouldn't it be sad to be a mockingbird and never have your own tune to warble?" Daniel whispers.

I nod, still looking up. Is he talking about me? Or himself? Or just a generic mockingbird? I close my eyes, not sure what to say. "Only a writer would use the word *warble* in a sentence."

He laughs softly. "Whether you win the contest or not, you're singing your own song now, Allie."

My eyes pop open. Okay, he's definitely talking about me. But "whether I win"? "I have to win."

"Why?"

"You may not realize it, but I used my severance pay to finance this little adventure. Losing isn't an option." So why am I sitting here playing the Audubon's Society's version of the Dating Game? I jump to my feet. "Not that I have time to sit around whining about it." My attempt at a smile feels more like a grimace.

He stands and drapes the camera strap over his shoulder, his answering smile obviously genuine. "I didn't know about the money. But, at the risk of spouting platitudes, God knows. And that's what matters."

God knew that my girls needed a father, too, but Jon still stepped in front of that car. There's no sense pointing out that logic to Daniel. "I'd better get back to work." My mantra these days.

"Don't work too hard."

Sorry, buster. I'm not making any promises. "See you tomorrow." I pick up the bottle of marking chalk.

"Even though you'll be pretending you don't."

"You've got me all figured out, don't you?"

He shakes his head. "Not yet, but I'm working on it."

Before I can come up with a reply, he's gone. But for some reason, the thought of him figuring me out makes for an unsettling afternoon.

# fifteen

How can one person look so beautiful and be so vicious? Blair Winchester smiles sweetly at the camera, enchanting viewers from ages nine to ninety-nine. Even I have to admit there are a couple of laughable moments in the other teams' clips today. Nothing like a rock wall falling down. But one prank among crew members. And one short interview with a guy who thinks a fellow worker is trying to suck up to the boss. Obviously staged. Just good-natured fun.

Then comes our turn. I sit on the bed, my feet tucked up under me, satisfied that there are no embarrassing moments on our tape for today. What will Blair do?

The clip plays—a nice shot of us building the wall, working together smoothly and efficiently. The image freezes on the screen beside Blair and she smiles. "TLC looks like they had a better second day, but rumor has it the whole project came to a screeching halt when one of the TLC crew members—socialite Victoria Worthington—broke a nail. Wonder if they called in a manicurist? Or simply rang up an ambulance to rush her to the nearest nail salon? What do you think, Shady Grove? Will TLC be able to *nail* this job? Tune in tomorrow to find out."

I slam my hand down on the pillow. Why does she have to do that? And worse yet, why did Daniel pretend to be all gentlemanly and turn off the camera if he was just going to tell Blair what happened anyway?

I have to put him out of my mind. The phone rings the instant the thought forms, and I grab for it, then jerk my hand back. No doubt it's him. I lean over and look at the caller ID. Not a number I recognize. But he could be sneaky. What am I thinking? Obviously, he is sneaky.

A ringing phone drives me bananas, so I snatch it up. "Hello?"

"Allie?" A male voice but smoother than Daniel's—more citified, as Lark's granny would say.

"Yes?"

"This is Trevor Wright."

Okay, I know this is awful, but a giggle bubbles up in my throat as I remember the Pinkies joking around about Mr. (W)Right. I put my hand over the phone and make myself cough hard. "Hi, Trevor."

"I don't know if Victoria mentioned it, but I saw her at the country club the other day. She said you weren't working at Coble's anymore."

"She did say she saw you." I try to think of what to say about my job situation. "I'm trying something different right now."

"Actually I just saw you on TV." His chuckle sounds a little embarrassed. For me? Or because he didn't admit that up front? "Interesting."

"Um, thanks." I hate phone conversations where I find myself wishing one of the girls will yell for me.

"I was hoping we might get together sometime soon."

I start trying to find an excuse, but then the realization dawns on me. What better way to get Daniel out of my mind than to go out with Trevor? "That sounds fun."

"Are you busy Saturday night?"

I was planning on working at the park until dark, but I didn't know a nice Christian businessman was going to call and ask me out. "Not really."

"Pick you up at seven?"

"Sure." I give him quick directions and hang up, immediately regretting my impulsive acceptance. I smack my forehead against my palm. What have I done?

Victoria, the marathon runner, decides that in order to avoid sore muscles, we all need to stretch every day before we start. Lark and I are game, but Adam balks, choosing to lean against the truck drinking his coffee while we gather around the old oak tree.

I don't want to get morale down, so instead of mentioning Blair's segment, I tell them about Trevor calling.

Lark puts her hands against the tree and leans in toward it for a calf stretch. "So Mr. Wright finally called. Is this a real, honest-to-goodness date?"

"I'm thinking it is." I reach toward the sky and lean toward the left.

"Are you excited?" Victoria bends over and deftly touches her toes without straining.

"Show-off," Lark mumbles.

"I don't know. This is going to sound crazy. . . ." I lean toward the right.

Victoria lightly balances herself against the tree and pulls her foot back to her hip with her other hand. "But you feel guilty about Daniel."

She knows me so well. "After he sold us out to Blair, how can I feel that way?"

" 'Sold us out' may be a little strong." Lark straightens and bends backward slightly. "In spite of my reservations, I kind of thought this morning was funny."

"Same here." Victoria snickers, switching feet. "I mean. . .me? A socialite?"

Lark and I just look at her.

"What?" She puts her foot down and frowns. "What are you looking at?"

"Oh, I don't know. . . ." I tap my chin. "A socialite maybe?"

Lark puts the back of her hand against her forehead in a mock swoon. "As I live and breathe."

"Is this hen party almost over or should I pour another cup of coffee?" Adam raises his empty cup in a salute to us.

We take the hint and get to work. I don't even turn around when Daniel drives up with his camera. I can hear Victoria and Lark joking with him about Victoria's manicure, but I just keep on digging holes and planting petunias.

A vaguely familiar female voice sounds behind me. "Honey, you know. . .if you put those marigolds in that bed with those petunias, in a few weeks you won't even be able to see the marigolds."

Still clutching my trowel, I wipe my forehead with the back

of my hand and look up at Tansy the walker, decked out in neon purple spandex today. "What?"

She motions toward the bright red flowers I'm so carefully spacing out in the soft dirt. "Those are wave petunias. They spread."

I'd bought them for that very reason, hoping that if we planted them early in the contest, by judging time our flower beds would look mature and colorful. Still, I hadn't really thought about them spreading over the marigolds. Of course, she was right. I'd need to make a terraced bed and keep a close watch on them.

I stick my trowel in the dirt with a vicious twist. "I'll keep that in mind. Thanks."

She's off again, but when I reach for another petunia, I almost grab a Nike-clad foot instead. Daniel squats down beside me. "Who is that lady? Does she work for you?"

"I don't think I'm required to keep you posted on our employee roster, am I?" I squint at him. "I didn't read the small print all that well, so if I'm wrong just let me know."

"What's wrong with you today?" He seems genuinely puzzled.

Okay, I'm the only person in Shady Grove without a sense of humor. The Pinkies thought the show was funny. Daniel thinks he's done nothing wrong. Am I overreacting? On the off chance I am, I lighten up. "Don't mind me. I guess I'm just a little stressed."

He peels a petunia from the six-pack and hands it to me.

I dig a hole and plant the offering. "Aren't you worried about losing your job? Technically you just helped me."

"Maybe that was just my way of telling you to stop and smell the flowers."

"When this contest is over, I will."

"Speaking of the contest being over, I'm sure you're too busy to go out right now. . . ."

Guilt burns my face, and I keep my gaze focused on the plants. I *am* too busy to go out. Why had I accepted the invitation from Trevor?

"But after the contest is over, maybe we can hit that Mexican place again?" He smiles and his dimple flashes. Have I mentioned I love dimples?

But I'm trying to get him off my mind, right? Not keep him front and center. "I normally don't make plans that far ahead."

He pushes to his feet and dusts his hands together. "Yeah, I noticed that about you. A real free spirit, aren't you?"

The sarcasm in his voice is good-natured, and when I look up, his blue eyes are twinkling. It didn't take him long to pick up on my slightly obsessive personality, did it?

Thankfully he lets it drop, and for the next thirty minutes, we work in peace, once again trying to be oblivious to his camera. A roaring engine makes me look up. A little red corvette screeches into the parking lot, sucking all the peace from the air. Blair.

I scramble to my feet and instinctively look over to the far side of the park, where Adam is unloading plants.

"Daniel!" Blair calls as she alights from the car with the grace of a model. "Come here."

Daniel drops his camera down by his side. "Excuse me." Without a backward glance, he strides across the park.

"Sure. No problem," I say to thin air. "Nice talking to you."

" 'Come here,' my foot. 'Come hither' would be more like it," Lark mutters from five feet away.

"It's a free country." I kneel back down in front of the plants.

"Probably had a few minutes to kill and thought she'd stop by and reel Daniel back in."

"Well, don't look now, y'all," Victoria says from the other side of me. "But she's got on her reporter face. I'm thinking she's trying to land another embarrassing moment for us."

Of course Lark and I both look. Sure enough, Blair, microphone in hand, is playing for a bigger audience than one.

As they reach us, she gives Daniel a "keep rolling" signal and turns to where I'm still on my knees. "So, Allie, tell us? How have the first few days been for TLC Landscaping?"

I stop to think about that, then smile up at the camera. "Wonderful." We're here, and in spite of my inexperience and my largely volunteer crew, with God's help we're doing the job. That's more than I ever dreamed. "We'd like to thank Channel Six and their viewers for giving us this opportunity."

She squats beside me and pretends to plant a petunia. "Are these those new wave petunias?"

"Yes."

"Aren't you afraid they'll take over the bed?"

Is this a coincidence or did Daniel trot over to tell her about the spreading flowers as soon as she got here?

"Why, Blair, you've been hiding your talents." Under normal circumstances, I'd say I don't even have claws, but she always manages to bring them out with seemingly minimal efforts. "I didn't even know you gardened."

I think she's actually at a loss for words, so I cut her some slack. "Actually, I'm going to do a little terracing with rocks and plant the marigolds higher. And it'll be the winner's job to be sure they're kept in control." I smile, even though my heart is pounding.

"Hopefully that will be us."

She stands, so I do, too.

She thrusts the microphone in my face again. "Does the camera bother you?"

I shrug. "Does a goldfish mind living in a bowl?" Let her make what she wants of that.

She motions Daniel to cut.

"Daniel, be a dear and run get my makeup bag out of the car, would you?" she purrs.

He lopes off to do her bidding, and I can't help but wonder if that's in his job description or if being at her beck and call is just something he does for fun. Not that I'm jealous, mind you. Just curious.

Blair moves closer to me, her eyes narrowed slits. Victoria and Lark automatically move to flank me. If Blair had a couple of girlfriends, I could imagine we were at an all-girl rumble. But it's just her.

And her tongue.

"Don't cross me, Allie Richards. I'm the one who does the editing." She puts her hands on her hips. "If you think your brother was the laughingstock of Shady Grove, just keep this up and see what I can do to you."

I hear a noise behind us and spin around in time to see Adam with a barberry bush in his hands. His face is ashen.

# Sixteen

"Blair, you—" But I can't think of a thing to say to her that I won't regret later. I take a step toward my brother. "Adam. . ."

His smile doesn't reach his haunted eyes. "No worries, sis." He sets the shrub down and nods toward it. "Watch out for this one. It might look beautiful, but underneath it's loaded with thorns."

Before I can respond, he's gone. A second later, his truck roars to life and out of the park.

"Adam's right. That is a nasty little shrub," Victoria drawls, giving Blair the evil eye.

"Yep," Lark says casually, but her fist is clenched around the trowel handle. "When the pretty colored leaves fall off, those barbs are all that's left."

Daniel shows up and hands Blair her makeup bag.

"Thanks so much. If you're ready with the camera, I've got a few questions for the workers," she says, her smile so sweet sugar wouldn't melt in her mouth, as Lark's granny would have said.

As she freshens up her lipstick, I lean over to Victoria and Blair. "Just get it over with and be polite so she'll leave. Please, guys."

While she barrages Victoria and Lark with questions, I can't help but be glad shy Rachel isn't here. The other two Pinkies are giving Blair a run for her money, though I doubt seriously this interview will ever be seen by Shady Grove viewers.

"So why did you two agree to do landscaping work?" Blair finally asks them.

"She made me an offer I couldn't refuse," Victoria says, grinning.

"Yeah, me, too," Lark chimes in. "Eternal gratitude." She turns first to one side and then the other. "Although being in front of the camera is kind of a kick, too. Which do you think is my best side?"

Victoria pretends to consider her question. "I'm not sure, honey." I'm in awe of how nice they're being, even though they're being silly, when Victoria finishes, "They say the camera adds ten pounds. I'm sure you know how hard that can be to deal with, don't you, Blair?"

While Victoria is talking, Lark waves her hands in the air behind her and mouths "Hi, Mom."

I put my hand to my mouth to stifle a laugh.

"Cut." Blair glares at my two goofy friends.

Daniel drops the camera, and I'm relieved to see he's grinning. Just when I think he's totally clueless, I see signs of life.

Blair sniffs and raises her nose even higher. She levels me with a hard look. "Next time I come back, I'll expect more cooperation. You did sign a contract."

"Aw, c'mon. You said you wanted to make us the laughingstock," Lark says, loud enough for Daniel to hear. "At least *we're* laughing." She pretends the trowel is a microphone and thrusts the handle end toward Blair. "By the way, Blair, the whole 'rushing Victoria by ambulance to the manicurist' thing was funny. Am I correct in guessing you don't write your own material?"

Blair ignores Lark and puts her hand on Daniel's forearm. "Walk me to my car, Daniel. We need to discuss some things." She looks back at us. "Privately."

Daniel hesitates, but I guess he figures he's on the clock, so what can he do? He follows her, but I notice he stays out of arm's reach.

I turn back around just as Lark and Victoria high-five each other. I bite back a grin. "You guys planning on taking that show on the road?"

"Depends." Lark nudges Victoria. "You firing us?"

"With Adam already gone? Not a chance." I nod toward the flowers. "Think you can handle this? I've thought of one more thing I want to say to Blair." If she wants the show to do well, she'd better lay off. Maybe appealing to her hunger for success will be better than trying to shame her into decency.

"Sure you don't need backup?" Victoria raises her arm and flexes her small muscle.

I grin. "Positive, Wonder Woman. But if you and Lois Lane could get this flat of flowers planted, that would be awesome."

As I walk away, I hear Lark say, "How come you get to be a superhero and I don't?"

I'm still smiling when I come up beside my SUV, which is next to Blair's little car. I have no intention of eavesdropping, but Daniel's voice comes across loud and clear before I can see them. "For the good of the show, maybe you should put aside your differences for now and just concentrate on keeping this light and funny," he says.

My grin grows broader. We apparently had the same idea. But I'm pretty sure she'll come nearer listening to him, so I grab a drink and head back to work without making my presence known.

By the time I stop by Rachel's chiropractic office that evening on the way home, I'm ready for an adjustment. I'm her last appointment of the day and the front desk girl is already gone, so she listens patiently while I recount the events of the day, including the fact that Adam never showed back up at work.

She pushes a button and raises the adjusting table. "Face down," she says automatically. I obey, and after the table lowers I feel her fingers pushing along my spine. "Now I'm nervous about my first day on the job tomorrow."

"Oh, Rach, don't be silly." My voice is muffled against the headrest paper. "Besides, are you sure you want to work on your day off?"

She hits the air strip with her foot and pops the table up under me in that way that always startles me. "Positive. Unless you don't want me?"

"Want you? I don't know how I'd make it without you. But I just hate for you to work so hard."

"That's up to me, isn't it?" she says, then sweetly and forcefully adjusts me, intent on "removing the nerve interference so that the brain can communicate with the rest of the body." I don't know how it works, but my brain needs all the communication help it can get. And the rest of me feels pretty doggone good too by the time she finishes.

I slide off the table.

She keeps one hand on my shoulder. "Feel better?"

"As loose as a goose."

Rachel recognizes the phrase as being classic Lark's granny, and we both laugh.

"Thanks, Doc."

"Anytime."

I know she means it. And not just for me. Day or night, Saturday, Christmas, it doesn't matter. If someone needs her, she's there. Her dedication to her profession amazes me. I'd like to see her face light up over a man like it does when she talks about releasing the innate ability to heal itself that God has put into our bodies. Sometimes I think she feels safer with the doctor/patient distance between her and everyone else on earth, except maybe the Pinkies. "Want me to stay around while you lock up?"

"Sure. What's this I hear about you having a date with Mr. Wright?"

I grimace as I follow her from room to room. "They text-messaged you, didn't they?"

She laughs. "Actually Victoria called and left a message on my private voice mail. Marked urgent." When she turns off the nature sounds CD, the office is so quiet you can hear a pin drop. "Kind of surprised me."

"That I was going out?" I've not been *that* much of a hermit.

She shrugs and locks up the medical file cabinets. "I figured your next date would be with Daniel Montgomery."

Heat floods my cheeks again as I remember Daniel's invitation from earlier. And my reply about not making plans in advance. "I told y'all I wasn't interested in him."

"I wasn't paying a lot of attention to your words." She opens the tiny refrigerator in her break room and tosses me a bottle of water. "I was listening to your heart."

"Yeah, well, my heart's not in charge."

She grins and toasts me with the water bottle. "Here's to famous last words."

I think about Rachel's teasing as I drive home. Even the Pinkies don't realize how important it is to me to make wise choices. My pride won't let them know how badly we're struggling financially. So they don't understand that I have to stay focused on making a better life for the girls without letting my heart distract me.

Mama is keeping the girls at my house, but I bypass the carriage house and go straight to her place in search of Adam—the perfect example of what can happen when you start letting your emotions govern you. I find him lying on his bed playing video games. The door's open, but I tap on it anyway. "Can I come in?"

"Sure." He doesn't look away from the screen.

After I'm in, I'm not sure what to do. Finally I collapse on a hunter green beanbag near the bed. He tosses me a control without taking his eyes off the screen. "See how fast you can get to the dungeon and rescue the prince."

"Prince? Isn't that supposed to be princess?"

He looks over at me and raises an eyebrow. "This is gender specific. If you're a female, you rescue the prince."

For the next half hour, we play. And even though I don't stand a chance, it's a blast.

When GAME OVER flashes next to my icon, I hand him the control. "Cool game. You planning on coming back to work?"

"If you'll still have me. I'm sorry about today." He flashes me a rueful grin. "I had visions of her lying in wait for me with the camera."

"She hurt you really bad?" We never really talked about Blair before. Zach's betrayal of Adam and then Dad's death seemed so much more important. But it hadn't occurred to me she might have broken his heart.

"Nah, just bruised my ego a little. I knew almost from the start that she wasn't the one for me. But she's right about one thing. I've had enough of being made to look stupid." He pushes up to a sitting position and sets his own game control on the bed. "So don't expect me to be front and center when the camera is there, okay?"

"Gotcha."

He stands and helps me to my feet. "You can count on me. I want you to win."

"Thanks, Adam. I want *us* to win."

I have a deep, dark confession. I've been known to participate in an occasional boycott. Give me a real reason not to buy a product or support a company and you can count on me to stick to it. And Blair was hateful enough yesterday that I feel totally justified in boycotting her show. So I'm not watching. But that doesn't stop Victoria, Lark, and Rachel from talking about it. No mention of Adam at least. Just a little clip of Blair kneeling beside me in the dirt and discussing the pros and cons of wave petunias, followed by an edited version of Lark and Victoria saying that they're helping out a friend. The rest is just film of us working hard. The other teams are coming along well, according to the Pinkies, but not any better than we are.

My mood can only be described as buoyant while we work Thursday. I'd hate for Victoria and Lark to know it, but having Rachel around helps. She's done a lot of gardening, but she also has a calming spirit that balances the fact that Daniel's presence distracts me. I'm starting to get used to that kind of buzzing feeling when he's around. No doubt pure infatuation, even though I'll never tell a soul. Way too junior high-ish to talk about.

I'm up to my elbows in potting soil when the cause of my agitation stops by where I'm working.

"Got a minute?"

A cautious glance reveals no camera. "What's up?" I dust off my hands and turn to sit on the grass.

He sinks down beside me. "I'm done for today. Just wanted to tell you the park is shaping up. You're working wonders."

"Thanks. I've got a lot of help."

He plucks a piece of grass and rolls it around between his finger and his thumb. "I know we talked about how busy you are during the contest, but keeping in mind your aversion to making plans in advance. . ." He grins. "I thought you might like to go out Saturday night?"

What do I say now? Um, sorry, Daniel, but I'm going out with Mr. Right Saturday night? "I've already got plans for Saturday night. I'm sorry."

He flicks the grass away. "It's hard to find that window with you between not making plans in advance and asking too late, isn't it? Is there another night that would be better?"

"Actually, considering our professional relationship, I think we should probably just stick with being friends."

He reaches over and brushes his fingertips across my hand.

I catch my breath.

"You had some dirt." He pushes to his feet. "Why do I scare you so badly?"

I jump up. "You don't scare me." Okay, that might be a lie. "Much."

He grins at my last-minute attempt at honesty. "Someday you're going to run out of excuses, Allie. Then what?"

"Maybe by that time you'll lose interest." I can't imagine why he hasn't already. But even though my knees are trembling, I can't help but take comfort in that puzzling fact.

"Don't count on it." He turns and walks away without saying another word.

And coward that I am, I let him go.

# Seventeen

Friday morning, I'm sitting on the bed finishing up my Bible study for the day when Miranda comes in, still wearing her pajamas, and climbs up beside me. The second she stretches out against me, I realize how long it's been since she's done this.

I smooth her long dark hair with my hand. "You okay, honey?"

"Yeah." She rolls over to the wall and says something I can't hear.

"What?"

"I don't like you getting home so late. I miss you."

Tears spring to my eyes. I guess in my natural insecurity, I assumed my mama would be more than able to take my place with the girls. Especially Miranda, my has-it-all-together oldest daughter. I blink hard and keep my voice even. "I miss y'all, too. But once the contest is over, it'll be different." Either I'll be working for someone else or I'll be my own boss and able to get home at a decent hour.

She turns over and I can see her own eyes are red-rimmed.

"Are we still going to get to work with you Saturday?"

"Sure. I can't wait! And guess what?"

"What?"

"I have a date Saturday night, so when we get home from work, you'll have to pick out something for me to wear and help me get ready." Unlike sitcom kids, my girls have been really excited the few times I've had a date. I don't probe the why of that too much, partly because I'm afraid of what I'll learn. Are they hoping that some wealthy prince will sweep us away to his castle, where things like pot pies and generic brand jeans will just be a distant memory? Or is it simply that they want a father to take the place of the daddy they barely remember?

"Who is he?"

"A man I met when I worked at Coble's."

She pushes herself up against the pillow. "And you like him?"

I think of Trevor, seemingly perfect in so many ways. Do I like him? He's fine, as far as I know. But that's not an answer, is it? "I don't know him very well, but the Pinkies think it's hilarious that his name is Mr. Wright." Mothers never realize how fast their kids are growing up, a fact hammered home when I open my mouth to spell his name and explain the joke and am interrupted by her laugh.

"This must be the one then, huh? Mr. Wright?" Her grin is more mischievous than hopeful.

"Must be." Could be. Should be. Then why do I keep thinking about Daniel?

I answer my own question when he drives up at the park midmorning. *Because he's always there.* No doubt that's the reason he's constantly on my mind. A weekend away from him, a date with someone else. That's what I need. And that's what I'm going to get.

Maybe sooner than I realize. Whether by design or by accident, our paths don't cross much at all by the time he leaves two hours later. I lean toward design since the park is not that big. As he's loading up, I have to force myself to keep from casually walking over to his van. I've always hated it when girls—and guys—act interested in someone one day and not the next. Now I'm starting to sympathize. I'm not fickle. Just confused. I'm a good girl, though, so I just keep working until it's too late to speak to him, unless I chase the van down the park's road waving my trowel. And I'm not about to do that. Yet.

At quitting time, Victoria and Lark corner me. "What's up with you and Daniel?" Lark asks.

"I wish I knew." That about sums it up.

"Why not just give this a chance, Allie, and see where it goes?" Lark has never been anything but blunt.

"Look. I'm having a hard enough time not going gaga over this man, and I haven't even dated him."

Victoria frowns. "What about that one time at the Mex—"

"That wasn't a date."

"You don't have to bite my head off, shugah. Did he pay?"

"Yes."

"Then it was a date."

Hard to argue with Victoria's Southern logic.

"I have a real date tomorrow night, remember?"

"How could we forget Mr. Wright?" Lark asks. "Do we need to come over and help you get ready?"

"No, I promised that honor to Miranda, but thanks."

"See you at the game tonight?" Victoria calls as they walk to their car.

"I'll be there."

I hit the ground running when I get home. Thankfully Mama is ready and has the girls dressed in their red and white soccer uniforms, so after I get a quick shower and pull on some clean jeans and a T-shirt, we're good to go.

"Y'all look so cu—" I catch myself just in time and cover the faux pas with a cough. "Professional."

"We're twins," Katie says, bouncing from one foot to the other.

"You are, aren't you?" Mama looks like she wants to use the c-u-t-e word, too, but knows better.

"We are *not* twins." Miranda's words, aimed toward her younger sister, drip with disgust.

I physically step between the girls. "She just means you're dressed alike."

"Not my choice," Miranda mutters, but we make it out to the car without a fuss.

We arrive at the park just as our team is taking the field for their warm-up. Miranda grumbles about being late, but Victoria pulls in right behind us, so I don't feel too bad. I know it's probably awful when you judge how late you are based on how many people show up after you, but in the South that's how we do it.

When Mama, Victoria, and I get to the bleachers, the first person I see is Daniel, with Blair on his left and some other woman on his right. My mood sours.

"Who is that woman with Daniel?" Victoria whispers.

I shake my head. "How would I know?" Or why would I care?

Adam slides in beside us just as the game starts. Once the whistle blows, I almost forget about Daniel and the women on each side of him as I watch my girls work together to get the ball down the field. This year will be good for them, hopefully.

Miranda scores and Victoria, Mama, Adam, and I jump and scream like teenagers at a rock concert. I notice Miranda and Katie share a high five. Things may be looking up at the Richards's household.

We yell plenty the rest of the night, and the Hornets fight valiantly. But the other team has older players, and in the end we lose one to three.

"What a goal!" Adam calls to Miranda as he and Mama head to his truck. "I thought sure you were going to win."

Miranda shoots a look to where Katie and Dylan are goofing around with a couple of other kids their age, then rolls her eyes at her uncle. "If we had older kids instead of these babies."

"Miranda!" I point my finger at her, grateful that Katie didn't hear.

"Can we go eat pizza? Can we go eat pizza?" Katie and Dylan come bouncing up to Victoria and me. What brought this on?

Before I can ask, Daniel appears in front of us, the woman who is not Blair beside him. "Allie, this is my sister, Candice. Elijah's mom."

"Nice to meet you." The dark-haired woman's eyes twinkle, and her smile is sweet. I'm pretty sure she can tell I'm still computing the fact that she's Daniel's sister and not his date.

"You, too."

Daniel motions toward the swarm of Hornets. "We were hoping to take the team out for pizza. How about it?"

I want to say no. I should say no. Pizza is not in our budget. But the kids would be so disappointed. Plus this way I won't have to fix supper. None of these reasons have anything to do with Daniel. I smile at Candice. "Sounds good." So, I'm weak. I never claimed otherwise.

At the Pizza Den, Victoria and I find chairs as far away from the rowdiest kids as possible. I end up by Candice, who is next to Daniel. No big surprise that Blair is on Daniel's other side, clinging to his arm like he's her homecoming escort.

Leaning across him, she fake-smiles at me. "Allie, have I told you how happy I am that you're a finalist? It took me awhile to convince them that, since the other two competitors are professionals, your team would provide a little more fun for the audience. But everyone can see I was right now."

I pretend I don't get the fact that she's saying TLC Landscaping was chosen for the comic relief. But I blink hard against the tears stinging my eyes. "Thanks for the vote of confidence, Blair. Anything for the ratings, right?" My laugh may be a little strained, but at least it's not a sob.

Candice turns toward me. "I'm really enjoying watching you. I bet you'll be getting fan mail soon."

Blair shoots her a hard look. Now there's something she hadn't considered, I'm sure. Neither had I, for that matter, but it sounds good. "Thanks, Candice. Won't that be cool?"

Daniel gets up to go check on the kids, and Candice scoots over next to Blair. "I guess you get quite a bit of fan mail," she says.

As Blair shares the highlights from some of her more gushing viewer letters, I'm feeling betrayed by Candice's defection. But when Daniel comes back and slides into the chair next to me, I get the feeling the brother/sister team orchestrated that little musical chair game on purpose. Especially since Daniel winks at me.

Victoria leans forward in the middle of Blair's monologue about her fans singing her praises. "So do you ever get any hate mail?"

Blair pauses, then laughs. "Not yet. Are you thinking about sending me some?"

Victoria pushes a napkin down the table toward her. "Hadn't really considered it. You can give me your address, though. Just in case."

"You know, ladies." Blair's voice grows serious. "The 'Get Real, Shady Grove' segment is only a job." She flashes me her sweetest smile. "Daniel and I would hate for you to think of us as the enemy. It's nothing personal. When we're out like this, I like to think of us as just fellow soccer moms."

Before I can bristle at the way she neatly made her and Daniel one entity, Daniel says, "Speak for yourself, Blair."

"What do you mean?" she asks, obviously puzzled.

"I never think of myself as a soccer mom." He looks at me as if I'm the only person in the room. "And I'd just as soon you didn't either."

Everyone laughs, except me. And a certain TV anchorwoman.

# eighteen

The next morning, I awake to whispering.

"Should we wake her?" Katie.

"Not yet." Miranda.

I open one eye and squint into their alert faces. I raise my head and grab the alarm clock, pulling it close enough to read through my bleary vision. 6:30 a.m.

"What are you doing up?" Miranda, I can understand, even on Saturday, but Katie? Fear snatches away the last remnants of sleep, and I push myself to a sitting position. "What's wrong?"

"We're ready to go to work." Katie pirouettes next to my bed to show off her jeans and shirt, complete with a floppy hat she undoubtedly fished out of the beach bag.

I reach over and turn off my alarm. "First we have to get breakfast."

"Check." Miranda grins. "We had cereal and milk."

Katie reaches up for a hug and I pull her close. "Who are you and what have you done with my youngest daughter?" I growl against her neck.

She giggles, and over her shoulder I see Miranda watching. Who cares if she thinks she's too mature for such silliness? I grab her with my other arm. "You I recognize," I say in a silly voice and am rewarded with a laugh I haven't heard in quite a while.

They break free and run toward the kitchen. "Hurry!" Katie calls over her shoulder. "We want to be the first ones there."

When we pull into the park forty-five minutes later, we are definitely the first ones there. "Y'all want to stretch?"

"Sure." Miranda wraps a bandanna around her hair as we get out of the vehicle.

My mockingbird friend chirps hello from a high branch of the oak tree. I point him out to the girls and we stand in silence for a minute, appreciating his varied song.

Some of us tire of nature appreciation faster than others.

"I thought you said we could stretch." Katie bounces around the tree.

It doesn't take them any time to catch on to the stretching routine Victoria taught us. When we're all warmed up, I assign them different areas with a safe distance between them. They seem to be getting along some better, but no sense borrowing trouble.

"We'll swap areas later."

As we get started, the rest of the crew straggles in. Adam and Mama followed quickly by Rachel, Victoria, Dylan, Lark, and Craig. I check my job list and point each person in the direction they're supposed to go.

"Hey, sis. It's Saturday. Cut us some slack." Adam salutes me with a half-eaten donut.

Miranda places her hands on her hip and gives her uncle a stern look. "If we want to be done by four, we can't afford any slack."

"Oh no, Allie Junior." Adam shoves the last of the pastry in his mouth. "One of you was bad enough."

Miranda just grins and starts to work, but I think about what Adam said as I double-check my list. I always thought she inherited her super-organizational skills from Jon and his family. Did she get that bossy attitude from me? Am I a bit of a control freak? Maybe. Something to think about later.

Midmorning, Craig hollers, "Hey, Allie. Come look at this."

I look up from where I'm patting down the soil around a freshly planted holly. "What?" I say automatically as I walk over to him.

He brushes back some junk and motions toward a dirt-covered pipe. "Did you know there used to be a fountain here?"

"No." Suddenly I do remember when we were kids. . .we called it the wishing fountain. "Yes. I did know it. But I'd forgotten."

"When we were cleaning up this debris. . ." Lark motions to a pile of broken bricks and old mortar. "Craig found the plumbing."

I take in the excitement on their faces. And it hits me. "Are you saying we could make it work again?"

Craig nods. "I'm pretty sure."

A rustling calls my attention to Tansy, power walking, a few feet away, her neon green spandex not even coming close to blending in with the trees. Call me paranoid, but I lower my voice. "I'd have to get approval from the contest board, but let's keep it to ourselves for now, okay?"

They follow my gaze and nod.

"Mum's the word of the day." Craig makes a zipping motion toward his lips.

Lark's smile looks a little forced for some reason, but she nods. "We won't say anything."

136

As I walk away, I hear Craig say, "C'mon, honey. It's just an expression."

"Maybe I'm tired of your expressions." The sharpness in Lark's tone surprises me.

Who knows what that's about? Usually those two are so much on the same wavelength it's hard to hack into their signal. But today you can almost feel the static between them.

"Honey," Mama waves at me. "The holes y'all dug for these shrubs aren't straight."

"They're staggered on purpose."

"Why?"

"It just works better that way. Trust me."

"Okay, then. In that case, Katie girl, let's get these planted."

I spend the next hour walking around the park, solving problems and answering questions. Tansy is walking late today and apparently decides to have a picnic lunch. Just my luck. We grab a bite to eat, too, then get back to work. When I see Tansy climb into her luxury car, I hotfoot it back over to Lark and Craig. "So tell me about the fountain."

Craig draws out a rough circle on the ground, and we work together to clean it out. "I'm pretty sure this is where the original fountain was."

"Can't you just see it?"

"Yep, but if you still want to keep it hush-hush, we might want to stop looking," Lark says. "Looks like camera boy is here."

I swing around. Sure enough, Daniel and his nephew are walking toward us. "What's he doing here?"

"Working overtime?" Lark dusts off her hands.

Katie and Dylan run over to greet Elijah.

Hard for me to believe he'd spy on us for Blair on a Saturday, but who knows? "Just in case, let's move away from this area." I kick a few brick pieces over the exposed plumbing. "I have a crazy idea of unveiling a surprise fountain right before the judging, and the last thing I want is Blair's mole to find out about it."

"A fountain is a lot of work," Craig says softly. "That might be hard to hide."

"Allie knows what she wants," Lark snaps. "Let her decide what's best."

Craig nods curtly. "I think I'll go see if Adam needs any help."

"Thanks, Craig." When he's gone, I nudge Lark. "What's wrong with you today?"

"Nothing worth talking about."

"Yeah, right. We'll talk later." I know her. She can't keep a secret. And something is definitely wrong.

I walk to where Daniel is squatting down to help Mama hold a holly shrub straight as Katie packs the dirt around the base. "Hi."

He looks up at me. "Hey, Allie. How's it going today?"

"Fine." Would it be rude for me to ask him what he's doing here? Probably. "How about you?" There's a nice compromise—inquisitive, but polite.

"Pretty good. Katie told Elijah y'all were working today. We were on our way to get some ice cream." He nods toward the little ice cream store on the square. "Thought you might let the kids walk over with us."

Ice Cream Heaven is as famous for its ice cream as it is infamous for its high prices. I have five dollars in my pocket, but I hadn't planned on blowing it on ice cream. It always seems to come down to money.

"My treat, of course." Does he read my mind?

"The girls can go, but I'll get you some money." If it's more than five dollars, he can make up the rest, but I don't intend to be a charity case. "Thanks for asking them."

He shrugs. "Elijah will love having the company."

Katie bounces up with Dylan and Elijah in her wake. "Dylan's mom said yes." She glares at Miranda, who is on her knees spreading mulch twenty feet away. "Miranda won't go."

"Why not? She loves ice cream."

"She says she can't leave. 'This is a job. Not a game.'" She uses her fingers for quotation marks. On Blair, air quotes are annoying. On Katie, they're adorable.

At the same time I'm exasperated, I'm also proud of Miranda's work ethic. "Why don't you bring her some back in a cup?"

Katie touches Daniel's arm. "Is that okay, Mr. Daniel?"

He smiles at her and I'm amazed by how quickly she's taken up with him. Usually both of my girls are more reserved with grown-ups they don't know well. "Sure, that sounds great."

I tuck the five dollars in Katie's hand. "You pay for yours and Miranda's."

"Okay."

After they're gone, Lark and I go back over to the fountain area and rake the rubble into a pile on the side. When we're almost done, Craig shows up beside us. "You got some paper?"

I give him my notebook and pen and he sketches out the schematics of a simple fountain.

"How much is this going to cost?"

He names a figure I can live with. *If* we cut back even further at home. The girls and I will just have to pretend we're under siege and have to make it with what we already have. For three weeks we can surely survive. "Can you make a supply list?"

"Sure." He scrawls out words in the notebook.

I strain to read over his shoulder but can't decipher his chicken scratch. "Can we rock the outside of it with the extra rocks I have and make it look like it's just going to be a big round flower bed?"

Craig doesn't look up from his writing. "I don't see why not."

"What do you think, Lark?"

She shrugs. "If the expert says it'll work, it should. I'm going to go help Rachel for a while and let y'all figure it out."

I leave Craig working on the list and run after her. "Lark."

She stops. "Yeah?"

"You sure you can't tell me what's wrong? This is really weird."

Her smile doesn't reach her eyes. "Sorry, Allie. You can't fix this one."

My reputation as Miss Fix-It precedes me. "I know Someone who can. I'll be praying."

"Thanks."

"Who wants a chocolate shake?" Daniel calls from the park entrance. He and the three kids have their arms full of cups. I'm pretty sure my five dollars didn't cover that. But my ham and cheese sandwich played out long ago and cold chocolate sounds delicious.

We all collapse on the ground in the shade of the big oak tree and watch Daniel and the kids toss a Frisbee around. Katie makes a wild throw to Daniel, and I snatch the flying disc just before it hits Mama in the head. She never even looks up from her conversation with Victoria.

I stand up and meet Daniel halfway with it.

"Wanna play?" he asks.

*Where were you when I was young and had no responsibilities?* Oh, yeah, he was getting kicked out of school. There's something to be said for not being impetuous. "Better not. I have to work."

He throws the Frisbee to Elijah and turns back to me. "How did I know you were going to say that? At the risk of using a cliché, 'All work and no play. . .' "

"Makes Jane a successful business owner?" I push my sunglasses up on my head. "Thanks again for the ice cream. And for taking Katie."

"I enjoyed having her. Never a dull moment."

I cringe. Katie is my "tell-all" kid. Her Sunday school teacher once told me that it was a good thing I didn't live a wild life or the whole class would know about it. With Katie, it's all in the details. "Oh no. What did she say?"

He takes a step closer to me. " 'Fraid she spilled your deep, dark secret?" His blue eyes sparkle.

Right now, how I feel about Daniel would be my deep, dark secret, and Katie definitely doesn't know that. So. . . "Not really. I just know her propensity for dramatizing everyday life." I take a step back.

"Sounds like a writer in the making."

"You should know. How's that going?"

"Great. I got another rejection this week."

"I'm sorry."

"Don't be. With you around, I'm getting used to rejection."

"Ouch. That was a low blow."

He grins. "The truth hurts. But look at it this way. . .I'm also learning not to give up."

Deep down in my heart, I'm afraid I'm counting on that.

## nineteen

So are you really going out with Mr. Right, Mom?" Katie hands me a silver earring with dangling charms and watches as I fasten it.

The teenage girl who baby-sits for me occasionally is in the kitchen, baking a pizza for their supper. Usually the girls don't give me a second glance when Amber's here, but tonight, fascinated by watching me get ready for a real date, they only have eyes for me.

I smile at Katie in the mirror and put in the other earring. "It's Mr. Wright with a W, honey. It's just his name."

"Tonight might change all that, though." Miranda holds her hair up on top of her head and purses her lips toward the mirror. I'm struck for the first time by the similarities in our reflections. My oldest daughter is an enigma to me. Part child, part woman. Part me, part her father. I'm clutched by a sudden yearning to cancel the date and stay home with her and Katie, holding them tight before they grow up and are gone.

I'm not sure how much of that desire is born of mother love and how much is from first-date nerves. But the doorbell rings and I don't have time to analyze further. Probably a good thing.

"I'll get it!" Katie yells and takes off for the door.

Miranda's eyes widen. She spins on her heel and runs out of the room after her sister. "No, I will! You'll scare him!"

At the sound of a scuffle in the foyer, I look in the mirror and laugh. Trevor is in for a surprise. This welcoming committee may not be exactly what he's expecting. But if he's interested in me, he might as well get used to it. We're a package deal.

I hear a masculine voice, so I'm assuming he managed to get in the house without bloodshed. A second later, Katie pokes her head in my room. "He's here." She disappears back down the hallway.

I smooth down my peasant skirt and take one last look in the mirror. Casual gypsy is my look for tonight because that's the only outfit I have that'll fit in almost anywhere. Trevor didn't mention where he was taking me, and I didn't ask, but I'm guessing we're not going bowling. And if I'm wrong, who cares? At least my red, yellow, and blue skirt will go with the shoes.

Trevor is seated on the threadbare couch, Katie beside him. Miranda is sitting in the old wingback chair, looking like she's the lady of the house interviewing for a nanny. I can't hear what they're saying, but Trevor stands when I enter the room.

"Allie, you look beautiful."

"Thanks." *Now what should I say? You do, too?* Truth is, he does. From his runner's frame, slim but muscular, to his shiny hair, trimmed neatly, just the way I like it, he's the epitome of tall, dark, and handsome. His wire-rimmed glasses only serve to emphasize the intelligence in his chocolate-colored eyes.

So why do I long to see a knife scar or a bit of a crook to his perfectly straight nose? Some people are never happy. I'm starting to wonder if I fall into that category.

As we step out on the porch, Trevor wipes at his pant legs and motions to Buddy, who is barking like a wind-up toy that's been wound too tightly. "Judging by the golden hair on my pants, I take it he stays in the house part of the time."

*Ack.* I meant to vacuum the furniture, but between working today and getting ready, it never happened. "I'm sorry. We put him out when company is coming. He's way too hyper." I turn back toward the door. "Do you want me to grab the lint roller?"

"No, that's okay." He slaps at his pants leg again. "I think I've about got it."

I shoot Buddy a glare, then immediately feel guilty. It's not the dog's fault I didn't vacuum.

An hour later when we're cozily ensconced at a table in the corner of Chez Pierre—the only white-tablecloth restaurant in a twenty-mile radius—the dog hair incident is largely forgotten, and I'm happy to discover that, even though he's a little obsessed with the greeting card business, Trevor really is good company.

Finally we exhaust the topic of greeting cards and party favors, and Trevor leans forward. "Do you date much?"

I think of Daniel and shake my head. "Not really. You?"

"Not for pleasure."

My mind races through all the other reasons a man might date, but I'm drawing a blank.

He smiles. "Sometimes I need a date for business functions."

"I see." Sort of.

"I've been wanting to ask you out for a while, though. And that has nothing to do with business."

"I'm glad."

He reaches toward my hand and I'm torn. My girls deserve a

father who can provide for them. If I let my childish infatuation with Daniel stand in the way of that, what kind of mother am I?

It turns out he's just straightening a small wrinkle in the tablecloth. Can you say moot point? I grab my water goblet to give my empty hand something to do. And knock it over.

Horror-stricken, I stare as cold water streams across the tablecloth around tiny ice cube dams, beading up like rain on a freshly waxed car, and tumbles into Trevor's lap.

He jumps to his feet and shakes out his burgundy cloth napkin.

I stand, too. "Oh no. I'm so sorry."

"Don't worry." His smile is polished, but I can't tell if he's really upset or not. He brushes at his pants with the cloth. "My napkin bore the brunt of it."

He raises a single finger and the waiter comes scurrying over. Within seconds everything is back to normal, the offending water goblet removed and a new full one in its place, along with a new napkin for Trevor.

"If one of the girls did that, I'd probably make them have a half glass this time." I grimace. "I really am sorry."

He lifts his shoulders in a graceful shrug. "I'm just glad it was water and not tea." He smiles and it seems genuine. "That could have been a sticky situation."

I grin. "Water really is better for you, isn't it?"

The waiter appears with our salads. A frown mars Trevor's handsome face. "I asked for my dressing on the side, please."

"I'm so sorry, sir," the waiter says, whisking away the salad and hurrying away to the kitchen.

"He's going to be glad to see us go," I joke.

His brows draw together. "Why?"

"Between cleaning up my spilled drink and replacing your salad. . ."

"It's his job to clean up messes and as far as the salad goes, he should have checked in the kitchen to be sure it was done correctly."

"Oh, I know, I just feel. . ." I stop myself. There's no point.

The waiter returns with a new green salad, pristine and dressing-less.

"Thank you," Trevor says, with a smile.

Glad that the whole incident is passed, I relax and enjoy my salad. "This is delicious."

He finishes chewing and wipes his mouth with his napkin. "It could use a few more spinach leaves and romaine and a little less iceberg, but it is good."

At the risk of alliteration overload, picky people are my pet peeve. "Nothing's perfect, I guess."

"But that doesn't mean we should settle for mediocrity." He sips his drink. "That's the problem with our world today. Too many people are afraid to seek perfection. They're too willing to settle."

Daniel's face flashes through my mind. I'd been seeking perfection when I met him. Had I almost settled for less? I look across the table at Trevor. Whose standard am I going by?

"I think you're right. But the only place you can find perfection is through Jesus." I'm stunned by my words. I remember what Mama tried to tell me the day she was asking me to hire Adam. Have I been looking for perfection in all the wrong places?

"That's true." He smiles. "I'm sorry if I sounded like I thought perfection was attainable without Him. In my line of work, I just get tired of seeing people give less than their best."

The waiter takes away our salads with one hand and places

entrees in front of us with the other.

"So do your daughters always interview your dates?" Trevor asks. I almost choke on the bite of steak in my mouth. "Oh no. What did they ask you?"

"Just normal things. Like do I like dogs and children? And does noise bother me? Oh, and if I like Rocky Road ice cream." He makes a face. "I was doing fairly well until then. But they didn't seem very impressed that I'm lactose intolerant."

"I'm sorry. I'm sure they were just making conversation."

He laughs. "Don't kid yourself. Someday when they're old enough, I'll hire them both in our personnel department."

I give him a weak grin. What made me think those little scamps needed my help to ensure their future?

A little later, I relax into the leather seat of Trevor's sports car while he walks around to get in. The date's over, and aside from a few mishaps—like me dumping my drink in his lap—I think it went well.

Until he climbs into the driver's seat and looks at me in the moonlight. "So how about getting a cup of coffee at that new place?"

A million excuses pop to my mind. I open my mouth to give just one. But before I can, he speaks again.

"I promised the guys at the club I'd let them know how good it is." He grins. "The coffee place, I mean. Not our date."

"Oh, good. You didn't strike me as the type to kiss and tell." Heat rushes up my face. Where had that come from? "I—I didn't mean it like that," I stammer.

He takes my stammer for assent and laughs as he puts the car in gear. "You're right, though. I'm not."

Time for a new subject. On the way to the Coffee Central

Bookstore, we chat about the weather (it's been unseasonably warm this spring), Shady Grove (wonderful place to settle down), and the impact of the greeting card factory on the town (very positive according to Trevor). But all I can think about is Daniel. What will I say if he's there? I vacillate between heaping guilt on myself for going out tonight and reminding myself that Daniel has no hold on me. Not officially, anyway.

I could just plead tiredness or even say I'm not in the mood for coffee. But in good conscience, how can I knock Daniel out of a whole new group of customers? Besides, what are the chances of him being there on Saturday night? Even as I think that, the phrase "famous last words" resounds in my mind.

All my angst turns out to be for naught when we get there. Daniel is nowhere to be seen when we walk up to the counter.

I order my usual white chocolate latté, then step back for Trevor to order.

"Can I see a list of ingredients?" he asks the redheaded girl behind the counter.

Her eyes widen. "Sir? Which ingredients?"

"Of your drinks."

I promise she's about to cry. "Of all the drinks?"

I lean forward. "Trevor, maybe if you pick out two or three choices she can get you the list of ingredients for those."

His mouth tightens a little, but he nods and chooses three drinks. While she's gone to get the ingredients list, he looks back at me. "These places have to have that information available. When you're lactose intolerant, it's imperative to know whether a product has hidden dairy or not."

Hidden dairy gives me visions of black and white cows with

trench coats and dark glasses slipping around to meet Farmer Brown. If I smile, Trevor will think I'm not taking his problem seriously, and nothing could be further from the truth. So I run my thumb and forefinger over the corners of my mouth, forcing down my grin—a precaution that proves unnecessary when the redhead comes back, with none other than Daniel behind her.

"Can I help you?" he asks Trevor.

I'm slightly behind my date, and if he were a bigger man maybe I could hide there, but even I'm not that naïvely optimistic.

I brace myself and step out to face the music.

To my surprise, Daniel keeps his focus entirely on politely explaining the ingredients list to Trevor. After he finishes, Trevor thanks him and places his order. Daniel exits stage left without so much as a glance at me. I'm not sure if he didn't see me or didn't want to see me. Or plain old didn't care. Talk about anticlimactic.

After we finish our drinks, Trevor delivers me back to my house and walks me to the door. I remember my remark about him "kissing and telling" and my face reddens all over again. Before I can decide how to handle the inevitable front porch two-step, he drops a quick kiss on my hot cheek.

"I enjoyed tonight, Allie."

How sweet. "Me, too."

"I'd like to get together again. Is it okay if I call you?"

"Sure. But until this contest is over, phone calls may be all I have time for."

"I understand. But it won't hurt to ask." He starts back to his car. "You can always say no."

I grimace as I slide the key into the doorknob. *No* is one word I'm getting good at. Just ask Daniel.

# twenty

After worship Sunday morning, Katie nudges me. "Elijah's here. I just saw him."

She's right. From the double doors on the other side, the congregation is streaming out into the foyer, and there he is with Daniel and Candice. Candice waves at me and turns to speak to Daniel. I return her wave and keep moving toward the main exit. After last night, I'm not sure what to say. If by some freak of nature he didn't see me, I don't want to point out to him that I was on a date at Coffee Central. But the idea of not mentioning it feels incredibly awkward.

The girls and I step out into the bright sunshine.

"Hi, Allie."

I turn to greet Candice. "Candice, it's great to see you. Have you been coming here long?"

She shakes her head. "We've always gone to the downtown church, but this is closer. Plus, Daniel likes the early church service, don't you, bro?" She glances behind her and frowns. "Where did he go? He was here just a few seconds ago."

My heart sinks. Of course he saw me last night. He must have disappeared when he realized his sister was seeking me out. "That's strange. I guess I'd better run, too. We're really glad to have y'all here."

The girls and I always go to Mama's for lunch on Sundays and most often, like today, Rachel joins us. Her parents live ten minutes down the road, but she doesn't see them much. After we eat, the girls and Mama go out to play catch, while Rachel and I do the dishes—which works out perfectly because it gives me time to catch her up on the latest events in the saga of "As Allie's World Turns."

She rinses out a bowl and puts it in the top rack of the dishwasher. "Since your biggest concern is whether or not Daniel is mad, I take it the date with Mr. Right wasn't fantabulous?"

I shrug. "It was nice."

"As in knock-your-socks-off nice or as in finding-an-extra-ten-dollar-bill-tucked-in-the-back-of-your-wallet nice?"

I laugh and hand her a plate. "Probably more like an extra ten."

She mock-frowns and shakes her head as she runs the plate under the water. "That's not good."

"Hey. These days I'd probably rather have the money than the thrill."

"Somehow I doubt that." She closes the dishwasher and starts it.

"Speaking of money, I'm getting ready to spend some more." I rinse the dishcloth and squeeze it out.

"On the fountain?"

I nod as I wipe the table. "I called Paul Wilson, the city council chairman, yesterday after we left the park. He said we don't need approval for that fountain as long as it fits into our budget."

Rachel plops down in a chair. "Wonderful. I'm surprised, though. Why?"

"Apparently it's 'grandfathered' in. There's always been a fountain there until about fifteen years ago when a big tree fell across it." I sit next to her and dry off the table with a towel.

"That's fantastic. Saves so much hassle."

I nod. "Now if I could just get my personal life to work out so smoothly."

"Yeah, well, we're working on that."

Sad when salvaging your social life takes a group effort. But such is life. My life anyway.

The next morning I take a break from my TV boycott to see what Blair is up to. One of the other teams has a muscular, tanned man who is obviously a ham. He plays to the camera, and I keep expecting him to break into song any minute. The audience must like him, though, because the whole clip is of him, shirtless and sweaty. Next comes the other landscaping crew. They're so professional that I think Blair has given up finding anything silly about them. Two of the workers show how to plant a tree in exaggerated steps, actually talking to the camera as they do it. Then comes us.

For a second, I can see why they need us as comic relief. But that doesn't mean I like it. Especially when the clip shows each of us tripping. Not that any of us fall, but just a little stumble when we're carrying plants or rocks. Like the original rock-wall scene,

Blair has edited it to make it look like we're tripping one after another, first Victoria, then Lark, then Rachel, and finally me. I'm not sure if Adam didn't trip or if she actually had the decency not to humiliate him further. Probably he just didn't trip.

Blair freezes the clip with me in mid-trip on the big screen behind her.

Nice.

When she speaks, I quickly forget that my image is frozen in an awkward position for all of Shady Grove's viewing pleasure. "Rumor has it that Allie Richards is counting on a top-secret project to keep TLC Landscaping afloat in the contest. Let's just hope this latest venture doesn't land them in hot water as far as city ordinances."

I growl. Out loud. The fountain. The water references are unmistakable. How could she know about it? I'm not surprised that Daniel figured out what Craig was drawing on the ground when he showed up Saturday. But could he have been mad enough at me to sell me out to Blair even when he was off the clock? Maybe it was guilt at his traitorous actions that made him avoid me yesterday after church.

My only consolation is that she's wrong about city ordinances. So there. I make a face at the screen just as Miranda walks in.

"Did you just make a face?" She's obviously incredulous.

"Maybe." I sigh. "Yes."

"At the TV?"

I nod. "Sorry."

She shrugs as she walks to the bathroom. "Your business."

She's wrong. Since I've started this contest, thanks to Blair, nothing is strictly my business.

The workday goes well, considering Daniel and I both stay completely away from each other. I'm assuming Lark, Victoria, and Adam all saw the show, but no one mentions it. We actually get a lot done. I stay late and work on moving the rocks to the fountain area. Since Blair knows about it, I might as well go full-steam ahead.

I drag in just in time to shower, fix supper, and referee a fight between the girls.

"Mom! Why does she always get the computer just because she's the oldest? I want to play my game."

I step from the stove to the doorway of the dining room, where our computer resides on a corner desk.

"I'm working on something for school," Miranda says, barely looking up.

"Yeah, a list of the cutest boys."

"Tattletale!" Good thing Miranda doesn't have laser vision, or Katie would have a black hole bored through her.

"Miranda, it's Katie's turn on the computer."

"You always take her side. Just because she's the baby." Do parents with more than two children hear this constant refrain? You like her best just because she's the middle child or just because she's the second-oldest doesn't have the same ring to it.

"Girls, you're being ridiculous. I expect you to take turns."

Katie, apparently deciding that I do indeed like her best, sticks out her tongue at her sister. "Katherine Marie, that's it. You're both grounded from the computer until further notice."

"What'd I do?" Miranda whines.

"We'll talk about it in a minute. Go wash your hands right now. Supper's ready."

When we all have our plates full, I offer thanks for the food, then send up a silent prayer asking for wisdom in handling the girls. One of my constant prayers these days.

"Miranda, you asked what you did. Here's the deal, girls. It's the attitude. You both need to get a new one."

Miranda mumbles something.

"What did you say?"

"I just said you aren't around enough to know what kind of attitude we have."

Ouch. "I'm around now."

"But you never go to soccer practice anymore. And it's almost dark when you pick us up at Memaw's." She sticks out her lower lip, and I can see we're about to get to the root of the problem. "You didn't even ask how practice went today."

Was I really that tired? Maybe so. I'd just thought of getting a shower and fixing supper so we could get to bed. "How did practice go?"

"Miranda made a goal," Katie says.

"Good job, Miranda. Katie, how did practice go for you?"

"Great. Except I wish you could have been there. I got an assist."

"I wish I could have, too, honey, but your memaw and I agreed that she'd take you to practices, and I'd take you to games." I push the green beans around on my plate. I'm almost too exhausted to eat. "With this contest, I have to work extra-long hours. We talked about that, remember?"

"You talked about it. We listened," Miranda says from where she's slumped in her chair.

"Are you having a bad time at Memaw's in the afternoons?" I know better. The kids love staying at my mother's. But I want to give her a chance to voice her real complaint.

"No."

"Then what's wrong?"

She cuts her eyes at Katie. "Nothing."

In other words, nothing she wants her little sister to know.

I change the subject and we finish the meal in relative peace.

After they're in bed, and I've heard Katie's prayers, I tap on Miranda's door.

"Come in."

She's sitting on the bed, a pillow clutched to her stomach, her face red and blotchy.

I sit down beside her, determined to be casual. Too much attention is as bad as not enough when you're almost a teenager. I do remember some things. "What's up?"

She shrugs and sniffs.

"Something happen at school?"

Another shrug.

Mothers should be recruited for interrogation positions with the FBI. After you've managed to pry information out of a moody preteen, you can get anybody to talk. "Did you and Lindsey have a fight?" Lindsey is her new best friend, and I'm not completely sure I approve. She just seems so much more mature than Cassie, Miranda's best friend since kindergarten. And I don't mean that in a good way. Still, there's nothing I can put my finger on. She's a nice enough girl.

"Not really a fight."

I let the words hang in the air.

"I told her a secret, and she told someone."

"That's hard to get over. Was it a big secret?"

She nods and pulls the pillow up under her chin, seemingly ready to smother her words with it if she starts telling me too much. "I told her I like Brett. And she told him."

The biggest secret of all. Miranda has liked him for at least two years, but as far as I know Cassie is the only one she's ever told. And Cassie never told anyone. I resist the urge to explain that this is why she should have stayed friends with Cassie. "Sometimes girls think they're helping by telling a boy that their friend likes him. Maybe she thought you were just too shy to tell him and this would get him to notice you."

The tears well up in her blue eyes and bounce down her already blotchy cheeks. "She asked him if he liked me and he said 'as a friend.'"

Far be it from me to point out that at twelve, that's a good way to be liked. I pull her into my arms, and to my surprise she snuggles against me like she used to. "He might have been embarrassed to admit his real feelings."

"You think so?" She pushes back and looks at me. "His friends *were* all there."

"Then I'd say that's a really good possibility."

She hugs me again and whispers, "I think Lindsey likes him and that's why she did it."

"Could be. It's hard to be friends with someone you don't trust." Daniel's face flits through my mind. Who else could be telling Blair everything? Do I really want to be friends with someone I don't trust? "You'll have to decide that for yourself, though."

Miranda swipes away the last of the tears. "I'll think about that."

I don't say it aloud, but so will I.

# twenty-one

After yesterday's tripping bonanza and snide remarks about our secret project, I not only stay away from Daniel again today, but I'm back to my boycott of "Get Real, Shady Grove." According to the Pinkies, though, Blair hardly focused on us at all on this morning's show.

At noon when Adam goes to get some plants, Lark, Rachel, and I relax beneath the big oak with our lunch.

"What's Blair's deal, do you think?" Lark asks.

I cut my ham and cheese into triangular halves and pour myself a cup of water. "I really don't know. Why didn't she just spill the beans about the fountain? It's as if she's toying with us like a cat with a mouse."

"Do you think she was one of those mean girls in high school?" Lark takes a drink. "Or did her life just go so terribly wrong at some point that she turned?"

Victoria wags her sun-dried tomato turkey sandwich at us and shakes her head. "Nobody gets that bad without having some pretty hard knocks, surely."

"So I guess we should feel sorry for her."

They look at me like I'm crazy.

"Well, if she 'turned' because of some awful thing that happened to her, shouldn't we?" I pour some chips onto a paper plate.

"Feel sorry for her all you want to, shugah. Just don't trust her."

"You got that right." Lark picks at her tuna sandwich.

"Are you sick?" I blurt out, without thinking.

She looks up, startled. "Me? No."

"You haven't been eating much lately."

"Got a lot on my mind."

"You know, honey," Victoria drawls, "a burden shared is a burden lightened."

Tears glisten in Lark's dark eyes. "Not this one. Not yet. But thanks."

We let it go. At least she's not sick. That's a relief.

When Craig comes by a few minutes later in his plumbing truck, she goes out to talk to him, and Victoria looks across at me. "We need to be having some serious Pinky prayer for that girl."

I nod. "We have to tell Rachel."

"I'll leave her a message on her voice mail." She picks up her cell phone and walks toward the far side of the park.

I can breathe easier since the others are praying with me about Lark. A burden shared is a burden lightened. That sums up the Pinkies in one sentence.

The next few days are uneventful, unless you count the fact that not speaking to Daniel is making me tired. I hadn't realized how much I've grown to rely on his friendship.

Thursday, I'm sorting the new plants into the right areas when he walks up to me. "Hi."

"Hi."

"Any particular reason why you're not speaking to me?"

Leave it to him to get to the point. In a way, I'm surprised he didn't do this sooner.

"Maybe because you started it?" Leave it to me not to be able to think of a mature answer.

"How did I start it?"

"Sunday after church when you saw Candice was coming over to talk to me, you disappeared."

He raises his eyebrow. "Brother Jamison called me back into the building to ask me if we were enjoying worshiping there. When I got out, you were gone."

I'm dumbfounded. "You weren't mad about Saturday night?"

He runs his hand across the back of his neck. "Jealous maybe. But not mad. Why would I be? You told me you had plans." He gives me a rueful grin. "I admit I panicked a little when Katie told me you had a date with Mr. Right."

My turn for a rueful grin. At least he doesn't know how we teased about Trevor being Mr. Right. "You didn't speak to me."

"I wasn't sure I could pull off casual. And I didn't want to look like a jealous idiot and ruin your date."

How am I supposed to resist his honesty? Besides being flattered, I feel like the idiot. But obviously that's no one's fault but my own. Still there is the matter of Blair's informer. "So if you weren't mad, why did you tell Blair about the fountain? Is spying in your job description?"

Either he's a consummate actor or genuinely bewildered. "I don't tell Blair anything. I just deliver the tape."

Pull out the Arkansas oceanfront sales brochure and call me gullible. I can't help but believe him.

Friday morning I wake up excited to go to work. The black cloud that's been hanging over me since Trevor and I ran into Daniel Saturday night has dissipated. It's probably a sad commentary on the state of my heart that making up with Daniel makes me feel this energized and ready to go, but there it is.

I even flip on the TV in time to catch the end of the "Get Real, Shady Grove" segment. Zoom in on Blair: "TLC had their version of a full crew today. . . ." Pan out to the clip behind her shoulder to show Adam, Victoria, Lark, and me working. "Such as it is. But according to reports, Allie Richards may have gotten overambitious with her plan. Even though the other two teams seem to be a little ahead of schedule, I'm pretty sure TLC doesn't have a day to spare." She gives her most saccharine smile. "I guess we'll just have to hope it doesn't rain."

Yeah, right. Hope it does rain is more like it. I glance out the window. Sunny skies and last I heard, that's what the forecast calls for.

Unfortunately, Blair must have an in with the weatherman, because right before noon, the drizzle starts. I can't believe it. There wasn't a cloud in the sky twenty minutes ago. Now it's solid gray. And that's not good. I can remember watching the clouds with my dad when I was young. He'd point out broken clouds and say, "If it showers now, it won't last. But if there's a solid bank of clouds, you might as well find something to do inside."

Daniel is over at his Harley putting the camera away when the first drops start. "I'm going to try to beat the rain home," he hollers with a wave. "See you later."

So much for me thinking he might ask me to lunch. Of course I was going to insist we take the SUV. I might be slightly infatuated but not enough to be talked into riding a motorcycle.

"Are we quitting?" Adam asks from behind me.

I clutch my shovel handle and swipe at the raindrops on my face with my shoulder. "Y'all go ahead. I'm going to try to get a few more of these shrubs planted."

"I'll stay, too." He goes back to work.

Five minutes later, it starts to pour. Lark and Victoria wave and run for the vehicles.

Adam trots over to me and holds a plastic bag above my head. "It's lunchtime anyway, sis. Why don't we go home and if it stops later we'll come back?"

I nod and take the bag. "Thanks."

If I believed in jinxes, I'd say Blair did this, but I know better.

By midafternoon the rain shows no signs of quitting. It lets up occasionally, then starts again just as I get ready to head over to the park. As if I don't have enough uncertainty in my life.

I meet the girls at Mama's car with an umbrella. Their excited chatter as we slop back up to the house almost makes this impromptu day off worth it. Almost. Until I think of all the things left to get done at the site.

As soon as we get in the house, the soccer coach calls. Big surprise. Tonight's game is cancelled.

"Oh no!" Miranda flounces onto the couch and crosses her arm.

Katie's a little more philosophical. "Oh well. We'll make it up later."

"Of course you don't care. That's because you're a—"

I don't know for sure what Miranda was going to say because Katie throws her hand over her sister's mouth.

Miranda peels Katie's fingers away from her mouth. "MOM! She did it again."

This habit has gotten out of hand. No pun intended. Katie feels frustrated, I think, by not being able to keep up with her sister in a war of words, so she always resorts to trying to physically stop Miranda from talking. "Katie, go to your room. No TV, computer, video games, or even books for thirty minutes. I want you to think about why you're not to put your hand on your sister's mouth."

"But she was going to say—"

I hold up my hand. "I don't care what she was going to say. The point is you know better than to do that. Go to your room."

She goes.

And I turn. Just in time to see a smirk cross Miranda's face.

"Miranda!"

Immediate guilt. "What?"

"You know what. Were you going to call your sister a baby?"

She shrugs. "I guess."

"You go to your room for thirty minutes, too. Same rules apply."

"Why? What did I do?"

I narrow my eyes. "You're intelligent enough to know the answer to that."

She huffs away to her room and stops just short of slamming

the door behind her. Instead, she closes it extra gently at the last second. Like I said, smart girl.

And I'll go to my room and think about why I shouldn't worry about the weather, since I certainly can't control it.

I stretch out on my bed and try to relax. My gaze lands on my well-worn Bible on the nightstand. The last few days I've been too rushed in the morning to read my verses. And too tired at night.

Maybe the rain is just a time of much-needed respite for me to bring my life back into focus. Or maybe it's just weather patterns, but I can still use it for respite, can't I?

I turn over on my stomach and slide the leather-bound book toward me. As I flip through, I run across my verse from that first day after I didn't get the bank loan.

*"Do not be anxious about anything, but in everything, by prayer and petition, with thanksgiving, present your requests to God."*

That day I'd been really hung up on being anxious for nothing, but today the next verse jumps out at me. *"And the peace of God, which transcends all understanding, will guard your hearts and your minds in Christ Jesus."*

I'm so tired. The thought of a peace that transcends all understanding sounds wonderful. *Oh, Lord, I want that peace.*

When I wake, Katie is calling my name.

"In here." I push myself up and close the Bible.

She comes into the room and hugs me. "I'm sorry, Mom."

"Okay, sweetie."

I sit on the side of the bed and get my bearings. "What do you want for supper, kiddo?"

Miranda walks in before Katie can answer. "Pizza?"

I open my mouth to remind her that we can't afford pizza when she says, "I mean frozen."

"Sounds good."

The three of us walk together to the kitchen, but the phone rings as we're walking by my desk. I glance at the caller ID. A cell phone number I don't recognize.

"Hello?"

"Hi, Allie. It's Daniel."

I sink down onto my chair. "Hi. Did you get your baby home without getting it too wet?" I wind the cord around my fingers and smile.

He laughs. "Yes. Sorry I was in a hurry. I was hoping you heard me holler good-bye."

"I see where your priorities lie." Hold the phone. Am I flirting? What am I thinking?

I look up to see the girls watching me, apparently fascinated by my transformation.

"Who is it?" Miranda mouths.

I shake my head and swivel until my back is to them.

"I've got a problem." His voice is deep and solemn.

"What's wrong?"

"I guess you know the soccer game is cancelled. Candice pulled a weekend shift in the ER, and Elijah and I are at loose ends tonight."

"Really?"

"I thought we might pick up you and the girls and go out for a burger. Our treat."

"Oh. . ." Yes, yes, yes. I think the rain has fogged up my brain. I can't think of one reason not to say yes.

"As friends, of course."

See? He knows it's not a date. So what's the harm? "That sounds good. What time?"

"Can y'all be ready in half an hour?"

"No problem." If I move at the speed of light. "We'll meet y'all outside so you don't have to get out in the rain."

I hang up and explain to the girls.

"Yippee!" Katie whoops.

"So you're going out with Mr. Daniel," Miranda says, her eyes twinkling.

"As *friends*," I stress.

Miranda grins. "You did sound awfully friendly on the phone."

I smile at her. "Hush and go get ready."

# twenty-two

W'e're waiting on the porch when they arrive in Daniel's extended cab truck. He jumps out with an umbrella and ushers the girls into the backseat with Elijah. Since I have my own umbrella I go around to climb in, but before I can, he's there opening my door and giving me a hand up into the front seat.

For that few seconds while he is going back around to his side, I stare at the windshield wipers swishing away the rain. In spite of the kids rattling away in the back, this feels more intimate than my "date" with Trevor. Especially when Daniel climbs in the cab and looks across at me, rain dripping off his hair and running down his face. He picks up a hand towel from the seat and dries his hair off. "Hi."

Did I mention his eyes are so blue?

"Hi."

He gives me a slow smile and puts the truck in gear. "You look nice tonight."

I look down at my damp jeans and tee. "For a drowned rat, maybe."

He glances at me. "You're going to have to learn to take a compliment."

How many times have I heard that before? "You're right. My friends always say the same thing."

"That you look nice?"

I laugh. "Hardly. Anyway, thanks."

"You're welcome. Is this rain going to mess you up at the park?" he asks, but I'm glad to see he's keeping his attention on the wet road.

I look out my window at the small stream flowing down the side of the highway. "Only if it doesn't stop by tomorrow."

"Too much of a good thing, huh?"

"Something like that."

When we pull into Burger Barn, Daniel insists on letting us out under the awning, so the kids and I go on in and get a table for five. By the time we're seated, he joins us. We study the menu, then all order cheeseburgers and fries. As soon as the waitress is gone, the kids beg for quarters for the retro arcade games. I give each of my girls a dollar bill—the last two in my purse—and they head off with Elijah to play Pac-Man.

Daniel picks up the saltshaker and passes it from hand to hand. Nerves? For some reason the thought makes me feel better about my own pounding heart. "Between Candice getting called in to work and the soccer game being cancelled, Elijah and I were pretty lonesome. Thanks for coming."

"Thanks for inviting us. Candice is an RN, right?"

He plunks the shaker down on the table and it tips over, spilling a little salt. "Oops." He sets it upright and smiles. "Yeah, she hates weekend shifts, but occasionally she ends up with one."

"She seems so down-to-earth. I bet she's really good at what she does."

He nods. "She has a calming way about her that patients love. And it doesn't hurt at home either, especially with Carl over in Iraq."

"Oh, I had no idea. I guess I just assumed she was a single mom like me."

"He just shipped out a couple of months ago. That's why when the opportunity came up, I decided to try my hand at the coffee shop/bookstore combination. It isn't exactly my dream career, but it puts food on the table."

"Coffee Central looks like it's going to be successful. So your dream is to be an author?"

He nods. "Sounds crazy, doesn't it? That's why I don't tell most people."

"No crazier than me wanting to have a landscaping business. Do you know how many people have laughed at that?" Even Jon did, but I don't say that. "Why would a woman want to do that?" I shrug. "But it's my dream. And this is yours."

"Thanks."

"How did you get started writing?"

He sits back in his chair. "Once I learned my ABCs it was fairly simple." His dimple flashes. "Seriously, when I was young, I wrote stories to escape. Of how life could be if I were writing it. Everything was perfect in those stories."

"I can imagine."

"Then later, after I left here, I got into dark reality and wrote some out-of-control pieces I considered realism." He gives me a wry smile. "You might call them horror."

"Is that what you write now?"

He shakes his head. "No. Since I've met the true Author of Life, I hope I've found a balance."

I swallow against the lump in my throat. Here's someone who's been to the pits of despair with his family life and whatever came after, but he still came out of it filled with hope. And I let a little rain get me down?

The waitress returns with our drinks.

Daniel passes me a straw. "So, how is your park project shaping up? I don't know that much about landscaping, but you seem to be doing a great job." I could almost hear "no matter what Blair says," but at least he didn't say it aloud.

"Thanks. I really need to win. You know how important this is to me and the girls."

"I don't get a vote, but if I did, I'd vote for you."

"Thanks. But with Blair against us, though, we probably don't have a chance."

"Just for the record, Blair doesn't get a vote either. The judging is strictly confidential. I don't think it's influenced by anyone at the station."

"I appreciate knowing that. I figured she was a strike against us." I take a sip of my drink and almost choke at his next words.

"No. I've seen your stack of fan mail."

"You're kidding? Fan mail?"

"The station manager should be getting it to you soon. But it's there. Most of the viewers really admire you."

"Right. What's to admire?" As soon as I say it I realize it sounds like I'm fishing for compliments. "I mean—"

Daniel leans forward. "Don't sell yourself short, Allie. There's a lot to admire." To my amazement, he starts a list. A list! "Like what a good mother you are. Even when you have so much going on, you make it to their games. And what loyal friends you have. That says something really good about you. And that you still have faith in God—even after you lost your husband and your job. And that you look beautiful even when you're sweating over those plants. Oh"—he winks at me—"and that you haven't lost your cool and told Blair off even though I'm sure she deserves it. Need I go on?"

Well, if there's more. . . "No, I'm blushing already. But thanks."

"Just stating the facts."

"Mom, can we have another dollar?" Katie is hopping beside me.

I telegraph to her with my eyes that I don't have anymore and amazingly, she gets it. She slides into her seat without another word.

I'm guessing Daniel recognizes the look, too, because he waves to Elijah and Miranda. "Sit with us for a while. Our food will be here in a few minutes. And if you all eat a good supper, I've got some money in my pocket that's just dying to play Pac-Man."

With perfect timing, the waitress brings our burgers and fries. After we eat, Daniel makes good on his promise and gives the kids two dollars each.

When they're gone, I look up at him. Honesty is the best policy. We both know I'm broke. "I'll pay you back."

"You don't owe me anything. You rescued us from a night of total boredom."

"Yeah, like I believe you couldn't find something else to do."

He smiles at me across the table, and for a second, the noisy Burger Barn is the most romantic place in America. "Nothing I'd have enjoyed more."

Mr. Wrong? Maybe so. But I'm starting not to care.

Much later that night, I lie in the bed, cordless phone tucked between my ear and my pillow, and pour out my woes to Rachel.

"It's hard for me to think straight when I'm with him. Tonight when we got back here and the kids were watching a movie, we sat at the kitchen table and talked. It felt like we'd known each other for years."

"Haven't you?"

"I mean *really* known each other. Been friends. Close friends. Close friends who occasionally hold hands across the table."

She snorts. "Gotcha."

"We have more in common than you can imagine. He loves John Wayne movies, too. Did you know?"

"How can you go wrong with a man if he's seen *Big Jake* even half as many times as you have?"

I giggle. "He has all his movies on DVD."

"There's reason enough to marry him right there."

"Oh, Rach. When I'm away from him, I know he's not the one for me."

"How do you know?"

"That he's not the one? Easy. He wears jeans 24/7 and rides a Harley."

"So you're looking for a man who wears a suit and drives a Volvo, right?"

"Yes. No." A strangled laugh erupts from my throat. "You make me sound shallow."

"Not shallow, just cautious."

"I don't care what he wears or what he drives. Not really. The problem is *who* he is."

"A really sweet Christian guy who appears to be crazy about you."

"That's something else." I shift in the bed until the pillows are behind my back and clutch the phone with my hand. "That right there shows he doesn't think before he acts. Why would he be crazy about me? Especially so quickly?"

"Oh, yeah. I hate it when sweet Christian guys fall at my feet too soon."

"Rach! Be serious. You know what I mean. He's impulsive. He's liable to up and sell the bookstore tomorrow and roar off to parts unknown. That's who he is."

"I'm not as sure of that as you seem to be. I don't think you're letting yourself really see him."

"Why wouldn't I?"

"Maybe because it's easier to find someone like Trevor who appeals to your logic and good sense but leaves your heart alone? That way you don't have to worry about being hurt again if something happens to him."

Ouch. "I don't think that's it." But I don't intend to spend any more time analyzing. "We'd better call it a night. The rain's stopped finally. We're going to have a long day of work tomorrow."

"See you there. If it's not raining again."

"Bite your tongue."

She chuckles. "Hey, I don't make the weather. I just watch it on TV."

I hang up and resist the urge to get up and go check the NOAA weather Web site. Whatever happens tomorrow happens. My new motto.

# twenty-three

My new motto lasted as long as it took for me to get out of bed this morning to the sound of pounding rain. It's easy to say we won't worry about tomorrow, but when tomorrow becomes today, how do you keep from worrying then? Invariably when life gets complicated, I look to the simpler things for comfort. My old flannel pajamas, classic reruns, cinnamon sugar toast, hot cocoa from scratch. I'm hoping that this explains why I'm sitting here now in my nubby blue cloud PJs, wiping away crumbs of sugar and slurping chocolate heaven, while I watch John Boy and Mary Ellen make peace about which one of them Mama left in charge.

"Mama." It takes me a minute to realize the voice doesn't belong to Erin or Jim Bob, but my own real-life Katie.

"What is it, sweetie?" I murmur, my eyes fixed on the screen as if watching them solve their problems will magically erase my own.

"It's nine o'clock. Miranda says she thinks you're having a breakdown because it's raining and we can't work."

Am I? Maybe. But not if I don't admit it. "She's wrong this time. I'm okay."

"Why aren't you fixing breakfast?"

I keep my eyes on the screen and nod toward the stove. "Cinnamon toast for both of you. Hot chocolate in the pan."

"Oh. Okay. Thanks, Mom. You're the best."

A few minutes later I hear her telling Miranda that I made a yummy breakfast and am not having a breakdown. I can't hear her sister's reply. Probably just as well.

At some point, the girls join me in my Walton marathon. At noon I glance out the window. Either I'm delusional or the rain has really slacked off.

I push Katie off my lap and gently slap Miranda's leg. "Let's get ready and run over to the park, see if we can work a little. Y'all want to?"

They agree and hurry off to change. Before long, we're on our way.

To a big muddy mess. The rain has actually stopped completely by the time we get to the park. But the aftereffects linger. I make the girls stay on the pea gravel playground area while I slop around a little, taking stock of the situation. No permanent damage, but it'll be Monday before things dry out enough for us to work without making large ruts everywhere we step.

When I get back to the girls, Katie's at the top of the slide. I look at Miranda. "Sorry. We're not going to be able to work today."

"Oh no." An impish grin teases at the corner of Miranda's mouth. "Looks like we're stuck with the playground."

"It's too wet, isn't it?"

She turns to show me the seat of her jeans. "Katie and I are drying it off—one thing at a time."

They're already wet now. No sense ruining their fun. "That's so nice of you," I tease.

"We thought so. Wanna help?"

"Not really. But I do have a book in the vehicle." Left over from the pre-contest days. "Maybe I'll just sit here on the bench and read."

I grab the book, and since the sun is peeking out from behind a cloud, I pick up my sunglasses, too, and head back to the bench. An hour later the girls are done playing. I never got past the first chapter of the book. Too hard to concentrate when I'm fretting about the lost day of work—day and a half if you count yesterday.

"This was fun, Mom," Katie says as she loops her arm in mine. "We should do it more often."

I look toward the clear sky. When the contest is over. No more rainy days, please, until then.

Sunday morning dawns bright and sunny with enough wind to dry things out by tomorrow. I sing "Blue Skies and Rainbows" under my breath as I wrap my robe around me and search my closet for something happy enough to match my mood.

The sun is shining in more ways than one at our house. Maybe the girls take their cue from me, but even Katie hurries, and I actually get us to church on time.

We take our usual seats, and I shush the girls in anticipation of the beginning of the service. A slight scuff sound beside me draws my attention to Daniel and Elijah, standing at the edge of our pew. I smile up at him. This day just gets better and better.

"Is this seat taken?" My, he's formal today. Although judging by the twinkle in his eyes and hint of a dimple, maybe not.

I'll play along. "Actually, I'm saving it for a friend." I grin.

"Well, like they say, the only way to have a friend is to be one."

Mrs. McElroy in the pew in front of us turns and gives me a curious look. Unfortunately, even at church some people find fodder for gossip. I just hate to be the fodder. But I don't hate it enough to not have Daniel and Elijah sit with us. Besides, since Blair has taken on the mission of making me the laughingstock of Shady Grove, what harm can one more wagging tongue do? I shoot a steely smile toward Mrs. McElroy and open my mouth to reply to Daniel's quote with a witty little rejoinder. Of course, I draw a blank. He'll just have to settle for a warm invitation to sit with us. But my pause must have been longer than I realized.

"Don't worry about it. I see empty seats two pews up."

I jerk my head up. I embarrassed him. "Oh no, you don't!" Oops. That didn't come out like I meant for it to. But I blunder on. "I mean, you're welcome to sit here. Hurry. The service is about to begin."

Daniel looks a little dazed, as if he's unwittingly wandered into the Twilight Zone. But he allows Elijah to slide in beside Katie before he sinks down next to me. With his elbow brushing mine, I have to concentrate at the beginning of service. But I gradually become immersed in worship.

When the last amen sounds, I step into the aisle behind Daniel, determined that for once in our rollercoaster relationship I'm going to step up to bat instead of leaving all the work to him. Who knows? I might even knock it out of the park.

"Hey." Brilliant intro. Strike one. "We're having lunch." Duh. Strike two. "I mean, we eat at Mama's every Sunday after church, and she fixes enough to feed an army." Now I'm implying that he eats a lot. Foul ball. "We'd love to have you and Elijah join us. Rachel usually spends Sunday afternoons with us, and Adam's there, but that'll be all." Well, that was a hit. More like a little dribble straight to the pitcher, but it gets the job done.

"If you're sure there will be enough extra for two growing boys, we'd be glad to accept. Why don't you let the girls ride with us?"

"Can we, Mom?" That's Katie. I thought she'd gone out the other end of the aisle.

"If you think you're up for corralling three kids, go for it. I'll go on and get the table set." Oh, yes, and warn—tell—Mama that I invited company. Not that she'll care. Hospitality's her calling.

Sure enough, when Rachel and I get there, she has a complete, traditional "Sunday dinner" featuring Southern-fried chicken and all the trimmings ready to eat. All we have to do is set the table and put ice in the glasses. As I put the last fork on the table, Adam comes downstairs. A few seconds later Daniel and the kids arrive.

When we're all finished eating, Rachel, who always stays at Mama's from morning service until evening service, discovers an urgent need to go home. She's so obvious. Maybe Daniel won't notice the wink she sends my way as she waves. He acts unaware, but whether from tact or truth, who knows?

Adam excuses himself and goes up to his room. Probably having withdrawal symptoms from being away from his video games so long. At least I know his departure isn't staged to give Daniel and me time together.

As soon as Rachel and Adam leave, Mama claps her hands and looks at the kids. "Who wants to fly a kite?" Within minutes, Daniel and I are doing the dishes alone. Mama and Rachel went to the same subtlety class apparently. Or maybe they were both absent the day they covered that.

He rinses the dishes while I load the dishwasher.

"Mama's always had a knack for fun. Adam and I learned to fly kites about the time we learned to walk." I'm leaned over putting a plate on the bottom shelf when I remember how Daniel was raised. Nothing like rubbing it in. I straighten and smile. "Of course sometimes when she told us to go fly a kite, it didn't mean we were actually going to have fun."

He stops in the middle of rinsing a bowl. "You don't ever have to do that, Allie."

"Do what?"

"Try to make your childhood seem less than idyllic just because mine was."

I should have known he wouldn't let me get away with that. "Sorry. As soon as I said it, I realized. . . ."

"Candice and I had a lot of good times growing up." He chuckles. "Of course, time does tend to make the lens we look through more forgiving."

"You *are* a writer, aren't you?"

"Are you *always* going to accuse me of using different words just because I'm a writer?"

"Probably." I take the glass he passes me and our hands touch. Be still my heart.

Is he as aware as I am of the possible future implied in his word *always*?

I wake up Monday determined to make up for lost time. With the park, definitely. And maybe even in getting to know Daniel better. I haven't given up my reservations about him, but they're not as strong as they were.

A sure sign I'm weakening—Mondays don't usually rate very high on my list of favorite days. But this morning I'm raring to go, even though we'll be playing catch-up all day after the missed days last week. I choose to look at the bright side. If I run fast enough, I should just be a blur in front of the camera.

I get to the park early and test out the ground. We'll have to avoid some areas until at least tomorrow, but there's plenty of work to be done. Victoria, Lark, and Adam arrive right on time. After a quick stretch for the Pinkies and a slam-dunk cup of coffee for Adam, we start to work.

Tansy walks circles around us, thankfully avoiding the muddy areas and stopping occasionally to offer her opinion on things.

"Think the cameraman's not coming today?" Adam calls as he walks by where I'm pinching off marigold stems that were broken by the hard rain.

I'd like to say I hadn't noticed that Daniel is half an hour late. But I can't. "We could only be so lucky." Even as I say it, I know I don't mean it.

"Yeah, right." Adam's smile says he knows it, too. "Mama said he hung around most of the afternoon yesterday."

I try to straighten a flower stem, but it falls back over. "You'd have known for yourself if you hadn't run off to play games right after lunch instead of staying to visit with the grown-ups."

"A little testy today, aren't we?"

"Not me." Not until he started teasing me. Another sure sign I'm confused about my feelings for Daniel. Usually Adam's kidding doesn't faze me.

The roar of a motorcycle interrupts our semi-friendly banter. I keep my eyes on the flowers. No sense giving Adam ammunition.

A few minutes later a throat clears behind me and I smile. He came straight over to see me. So if there are feelings—*if* mind you—at least they're not one-sided.

"I thought you were in the business of planting flowers, not pulling them up."

I stand and brush my hands together. "The rain killed these, but it's up to me to get rid of them. I don't want a bunch of brown stalks when it's time for the judging."

"Sounds sensible."

"That's me. Sensible." Or at least I used to be. I'm not so sure anymore.

# twenty-four

We had so much fun yesterday, and it was one of the most profitable days we've had work-wise. So when I turn on "Get Real, Shady Grove" this morning, I can't imagine what Blair will find to taunt us with.

I finish dressing while she shows footage of the other two teams hard at work and offers her usual complimentary commentary. I pause in the middle of tying my shoe and stare at the TV. For our segment, she captured the split second where we're all laughing at something funny Victoria said. So we end up frozen, full-screen, with silly ear-splitting grins on our faces. "It doesn't appear that TLC is taking this contest as seriously as the other entrants are. Will they still have these cheerful smiles at the end of the contest? I guess we'll have to wait until the winners are announced to see."

Guess we will. How do you make something negative out of smiles and laughter? That woman has a real talent for nasty.

By the end of the day, I've all but forgotten Blair's unpleasant comments. Another great day for TLC Landscaping with a major amount accomplished. Nothing she can say can take that away from me.

I check in with Mama to make sure the girls are okay and then stay late to get things ready for tomorrow. We're on a roll now and can't afford to lose our momentum.

Before I know it, the sun is setting. I wash the dirt off my hands and plop down, exhausted, onto the bench, but murmuring a prayer of extreme gratitude. I'm going to have to make more time to spend with God. I know He understands I'm busy. But murmured prayers now and then are no replacement for daily Bible study and real time spent in praise and prayer.

Just as I stand, a motorcycle roars into the park entrance and pulls to a stop. Through the dusky light, I'm not sure if it's Daniel or a stranger. I mentally plot the quickest exit from the park and clutch my key ring with my keys poking out between my fingers. Then the rider takes off his helmet and even from this distance in the dark, I recognize Daniel.

My legs go weak with relief. I shove my keys in my pocket and sit back down on the bench, trying to look casual.

He walks toward me carrying a white plastic bag. "Hey, girl."

"Hey, yourself. What are you doing here?" Not that I'm complaining.

"I saw your truck here earlier and thought you might be hungry."

"Starving. Mama's feeding the girls at her house, and I'd already resigned myself to going home to a bowl of cereal and milk."

"How about a salad and garlic cheese breadsticks?"

"For real?" When I'd spotted the bag, I'd guessed a fast-food cheeseburger and fries.

"I figured with a sandwich for lunch, you needed green vegetables. For your health." He grins. "And the breadsticks are just for pleasure."

Wow. He's concerned about my health. How cool is that? "Yum. Thanks." He sits down beside me while I eat.

"This is really amazing, Allie, what you're doing with the park."

I swallow the bite in my mouth. "Thanks."

He leans back. "I've been to a lot of places, but I've never seen one any prettier than Shady Grove. My mama always called it God's Country."

"Do you like to travel?"

He nods. "Remember Mr. Breckenridge's history class? All those stories about Mt. Fuji?"

"Who could forget?"

"That's where I went on my first real trip. To Japan. After that the travel bug got in my blood."

"I haven't traveled much. I always wanted to go to Australia. You know, toss some shrimp on the barbie. Go for a walkabout in the outback. Maybe when they get older, I can take the girls. If they're still speaking to me by then."

"From what I can see, you're good with your girls. But hard on yourself."

"Maybe you haven't seen me at my worst. Just ask Katie when she's dragging in the mornings. Or Miranda practically anytime." I lay my fork down. "No, that's not fair to her. She and I actually get along pretty well, considering that she's nearing those infamous teen years. I guess I'm just preparing for the future by dreading it now." Dead silence. I shoot a questioning glance Daniel's way and meet blue eyes head on. "What?" I can see that my innocent remark has struck a chord with him.

"So, do you dread things by subject? Like, 'Today I'll worry about Miranda becoming a teenager, and tomorrow I'll worry about this contest,' and so on. If that's how you do it and you ever decide to worry about me, could you please move me ahead of Miranda's teenage years? Because I may not age gracefully, so I need to capture your attention while I'm still young and handsome." He grins. "And modest, of course."

How had I ever thought he was clueless? "Young and handsome? Whose mirror have you been looking in?"

"Ouch! Haven't you ever heard of the fragile male ego? Do you have any idea what you've just done to mine? My tender psyche may never be the same."

"I just meant the mirror might be a little cracked and you're not getting the true picture."

"Oh, so you think I will age gracefully. Good. That gives me hope."

"Actually I was referring to the young and attractive part. Maybe you're just half of that."

"Now how can I be half young?"

"I meant either young or handsome. And obviously you're not old."

"Boy, you sure know how to hurt a guy."

One thing I love about Daniel is his sense of humor. But I'm not going to use the word *love* in conjunction with Daniel.

"You know I'm kidding. How could I think anything but good about a guy who brought me a salad?"

"That's more like it. I don't care what you think about my looks as long as you like my heart."

I'm not about to tell him that he has nothing to worry about in either department. "Well, I really appreciate you saving me from starvation, but I'd better head home. Mama will have the girls in bed by now, but I can still get there in time to hear prayers if I hurry."

He stands. "Let me help you gather your stuff. And I guess we need to throw our trash away. Unless you want to have it all over 'Get Real, Shady Grove' that midnight snacks are a part of your park landscaping plan."

"By all means, let's clean up. Thanks." I begin gathering garbage as Daniel picks up my trowel and shovel. We work in companionable silence, then walk to the parking area and stash the tools in the back of the SUV.

Now comes the awkward part—the good night scene. I stiffen my spine and my moral resolve in preparation. Daniel takes the wind out of my sails and the starch out of my spine when he waits for me to get in the driver's seat, then says, "Get a good night's sleep." With a casual wave, he climbs onto the Harley and motions for me to go first.

I gun the motor. Isn't he quite the gentleman? I wasn't planning on letting him kiss me, but he could have at least tried.

I'm stunned by how great I feel when I wake up Wednesday morning. Good in every sense of the word—spiritually, mentally, physically. Unfortunately, it doesn't take a brilliant mind to surmise that the happy feeling stems mostly from my growing relationship with Daniel.

And that terrifies me. Especially because half the time these days, I'm wondering if my initial fears and doubts about Daniel are unfounded. Maybe I just need to loosen up and follow Lark's granny's "let go and let God" philosophy.

I'm in too good a mood to mar it by watching Blair, so I grab a bite to eat and head straight to work. My TV needs a good rest, anyway.

To my amazement I'm not the first one to work. When I catch a glimpse of Adam's fluorescent orange T-shirt in the park, I check my cell phone. Low battery, but the clock is still working. I put the phone on the charger and get out to see what's going on.

"Hey, sleepyhead, 'bout time you showed up." Adam tousles my hair, and I give him a friendly push.

Victoria walks up. "We thought you were never going to get here."

I put my hand to my heart. "As I live and breathe, socialite Victoria Worthington is up and dressed and it's barely good daylight."

She sticks out her tongue at me and we laugh.

"What earthquake got you up this early?"

"Earthquake Adam."

Lark comes up behind me. "Can you believe he called me thirty minutes before my alarm went off and rushed me out here, too?"

"Why?" If he wanted to start early today, why didn't he call me, too?

"To surprise you, silly." Lark grins.

"Come look at what we've done!" Victoria motions me.

I shoot my brother a questioning look, and, to my surprise, a blush spreads across his face.

I follow them over to the west side of the park. Wow! They've gotten a whole section of the border bed done. "I'm so impressed! At this rate, we'll have our lost days made up in no time!"

I high-five Adam and hug the Pinkies.

Adam clears his throat. "Enough of the mushy stuff. Let's get back to work." I stare at my brother. Who'd have thought a few weeks ago that he'd be a driving force, a go-getter, Mr. Responsibility even? Not me, I'm ashamed to say.

We fly into the job with new determination and focus. Although, I admit my focus is partly on keeping an eye out for Daniel's arrival.

When the TV van pulls up, my first thought is that Blair must be making another impromptu visit since Daniel didn't ride the Harley today. I keep working but cast a surreptitious glance toward the van as the door opens. No Blair. No Daniel either. Just a stranger carrying a camera. Several thoughts flit through my mind while I keep going through the motions of work.

Did Daniel ask to be assigned to another group? Is he afraid I'll read too much into our discussion last night? Then I catch myself. I'm being paranoid. Knowing Blair, she picked up on the growing friendship between Daniel and me and decided to remove him from harm's way.

When filming ends with no problems, I saunter over to the man who is storing his camera. "Hi. I'm Allie."

He looks at me as if no one has ever introduced herself to him before. "Joe," he grunts and turns back toward the van.

So much for my idea of striking up a casual conversation. Might as well come right out with it. "So where's Daniel today?"

"Daniel?"

"The usual cameraman."

"Oh, him. Motorcycle wreck on the way to work this morning. Not that I'm surprised. I always said those motorcycles are death on wheels."

twenty-five

Death?" The word comes out as a gasp.

Joe shakes his head. "Aw, I'm not saying *he's* dead. All I know is Blair said he was out 'cause he had a motorcycle wreck. She didn't say anything about him bein' dead."

"Thanks." I turn to walk away, not sure what to do.

I feel an arm around my waist. "C'mon, Allie. Sit down."

Victoria helps me to a bench and sinks down beside me.

"Did you hear what he said?"

She nods. "I'm praying."

"Thanks." As I say it, I realize that I'm thanking her as if Daniel is a part of my family. My heart obviously feels like he is, because there's no way I can stay here and work, no matter how important the contest is. I fumble in my pocket and retrieve my keys. "I'm going to the hospital."

"Wait." Victoria puts her hand over mine. "Don't you think we should make some calls? Find out where he is?"

"Who do you suggest we call? Blair?" I spit out her name.

"What about Candice?"

191

"Okay." I reach back in my pocket and frown. "My cell's on the charger." I start to stand.

She flips out her state-of-the-art phone and slides it into my hand. "Use mine, goofy."

"Thanks. But I don't remember her last name."

"Call the ER. Ask for Candice. Maybe you'll get lucky and there's only one who works there." I punch in the number for information again. They automatically connect me with the local emergency room, and I close my eyes and pray silently as I listen to the ringing. *Please let Daniel be okay.*

"ER."

"Yes, may I speak to Candice?"

"Jackson? Or O'Neal?"

"O'Neal." Of course. Why didn't I remember that?

"She's not working today."

"Okay, thanks. Her brother is a friend of mine and I just heard he was in an accident. Do you know if he's a patient there?"

"Ma'am, with these new privacy laws, I can't possibly give out that information." The woman's voice is friendly but guarded. "I'm sorry."

"I understand."

I break the connection.

Victoria touches my hand again. "At least we got her last name."

I hit redial and ask information for Candice O'Neal. Once again they connect me automatically, and I wait for the ringing to be answered. And wait.

I click Victoria's phone shut and hand it back to her. "No answer. I'm going to check at the hospital."

"Which one?"

I think if he was conscious, Daniel would go to Shady Grove General where Candice works. I'll try there first, then the other one if necessary. "Both."

"I'm going with you."

"Suit yourself, but I'm going now." The need to see for myself that Daniel is okay makes it hard for me to wait for anything.

Victoria hurries to tell the others while I start the engine. Within seconds, she and Lark are back.

"Is Adam going to go on home?" I ask absently as they climb into the SUV.

Lark shakes her head. "We asked him if he wanted to come with us, but he said he'd better stay and work. He said just call and let him know how Daniel is."

When we get to the hospital, I pull up under the front entrance breezeway and leave Victoria and Lark to park. As I approach the semicircular reception desk, it occurs to me that if I appear desperate I might not get any more answers in person than I did on the phone. I force a deep, calming breath and step up to face the pert little blonde with a smile.

"May I help you?"

"Yes. I'm here to visit a friend. Could you tell me which room Daniel Montgomery is in?"

"Room 2415."

I nod, relief making my knees weak. If he's in a regular room then he isn't critically injured. I'd been braced to hear he was in ICU, or in spite of what Joe said. . .worse.

The relief is quickly followed by anger at myself for getting involved with a man who takes chances as a matter of course.

I'd known better, but I'd gone against my instinct. Never a good thing.

For a second I consider walking out of the hospital and never looking back. But I can't. In spite of my new and total resolve that Daniel is not the man for me, I have to see him. Make sure he's going to be all right.

My heart strikes a compromise with my mind. See him now to verify that he's okay, then make sure from now on that we never progress beyond friends. Fair enough?

Deal.

Lark and Victoria come in just as I press the UP button on the wall outside between the elevators. They rush right past the blond at the desk and hurry over to me. "Do you know anything?" Lark asks.

"His room number."

We ride in silence up to the room. I think they're hesitant to say much until they figure out how I'm taking this. And since my own mind is a jumble of emotions, I don't feel like talking. Even with no words, I'm so glad they're with me.

I step off the elevator and freeze.

Lark bumps into me. "You okay?"

"No." What if he's worse than I think? What if ICU is just too full and they had to put him in a room? "I can't do this."

"Want me to go see how he is and come back and tell you?" Victoria offers.

Yes. No. "I don't know. I just don't want to be here. I don't want him to be here. I can't go through this again."

Lark puts her hand on my shoulder. "Allie, we're with you. And more importantly, God's with you. You can do this."

I take another deep breath. Slow. So I don't hyperventilate and end up in a hospital bed myself. "You're right. Let's go."

When we reach Room 2415, the door is partially open. A good sign?

Lark reaches out and taps on it.

"Come in."

My heart jumps. I'd know that deep voice anywhere.

They stand back and let me push the door the rest of the way open. I step into the room, prepared for anything. I think. Daniel is wearing jeans and a T-shirt, but he's propped up on pillows in the bed. And sporting a bandage on his arm.

Candice looks up from the chair next to the bed with a tired smile.

Even though I want to hug him, I force myself to stand still. At this point, I'm not sure I'd let go if I allow myself to put my arms around him. I feel sort of like I did when Katie was four and I found her after she got away from me in Wal-Mart.

"Allie. I tried to call you." He starts to get up and winces.

"My phone battery's dead." I motion him back down. "Don't get up on my account." I'm embarrassed to hear my voice break.

Candice stands. "Hi, Allie. Victoria. Lark." She smiles. "I'm glad to have some reinforcements. He keeps wanting to get up and move around, but he's supposed to be still until they get all his test results back."

"Candice, why don't Lark and I take you to get some lunch?" Victoria offers. "Allie, you'll stay here and make sure this big guy doesn't move around, won't you?"

Great. I'm ready to bolt from the room and she's just committed me to visiting for an hour. But a friend would definitely stay with him. "Sure."

Daniel smiles and his eyes are on me and me alone. "I appreciate you coming."

"Thanks." Still held by his gaze, I take two steps closer to the bed. Is there some kind of physics law about this? If there's not, there should be. Surely this draw is a natural phenomenon.

"See you two in a bit."

I look behind me to see Victoria, a little smile playing across her lips, waving from the door. Lark and Candice have already gone out apparently. I didn't even notice them leaving. How bad is that?

The door closes. And we're alone.

"So, what happened?"

Daniel pushes himself up on the pillows and winces again. "An old man ran a red light. I dodged him but lost control of the bike." A lock of hair has fallen onto his eyebrow.

I sit down in the chair and clutch my hands together to keep myself from reaching up to brush his hair back. "How badly are you hurt?"

"I'm a little hurt that you didn't hug me." He grins. "All the time I was in X-ray, I was imagining you, weak with relief, throwing yourself into my arms when you saw me."

I force a smile. "Dream on." Hopefully he'll never know how close I came to doing just that.

"Well, if you won't have mercy on a man in the hospital, I might as well confess. I just bruised my wrist. Can't use the camera, though, or the computer for a few days. And I strained the muscles in my back a little. Other than that, I'm fine."

"What kind of test results are you waiting for?"

He grimaces. "Candice made them check for internal bleeding. I told them I could go on home. But the doctor was too afraid of my big sister to let me go, I think."

Internal bleeding?

"Whoa." Daniel reaches toward me with his hand. "You look like you're going to faint."

"I'm okay."

"I am, too, Allie. No worries. I promise."

I try to laugh. "How can you promise not to have internal bleeding?" *Any more than you can promise that the next time this happens you won't end up in the morgue instead of the hospital?* My heart aches at the thought. I don't need this.

"I just know. I'm fine." He reaches over and takes my hand.

This time I let him. Just this one more time. His hand is so warm.

"You're cold. Are you okay?"

Frozen with fear. Does that count?

He squeezes my hand, and I squeeze back.

I don't want to let go. But I do.

The story of my life.

# twenty-six

"S o he did get out of the hospital this morning?" Rachel has her red hair in two long braids this morning, the top of her head covered by a wild lime green bandanna. Between her old denim overalls and the shovel over her shoulder, she looks more like Farmer Brown's wild child daughter than a well-respected doctor.

I nod. "As far as I know. He was supposed to. And he was right. The final diagnosis was a bruised wrist and some strained muscles in his back."

"If he knows what's good for him, he'll go see a chiropractor." She grins. "Oh, yeah, I'm off duty today."

"You're never off duty and you know it." I use the bottom of a black plastic pot to score a circle on the ground, then stand back. "Do your stuff, shovel girl."

"I imagine it scared you to death when you found out."

"Yep."

She pauses with the spade still in the dirt and looks up at me. "I guess you're determined not to have anything to do with him after this close call?"

"Yep."

She sighs. "I don't blame you. But he's a really good man. Not to mention gorgeous and funny."

"You're right. Who knows? Maybe you or Victoria will end up dating him. No use wasting a perfectly good man." I feel a stab in my gut at the thought, but I'm not going to be the type who doesn't want him but won't let anyone else have him either.

She snorts. "Yeah, I'm sure you'd be fine with that. I'm not looking to date anybody, thank you very much. My dogs are all the company I need." Then she reaches over and swats my baseball cap bill. "Besides, those blue eyes are firmly fixed on you. And only you."

"He'll forget all about me in no time when this job is over."

"Somehow I doubt that."

I meet her gaze. "He'll have to. Just like I will. There's no way it could ever work between us."

"Whatever you say."

I leave her to finish up and walk up to the truck to get some more shrubs. My freshly charged cell phone rings in my pocket. I flip it open. "Hello?"

"Allie. Trevor Wright here."

It sounds like "Trevor—Right here." I smile. "Hi, Trevor."

"I wanted to tell you again how much I enjoyed our date. I've been out of town on business or I'd have called earlier."

"Oh, that's okay. I told you I'm busy with the contest."

"Yes, I remember that. Are you almost done with it?"

"Actually no. We have another week of hard labor."

"Think you can squeeze in a little free time for the two of us to go out again?"

I laugh. Hopefully not too hysterically. "No, I'm afraid not right now. Maybe when this is over we can catch a movie or something."

"Actually I'm not a big fan of movies. I would prefer to take you to Memphis to a play. That new Broadway play is at the Orpheum for one more week. If I get tickets, will you go?"

Didn't I just answer that question in another form? "Sorry. I'm sure it would be fun, but this contest is really important to me and the girls. I can't just run off to Memphis right now."

"I understand perfectly. I think it's wonderful that you're so responsible. A good work ethic is something to be admired. Most people nowadays are so lackadaisical in their work habits that I find it hard to hire employees who really care about their jobs."

"Well, I'm really hoping this will be more than just a job. I'm hoping it will be a career."

"Of course, of course. You have few choices right now. I'm sure that under different circumstances you would be thinking only of being a good mother to your young daughters. Being the sole support of your family must be really difficult."

Is he being as tactless as it sounds? Surely not. "We manage fine. Really."

"So no time off between now and the end of the contest?"

Wow. He's persistent. I'll give him that. "Only for soccer games on Friday nights."

He doesn't reply immediately, and I'm about to say good-bye when he speaks. "Would you mind if I came to a game?"

Whoa. I actually stop in my tracks. He wants to come to the girl's soccer game? "I don't mind."

"Out at the school field?"

"Yep. At six-thirty."

"Okay, great. I'll see you there Friday night."

"Okay."

I hang up, feeling a little dazed. Whoever said persistence doesn't pay off?

Just as I reach the truck, the phone rings again. Ah, Trevor thought about loud sweaty kids and changed his mind. I should have known.

"Hello?"

"G'day, mate."

The accent may be pseudo-Australian, but the deep voice is pure Daniel. "Hi."

"I didn't fool you for a minute, did I?"

"Maybe for a minute." But then I woke up.

"I just wanted to call and tell you they let me out."

"Thanks for the warning." No, no, no! I'm not going to kid around with him. "I mean I'm glad. Are you feeling better?"

"Yes. Much. I hope to be back at work Monday."

"That's good." That'll leave me one week to get through without compromising my determination to just be friends with this maddening man.

"Will you be working late tonight?"

I sit down on the tailgate of Adam's truck. "I don't know." I rub the back of my neck. "Daniel. . .I just want to be friends."

"Again?"

"Yes."

"Why?"

It's out on the table now. We've both admitted our relationship has progressed past the friend stage. They say admitting the problem is half the battle. Might as well find out if that's true.

"I just can't get involved right now with someone who. . ."

"With someone who what? Rides a motorcycle? Has a knife scar? Is a writer?"

All of the above. "Daniel, I'd drive you crazy."

"You already are," he growls.

I'm glad we're on the phone and not in person. I don't think I could handle seeing the pain in his eyes that I hear in his voice. "Just trust me. You and I are better as friends."

"I don't see it that way. I'll have to take your word for it, I guess."

"I should really get back to work."

"See you around then."

"Okay. Bye."

I click the phone shut and stare at it. I was straightforward and, just as importantly, I was right. So why do I feel so awful?

Trevor is at the field when we pull up Friday night. He looks as if he just stepped out of GQ in his sharply creased khakis and polo shirt. I feel bland in contrast, but I *am* pressed and clean. Hey, I find the good where I can. I admit it's flattering to have a nice-looking man make a beeline for me as soon as I get to the field. Now if I could just muster up some interest.

"I haven't seen a soccer game in a long time. This should be good fun."

"It can be, especially for the parents." I always feel a bit artificial around Trevor. He's a very nice man, but for some reason, I find myself measuring my words during our conversations. Not a terrible thing for an occasional meeting, but not something I'd like to do for the rest of my life.

We get our folding chairs set up and Trevor turns to me. "Would you like some refreshments?" Spoken like a true Southern gentleman. "I haven't eaten yet."

"Me either. A hot dog would be great if you're going anyway. Want me to go with you?"

"No, you stay here with our chairs. I'll be right back."

While the teams warm up, I face facts. I'm in no shape to be contemplating another relationship. Even though I've given up on any hope of working things out with Daniel, I'm not going to be able to replace him with Mr. Right or Mr. Anyone Else. In a way, confronting that truth is a relief. I don't have to pretend to still be looking for a soul mate. I can just relax and enjoy this season of being my kids' mom, as Dr. Laura would say.

The game starts, and within seconds our team takes the ball down the field. Katie passes to Dylan, he passes to Miranda, and she scores. I don't know what comes over me. Giddy with my newfound freedom from a need for a relationship maybe. Or just proud of my daughter. I break Miranda's hard and fast rule—"Never yell, especially never ever yell my name." I cheer loud and long. She glances up. And I try to look innocent. But she flashes me a big grin. I'm not the only one who's changing.

"Hey, that was a great play. She must have inherited those athletic genes from her mom."

Will there be a time when that deep voice doesn't make my heart beat faster? I look behind me to see my friend looking fully recovered and as nice as ever in jeans and a T-shirt. "Hi, Daniel."

"Hi, Allie."

Great timing. Trevor comes up right then, carefully balancing two hot dogs in one hand and clutching two bottled drinks with the other.

"Here you go, Allie. One hot dog, just as you ordered. I wasn't sure what you wanted so I brought ketchup and mustard for you to choose from."

Could this be any more awkward? I don't know what to do.

"Well, I'll see you around, Allie. Trevor." Classy exit line. And Daniel follows it with a classy exit. He walks away slowly, and I make a conscious effort not to watch him leave.

After Allie's big score, the rest of the game is sort of anti-climactic. We win 1-0, though. While the coach is doing the after-game talk with the team, I take a minute to have my own talk with Trevor.

"It was really sweet of you to come."

"I enjoyed it. Maybe I can come again?" His smile probably cost his parents a pretty penny when he was a teen. But there's no dimple. And his nose is too straight. Who am I kidding? There's nothing wrong with his appearance.

Still I smile. "Actually, Trevor. . ."

"It's not me, it's you?"

I shrug. "Really. It is me. This just isn't the time for me to get involved." Because the only man I care about "getting involved" with is the wrong man for me.

He glances over my shoulder to where Daniel waits down the sideline for Elijah. "I understand." I seriously doubt that. But I'm not going to even try to explain further.

"Thanks."

He smiles and kisses me on the cheek, still the quintessential gentleman. "You win some, you lose some."

As he strolls away, I see the girls coming toward me and Daniel and Elijah walking in the opposite direction.

And sometimes you always lose.

# twenty-seven

"Mama, I had a bad dream, can I sleep with you?"

I open my eyes and squint at Katie's face. Really close to mine. I glance over her shoulder at the clock on the nightstand. 4:30 a.m.

Katie's occasional bad dreams are something I've learned to deal with, but it's been several months since she's had one. I'd been hoping they were over, but I guess everyone is entitled to a relapse now and then. "Sure, baby, hop in."

I pull the covers back and she crawls in. Her warm body snuggles against mine in that age-old way of mother and child. I can get a couple more hours of sleep before we have to get up.

The alarm buzzes. I hit the button to turn it off and look down at Katie's face, so relaxed in sleep. Should I call and ask Mama to come stay with her while Miranda and I go to work with the others? Probably not. If there's one thing I've learned with my children, it's that they like to be consulted about major schedule changes if possible. "Katie. . ." I shake her shoulder gently. "Wake up."

She opens one eye halfway. "Hmm?"

"Do you want to go to the park and work or should I call Memaw to come stay with you?"

Both eyes pop open. "I'm going with you."

"Okay, then. You'll have to get up and get ready while I'm in the shower."

She nods.

I prod her until both feet are on the floor. "Now don't lie back down in your room, you hear?"

"Um-hum."

"If you do, I'll call Memaw."

That wakes her up. As I head to the shower, I smile to myself. My mother would croak if she knew I was using her as a threat. But hey, it worked.

The girls and I are in the middle of stretches with Lark and Rachel when Victoria arrives at the park. Bearing gifts. She lugs a picnic basket up and sets it on the picnic table under the oak tree where Adam and Craig are drinking coffee. Adam lunges for it, but Victoria shoos his hand away. "Oh no, you don't. The contents of that basket are only to be used for a reward after at least three hours of work." Victoria and her rules!

Adam stands. "Time to go to work, guys!" he calls.

Victoria winks at me and I grin.

By noon, I'm almost wishing Katie had left *me* with Mama. Rachel, Victoria, Adam, Craig, and I are hard at work on the fountain while Lark, Katie, and Miranda spread mulch.

"Will we ever get this done?" I pant as I heave another rock into place.

"O ye of little faith." Adam shovels mortar on top of the rock with his trowel. "Look how far we've come."

I grunt. "Thanks, but that's hard to do when I can see how far we still have to go."

Craig looks up from where he's working on the plumbing. "We'll finish the fountain today, I think."

"Thanks, Craig. I feel bad that you had to give up your day off to help."

He pushes his cap back and scratches his head. "I don't recall anyone forcing me." He smiles. "Lark and I are happy to help you any way we can."

"I appreciate it, Craig."

Victoria and Rachel roll up with a wheelbarrow full of rocks. I glance up at them. "I appreciate all of you."

"You'd better." Victoria wipes a loose curl out of her face. "Eternal gratitude, remember?"

We laugh. But I know I'm incredibly blessed to have friends who sacrifice unselfishly so that I can have my dream. Just another reason I need to win the contest. So their sacrifice won't all be for nothing.

"The girls and I have all the bulbs planted in that bed." I turn to see Lark, Katie, and Miranda watching us.

"Wonderful." They look as tired as I feel. "Y'all ready for lunch?"

Adam lays his trowel down. "I thought you'd never ask."

We wash up and convene to the picnic table.

Victoria pulls a white tablecloth from the basket and spreads it on one of the tables. Then she begins producing goodies. Besides sandwich ingredients, there are deviled eggs, ham rolls, spinach dip, and crackers. Topped with sparkling water, this is a meal fit for a king. Or as Adam says, "A dinner fit for a winner."

"I do think you'll be the winner, Allie," Rachel says.

"You have to say that," Adam teases. "You're her friend."

"No, seriously, her plan to have flowers in bloom at every possible season is going to make this a beautiful place."

"What about in the winter?" Katie asks. "Will there be flowers in the winter?"

"Knowing your mom, if she gets the contract, she'll come out in the middle of the night after the first frost, by the light of the full moon. . ." Adam lowers his voice in a spooky way, and Katie and Miranda lean forward. ". . .and plant fake flowers in all the flower beds."

Everyone laughs, including me. "Yeah, right. I'm not quite that obsessive."

The Pinkies all look at me with matching grins that say they aren't so sure.

"Hey, if I don't take this seriously, who will?"

"We don't mind you taking it seriously," Rachel says. "As long as you know if you don't win, it's not the end of the world."

I just stare at her. I've had to accept that the only man I care about isn't the right one for me. Will I have to see my dream of having my own landscaping company die, as well?

The others go back to eating, chatting about other things, but I look out over the park. Rachel's right. Even if we don't win, we've gained so much from this contest. It's worth every tear I've shed and every aching muscle, and yes, even all the humiliation Blair has heaped on my head. At least right now it feels like it. Let's hope the feeling continues.

209

Deep down, I knew Daniel would show up tonight. As soon as the park was deserted except for me, I realized it. If I'm honest, maybe even before, when I let the girls go home with Adam.

In spite of our phone conversation and my "just friends" spiel, we'd left things unfinished. And Daniel finishes what he starts. Now, with twilight falling, I hear the roar of the Harley before I see it, but I know it's him. My gut clenches as I push to my feet and slip into the women's restroom to wash my hands and face.

When I dry my face, I run my fingers through my hair and lean in toward the mirror. My eyes are large with apprehension. Which am I more afraid of—that Daniel will be waiting when I get out? Or that I misheard the engine noise and he won't?

I push the door open and step outside. Daniel's leaning against the big oak tree, and I resist the urge to run back into the restroom. Might as well face this and put it behind me.

"Hi."

He smiles. "Hi. Long day?"

"You might say that." With every step closer to him, my heart pounds.

He motions toward the park. "Looks like y'all got a lot done this week."

I follow his gaze. "It's shaping up." I nod toward his wrist. "No bandage? Is your wrist okay? And your back?"

"My back's a little sore, but my wrist is as good as new."

"I'm glad."

"Feel like taking a break?" He pushes off the tree and walks toward me.

Pound. Pound. Pound. How can one little heart make so much noise? "It's time to quit anyway."

"We need to talk." He's close enough now to hear my heart, surely.

"I thought we already did."

He raises an eyebrow. "No, ma'am."

I start picking up my tools and am suddenly reminded of Tuesday when he helped me gather things up. I'd known then that going against my resolve was wrong, but I'd allowed myself to be weak. I won't make the same mistake tonight. "Go ahead and talk. I'll listen."

"I know you're scared of getting hurt again. And I don't know what the future holds. But I know how I feel. And I'm crazy about you."

I'm reaching for a shovel, but when he says that my knuckles whiten around the handle. He really does believe in telling it like it is. Unfortunately if I say I feel the same way about him, he'll never let me leave. So I straighten and meet his gaze.

His blue eyes pierce my heart. "I'm sorry, Daniel. You're a wonderful man. But I can't. . . ." I look up at the stars just beginning to dot the slate blue sky and blink against the tears. This should be the happiest night of my life. But I remember how I felt Wednesday when I found out about his wreck. My girls don't deserve to have to go through losing another dad. "I can't do this. You're too much of an uncertainty. Too impulsive. When you had the wreck. . ."

He runs his fingers through his hair and sighs. "I knew this was about the wreck. It was just an accident."

"Yeah, but the motorcycle. . ."

"I'll sell the Harley." He steps closer, so close I can feel his breath.

"Don't be crazy. You can't do that."

He wipes a tear off my cheek with his fingertip. "It's just metal. Nothing compared to you and the girls."

I shake my head and try to smile. "Like I told Victoria that first night at Coffee Central, it's not a condition, it's a concept. The Harley is part of who you are."

"You're not being reasonable, Allie." He gently grasps my forearm. "Tell me you don't love me."

"I—" My voice doesn't seem to be working. He's too close for me to think.

He leans toward me, but my feet are apparently in cahoots with my voice. They won't move.

Eyes wide open, I stare at him as he leans closer. When his lips claim mine with incredible longing and promise, I close my eyes and cling to him. He enfolds me in his arms and my heart soars. This isn't an infatuation. This is forever and always. Until death do us part. A picture of his motorcycle lying in a ditch, mangled and broken, flashes through my mind, and I push him away with both hands. "No!" I spin around for fear of what he'll see in my face. "This is a mistake."

"You're right," he says softly behind me. "But it's your mistake."

When I turn back around he's almost to his bike. Seconds later, he roars out of sight.

# twenty-eight

For the first time since the year Jon died, I'm tempted to skip Sunday morning church service. I go so far as to turn off my alarm and pull the covers over my head. It's not like I slept any last night. Might as well just stay here until my body gives up and decides it has to have sleep.

Half an hour later, Miranda knocks on my door and sticks her head in. The anxious look on her face heaps guilt on me. "Mom? You okay? Katie's up and we've had breakfast. She's dressing for church right now."

"That's good, honey."

"You want me to fix you a bowl of cereal? Or bring you a glass of juice?"

If you want to crawl into a hole and forget the world exists, don't have kids. They won't let you. I throw the covers back and swing my legs around. "No thanks, honey. I'll get my own breakfast. I'll be in there in a few minutes. You go ahead and get ready. I'm fine." She stares at me as if she doesn't quite believe me. I smile and toss a pillow toward the door. "Scram. I'll be ready to

213

go before you are at this rate."

That draws a grin and the door shuts quickly. As I look through my closet, my hand brushes the bright yellow dress I wore last Sunday to match my happy mood. If I was going to do that this week, I'd have to wear a black dress, complete with a veil to cover the bags under my eyes.

I settle on something neutral and before long, I'm ready to go. Katie, with shoes on and her hair brushed, waits by the door. I gape at her. My baby really is growing up. The girls aren't fighting as much as they used to either. Isn't it always that way? When things get dark, there are always a few silver linings around to cheer me up. I'll take them anywhere I can get them today.

As soon as we enter the church building, we run into Daniel, Candice, and Elijah in the foyer. Daniel's eyes are cool—a far cry from last night—as he looks at me. "Hello, Allie. Katie, Miranda."

Katie and Elijah take off for their classroom.

I nod. "Hi, Daniel. Candice."

Candice smiles, but it's not a smile that encourages further conversation. I take it her brother told her what transpired between the two of us. My cheeks grow warm. Hopefully not everything, but enough that she knows I can't be trusted.

*You're right*, I want to say. *I can't be trusted not to hurt him.* But instead I just walk on by. I called Victoria and Rachel last night and they promised to save me a seat. After all, I'm not here to see Daniel.

For the next two hours, I do a pretty good job of keeping my mind off him. But when worship is over and it's time to go to Mama's for lunch, I can't do it. The memory of Daniel and I doing dishes together there last week is just too fresh. I send the kids to her house and go home to take a nap.

As I curl up in my bed, it hits me. I *am* right. If I'm already having to avoid people and places because of my memories of time with Daniel, how much worse would it be if I'd allowed the relationship to progress and then lost him?

At some point, I finally doze off and don't wake until Mama taps on my door. "The girls and I brought you some supper. You okay, honey?"

I sit up. "C'mon in."

She sinks onto my bed beside me. "Rough week?"

"Yeah." I find myself telling her the whole story. Talking to the Pinkies is good, but talking to Mama is cathartic.

She pats my hand. "Have you prayed a lot about this?"

I feel heat creep up my face. Even my ears grow hot. "Not really, Mama. I've been so busy. But I know—"

She shakes her head. "Sweetie, our wisdom is foolishness to Him."

"I know. But I also know what my heart can stand." Surely as a widow she can relate to what I'm feeling.

Almost as if she reads my mind, she speaks, "I loved your dad, Allie. As much as any woman can love a man. But if I found someone else that I loved, I wouldn't worry about whether I might lose him, too. That's not in my control. Any more than this is in yours."

Okay, so much for cathartic. I'm feeling a little judged here. And the word *control* comes up in my conversations way too often. Not to mention that the thought of Mama finding another man to love kind of freaks me out. "Thanks, Mama. I think I have to

215

work this out on my own." Daughterspeak for "butt out." But at least I'm nice.

A smile tilts her lips. "I understand."

And I'm pretty sure she really does.

"We have five more days. Friday when we get done working, that's it. The judging is Saturday morning." I hold the plan on the picnic table with one hand, circling areas with my pencil. "The things I've circled are still left to finish."

"I know it looks like a lot, but we can do it." Lark's smile lights up her face today. Whatever problem she and Craig had, they apparently resolved it.

"It is a lot. But if we all work together and don't miss any days. . ." I won't even say the word *rain*. "Then I think you're right. With God's help, we can do it."

Adam claps his hand on my shoulder. "You know, Al. You should really consider becoming a coach. These little pep talks of yours are almost as inspiring as Victoria's attempts to motivate us with food." He raises an eyebrow at her. "By the way, Vicky, where's lunch?"

"Hush it, game boy," Victoria drawls and hands him a shovel. "Pretend this is a joystick and see if you can actually accomplish something."

He grins, but his face reddens. This is a reversal. I could give him some sisterly advice—if he's going to dish it out to Victoria, he'd better learn to take it. She's not going to let anyone get the upper hand. And certainly not my little brother.

But who am I to be giving advice? I think I'm braced for Daniel's arrival, but when he finally gets to the park. . .as a passenger in Blair's little red Corvette convertible, I want to run and hide.

By the time they reach us, they're already filming, with Blair keeping up a running commentary. Daniel never glances my way, except with the camera.

"Allie, I love what you're doing here. But do you really think you have enough time to finish?"

"Hi, Blair. So nice of you to stop by." I grit my teeth and smile at the camera, pretending the man behind it is a stranger. "I don't think finishing will be an issue." *Either we will or we won't.*

"So, Allie, we talked a little in the beginning about you, as a single mom, taking on such a big project as this contest. Now that it's almost over, how do you feel about it? Was it a bigger sacrifice for your family than you expected?"

I open my mouth to give her another pat answer, but I freeze. I'm dragging in every night so late that Katie and Miranda are either in bed or should be. Guilt is my constant companion. But I have to know that in the end the good will outweigh the bad. "Actually, yes."

She makes that little *O* with her mouth that I can't stand, but before she can say anything, I continue.

"The hours and hard work that this contest have demanded have been a huge sacrifice, not just for me and my family, but for my friends and their families, as well. But the thing that keeps me from giving up is knowing that all through history, people have made short-term sacrifice for the long-term good. This is a lesson to my kids and to me. That we have what it takes to buckle down and get a job done, even if it means giving up things temporarily."

"Well. Thank you, Allie."

Daniel gives me a thumbs-up with his free hand. I blink and look again, but he isn't looking at me. Still, I'm sure he did. Maybe somehow we can still be friends.

I smile at the thought. "You're welcome, Blair. Now if you'll excuse me, I really have to get back to work."

"Oh, certainly. Don't mind us. Just pretend we're not here."

Easier said than done. But I give it my best shot. After about thirty minutes of filming, they work their way back around to me and Blair says, "I think that's enough for today." Out of the corner of my eye, I see Daniel lower the camera. Blair puts her hand on his arm, reminiscent of the first night I met him at the soccer meeting. "Come on, Daniel. If we hurry we can beat the lunch crowd at that little Mexican place."

*Run, Clueless Man, while you still can.* It seems like at least a year ago since the night I first thought that. I should have been warning him about me as well as Blair.

I'm afraid he finally got the message, though, at least as far as I'm concerned. He walks beside Blair to her car and never even looks back.

What have I done?

Midafternoon, Lark comes over to where I'm working. "Allie, I hate to do this to you, but I'm going to have to go home."

I stand, alarmed. "What's wrong?" As happy as she looked

this morning, she looks proportionately miserable.

She shakes her head. "I have to go. Really."

"Are you sick?"

"No."

"Did you and Craig have a fight over the phone?"

"I have to go, Allie. I'm sorry."

"You're not sick. Pinky promise?"

"Pinky promise."

"Want me to go with you?" I have no idea where that came from. All I know is that minutes before, nothing was as important as getting this job done, but suddenly that seems insignificant.

"No!" Her smile is more like a grimace. "You keep working, missy. I'll be fine." She runs to her car and drives away.

"What was that all about?"

I turn to see Victoria behind me. I shrug. "She wouldn't say. She just had to go home."

"Is she sick?" Victoria's brown eyes mirror my concern.

"She pinky-promised she wasn't."

"Then it must be her and Craig. I thought things were better."

"Yeah, me, too."

"You ladies taking the afternoon off?" Adam says as he walks toward us carrying a small tree.

Victoria gives him a lazy grin. "Yeah, we thought it would be fun to just relax and watch you work."

He hefts the tree to one side and flexes his muscle. "I can understand the fascination."

"You wish," Victoria says, then looks at me. "Looks like he's going to have our help to get this job done."

I smile at their shenanigans. "Yep. It looks like it."

That night as I drag home just in time to fix a really late supper and put the kids to bed, I think of Blair's question again. Is this worth the sacrifice?

When the girls are finally settled into bed, I sink down on my computer chair. Like so many things in my life since this contest started, e-mail is a distant memory. But as soon as I reach for the mouse, the doorbell rings.

My gaze darts to the taskbar. 11:15 p.m. Too late for a friendly visit. My knees feel like sponge as I hurry to peek out the side curtain.

I yank open the door. "Lark? What's wrong?" In all the years we've been best friends, I've never seen her like this. Her eyes are red and swollen, but besides that, she looks out of control. And the suitcase in her hand shakes me to the core.

"I'm moving out." She nods behind me. "In." A helpless shrug lifts her shoulders, and she slams her suitcase down, barely missing my toes. "Out from Craig. In with you."

# twenty-nine

"You're leaving Craig?" I step back and let her in, but my mind is reeling. "Why?"

She plops down in the chair next to the couch and raises her chin. Not a good sign. "Just because."

I squat down next to her and rub her arm. "Your granny always said *because* was just a word, not a reason."

"Granny didn't know everything," Lark growls.

Icy fear works through me as I pull her into a hug. For Lark, that's the next thing to blasphemy. "What's wrong?"

"Nothing. Craig and I are just—" Her voice breaks and the next word comes out as part sob. "—through."

"Okay," I say into her hair. "You had a fight. . . ."

"No fight."

"No fight," I repeat like a mindless echo. If I had ever made a list of the top ten things least likely to happen, this event would have been at the top. I sink onto the sofa diagonally across from her. "Lark, did he cheat on you?"

"No!" She's outraged.

Is that a good sign? That she's defending his honor? I'll take all the possible good signs I can get right now.

"What did he do, honey?"

"Nothing." She shoves her tear-damp hair away from her face and meets my gaze with a stubbornness I recognize all too well. "I don't want to talk about it, Allie. I just need a place to stay, okay?"

"Okay." What are the Pinkies for if not to take you in when you're being completely unreasonable? "Let me fix a bed for you. You can have my bed. Or I can get Katie up and move her into Miranda's room." That won't start anything worse than World War III. Katie sleeps crossways of the bed. And Miranda doesn't like to be touched while she's sleeping.

"No. I'll take the couch."

I smother my sigh of relief. Tomorrow, if this tiff isn't over, I'll figure something out, but if I can let sleeping girls lie tonight, we're all definitely better off.

She sits mutely while I bring sheets, blankets, and pillows in and make up the couch. I'm half afraid to ask anything else. When she's settled in, her face turned toward the back of the sofa, I get over my fear. "Lark, think about everything we've been through together. Are you sure you can't tell me what's going on?"

No answer. We've slept over too many times for me to think she dozed off that fast. So apparently she can't tell me.

I go on to my own bed and fall asleep praying. For Lark, for wisdom, and that we all survive this week.

Soon after I climb out of bed, Miranda taps on the door and

comes on in. "What's Aunt Lark doing here?"

"She needed a place to sleep."

"What's wrong with her place?"

"I think she probably just needed some space." Suddenly I'm reminded of Lark's mother, who left to "find herself" when we were kids and never came back. Has Lark thought of that?

I turn on the TV in my bedroom and watch Blair make a mockery of journalism. Again. She must have made an A in Creative Editing. There she is, smiling at the camera. "So, Allie, we talked a little in the beginning about you, as a single mom, taking on such a big project as this contest. Now that it's almost over, how do you feel about it? Was it a bigger sacrifice for your family than you expected?"

I stand there open-mouthed, then I say, "Actually, yes." And the clip freezes behind her. Cut to her in the studio. "You heard it here, Shady Grove, straight from her own mouth. Allie Richards admits that this contest was a bigger sacrifice than she expected. One has to wonder—will she see it through to the end?"

I shrug. So my words of wisdom won't be recorded for posterity. I'm getting used to Blair's bull. At least she didn't say "straight from the horse's mouth."

When I enter the living room, Lark is as still as a lump of pillows under the cover, but I can see her black hair spiking out in every direction. Should I be quiet? Let her rest? She obviously had a rough night. Or am I better off to just brazen my way through this and act like it's business as usual with her sleeping on the couch? I flip on the overhead light and drop my tennis shoes on the floor. She stirs.

"Good morning, sleepyhead."

She moans.

"Are you going to be able to work today?"

She grunts. "Do you have any chocolate?"

"I think there's some leftover Easter candy in the freezer."

"That'll do."

I reach over and pull the covers back so I can see her face.

She throws her arm up to shield her eyes. "What?"

What? What? How can she ask me what? I take a deep breath. "What do you have planned for today?"

Her eyes are really bloodshot. "I don't think I can work today. Maybe tomorrow."

Half an hour later when I walk out the door, she's sitting cross-legged on the couch with a blanket over her, a box of candy on her lap, and the TV remote in her hand. I'm deeply worried about her. But I'm also terrified about my own future. What am I going to do with one less pair of hands when the judging is just days away?

On the way to the park, I punch in Craig's number on my cell phone.

"Allie. How are you?"

How *am* I? How am *I*? Besides being three days from the judging and having to leave one of my few employees lying on *my* couch eating bonbons and watching HGTV, I'm just peachy.

"I'm fine." I know I should just admit that I don't know what the problem is with him and Lark, but if I do, I'm afraid he won't tell me either. "But I'm concerned about what's going on with you and Lark."

"Me, too."

"So what are we going to do about it?"

Silence.

What did these two do? Take a vow of silence? Pinky promise not to tell?

Finally he speaks. "What did she tell you?"

Busted.

"Nothing, Craig. She's not talking to me. That's why you need to call her."

"Sorry, Allie. I can't."

"And you can't tell me what's going on?"

"No, that's up to her. I'll see you this afternoon to get that fountain going, hopefully."

I say good-bye and hang up before I scream in his ear.

Victoria and I halfheartedly perform our stretches while I tell her about Lark. She's as clueless as I am. "We'll have to pray harder."

"We'll also have to work harder," I mutter. I'm ashamed of my selfish worries, but that doesn't stop me from having them. After losing those two days to rain last week, I don't see how we can get it all done with a full crew, much less shorthanded.

When Daniel arrives to film, I cringe for two reasons—I dread facing him without Blair to keep us apart. And Blair will have a field day with our troubles. Victoria and Adam and I all work on separate projects while he's there, hoping to fool the camera into thinking there are more of us. Although I'm almost beyond the point of caring what the public thinks, if we can just win the contest.

After he loads his camera, Daniel comes back over to where I'm working on the walking trail. "You okay?"

"Yep." I keep my head down and continue working. "Why?"

225

*Just because you're bound and determined to turn my heart against me, and my future's crumbling before my very eyes. Why wouldn't I be okay?*

"You seem stressed."

I dig into the bag for another double handful of mulch. "A little." In the same way that the Amazon is a little stream.

"Allie."

The tenderness in his voice jerks my head up. I gaze into his eyes for five seconds, then look back at the suddenly blurry ground.

"Yeah?"

"About Saturday night. . ."

"I told you that was a mistake. I'm sorry—"

"That's what I wanted to tell you. It wasn't a mistake. If you change your mind, you know where I am." He turns to walk away.

"Daniel."

He stops and turns back toward me. "Yeah?"

"Can we still be friends?" If we can, maybe my heart won't feel so heavy.

He gives me a slow smile. "Allie Richards, I could never stop being your friend."

I try to smile, but it hurts my face. "Thanks."

After he's gone, I drop the mulch and sit back, letting the tears go. Who ever thought pursuing a dream would be so hard?

Victoria jogs over to me, and I swipe away the tears and brace myself for her sympathy.

She barely looks at me, though. "The school just called. Dylan has a hundred-and-one temperature. The nurse thinks it's the flu."

My heart sinks. "Oh no!"

"I'm sorry. I've got to go get him."

"Of course you do. Go now." I push myself to my feet and hug her. "I'll be praying. Give him a hug from Aunt Allie. Call me later and let me know how he's doing or if you need anything."

"Thanks, shugah. Love you."

"Love you back."

As she runs to her car, I stand amazed that I can say all the right things even when I'm having to force the words out around a lump the size of a pine cone. I'm not sure if that's grace or hypocrisy. I'm concerned about Dylan and I'm concerned about Lark and Craig, but at the same time, as my crew falls apart before my very eyes, my mind races for a backup plan.

Craig stops by shortly after but hits a snag in getting the fountain running. Naturally. He hands me a part number and the name and address of a place in Memphis that will have it and leaves.

"Looks like it's just you and me, sis," Adam walks over from a few feet away where he's doing some last-minute work on the fountain base.

"Why is this happening to me?"

He crosses his arms and leans against a tall poplar. "To you? Needing to control every detail kind of makes us think the world revolves around us, doesn't it?"

I push back my hair and push to my feet. "What are you saying? That I'm selfish?"

He shrugs. "You've changed since this contest started. I guess what I'm saying is you're so determined to use your head that your heart isn't getting equal time."

I glare at him. Maybe if he used his head more, he'd be doing something with his life instead of wasting it on video games. But he's the only employee I have left at the moment, so I have sense enough to not say that aloud. "Aren't you the philosophical one all of a sudden? Let's just get to work."

A few hours later, he comes back over. "It's six o'clock. I'm calling it a day. How about you?"

I shake my head. "You go on. I need to finish this before I quit. Tell Mama I'll probably be late."

"Okay."

Guilt, guilt, guilt. "Hey, Adam."

He turns around. "Yeah?"

"I'm sorry about awhile ago. Thanks for all your help."

"No problem. Thanks for the job."

Okay, everything isn't quite back to normal, but this is a step. "You're going to pick up that part Craig said we needed for the fountain at Memphis in the morning, right?"

"Right."

"They close at noon."

He gives me a thumbs-up. "Gotcha."

After he leaves, I force my mind to think of nothing but work, and the next time I look up the sun has disappeared, leaving the park hazy in the twilight. When did the lamps come on? I sink onto a bench and survey our job. If we had a full crew, we could get it all done by Saturday. Unfortunately, we don't. I take a minute to pray for mercy and grace, then drag myself to my vehicle.

The house is dark when I unlock the door except for a soft glow emanating from the living room. I flip on the overhead light, and Lark looks up from the couch. "Hey."

"Hi. The kids in bed?"

She shakes her head. "Soccer game."

Perfect ending to a perfect day.

# thirty

I stare at Lark. "A soccer game? This is Tuesday."

"It was the makeup game from Friday. Remember?"

I groan. "That's right. I forgot."

"They tried to call but you must have left your cell in the car."

"Oh no. I sure did. Why didn't they run by?"

"By the time they figured out you weren't coming, it was too late to go by the park. Your mama took them."

I grab my keys off the hook. "I'm sure it's over, but I've got to see if I can make it."

Lark nods.

I jerk the door open and step onto the porch just as Mama's car pulls into the driveway. Katie and Miranda climb out.

"Hi." I don't know what to say. Their faces are downcast as they walk past me like I'm not there.

"Did you lose?"

Katie looks at me. "No, we won."

"I'm sorry I wasn't there."

"Katie and I both scored." Miranda's words are too cold for

229

the balmy May night.

"That's fantastic." I pull Katie to me and for a second she relaxes against me. Then she pushes away.

"I have to take a shower." She heads for the house.

"Me, too." Miranda follows her in.

I turn to where Mama is standing taking it all in. "I really messed up."

"Yeah."

I don't know what I expected, but this wasn't it. "That's supportive."

"Honey, I've been supporting you. All of us have. But this contest isn't the only thing in the world. You're doing this for their future. But their present is important, too."

I sink onto the porch swing and she sits beside me.

I want to bury my head in her shoulder and cry my heart out. Considering her attitude, I resist the urge. "So I missed one lousy soccer game. . . . Candice had to work last time. No one made a federal case out of that."

"But you promised them you'd go to the games if I took them to the practices." Her soft voice makes my words echo harshly in the air. "No matter how lousy."

"You know I didn't mean it was lousy." I rub my temples with my thumbs. "I forgot tonight was a makeup game. People make mistakes."

"Tell them that. They'll understand. They're just disappointed."

My stomach rolls. What if they don't understand? What if I've scarred them for life? I stand. "Thanks for taking them."

"You're welcome." She walks back to her car, and I go in to face the music.

Lark looks up from the couch. "Sorry."

I nod. That seems to be the word of the day.

Since Miranda's room has a handmade sign on the door that says EXPLOSIVES AHEAD: NO LITTLE SISTERS ALLOWED and it takes an act of Congress to change her attitude about that, I choose Katie's room for our meeting.

I sit in there and wait for them. While I try not to think about the disappointment on their faces, for the first time I notice the total absence of pink. For the first nine years of her life, Katie lived and breathed pink. But about a year ago, Miranda declared it the most awful color on earth. Apparently for the last year, Katie has been quietly erasing any vestiges of pink from her room.

Katie sits on her bed, her blonde hair in damp ringlets. Miranda, her hair still up in a towel, plops down on the turquoise beanbag near the door as if ready to bolt at the first sign of trouble.

"Girls, I'm sorry."

Silence.

"I forgot there was a makeup game tonight."

"You forgot?" Katie purses her lip as if considering this.

I perch beside her on the bed. "Totally. I'm used to the games being on Friday night, and I left my cell phone in the car by accident." I run my hand over her hair. "What did you think? That I didn't want to come?"

Miranda repositions on the beanbag. "We figured you just got busy working and decided that was more important."

"I was busy, but I would have come to the game if I'd remembered. So do you forgive me?"

"Yes." Katie throws her arms around my neck. "But I still miss you."

I look at Miranda. "You forgive me?"

She nods.

"So tell me about the game."

For the next five minutes, they talk about their win, particularly the goals they made. I feel a keen sense of loss for not having been there. But I can't stand much more guilt, so I let it go.

"I'd better go dry my hair," Miranda finally says. She stands and hugs me without reserve before heading to her own room.

"Don't forget to hug Aunt Lark good night," I remind her.

"I won't." She sticks her head back in the door and lowers her voice to a whisper. "When you said she needed some space did you mean that space in front of the TV?"

I open my mouth to explain, and she grins. I grin, too. Even her sense of humor is growing up. "Smarty pants."

Katie hugs me again and I listen to her prayers, then go out to see if Lark feels like talking.

"No. I'm sorry, Allie." She clutches a pillow to her chest and pulls her gaze from the TV. "I should probably go to a hotel."

The idea of her alone in a hotel room mindlessly watching TV breaks my heart. I'm not sure why it's different, but it is. At least she's not totally cut off here. I reach over and pat her arm. "Don't be silly. We want you here."

"I'm so sorry about work. I guess I could try to go tomorrow."

Really? "Well, you can decide in the morning. If you think it would help you, that's fine. But if you don't feel like it, I understand." I almost laugh at the stupidity of that statement. It's all I can say, though. Unless I want to scream "I'm desperate!" at the top of my lungs. And I don't really see what that would accomplish. We've had enough drama around here to last for a while.

Lark is still on the couch when I'm ready to leave the next morning.

I flip on "Get Real, Shady Grove" on the kitchen TV before I walk out the door. There's a big deal with the company who is landscaping the courthouse grounds. An anonymous caller told Channel Six that the owner is spending more than allowed of personal money. Blair made a personal appearance at the site to confront him on camera. The guilt on his face is obvious, but he tries to smooth it over with his good ole boy charm. She's not buying it, though. If it proves to be true, he will be required to remove the things bought with the money or withdraw from the contest. I feel a twinge of pity for the man.

The other team—Blair's obvious favorite—is doing great, according to the footage. The shirtless muscular man who has appointed himself their spokesman flirts shamelessly with her.

When she plays our clip, I grab a chair and sit down. Blair has managed to find the perfect shot of Victoria and me both on our knees working hard, while Adam leans against a tree drinking water. As it freezes on the screen behind her, Blair says, "Call me old-fashioned, but isn't there something wrong with this picture? It almost makes one wonder if Allie would have been better off to look outside the family for her only paid employee."

I snatch up a plastic fork and throw it at the TV.

"Still feel sorry for her?"

I look up to see Lark standing in the doorway.

"Did you see that?"

She nods. "She's pure evil."

"I'm just afraid she'll show up at the park again today."

Lark frowns. "I'd better go with you then. With Adam gone

233

to Memphis and Victoria home with Dylan, she'll get a real kick out of you being the only worker."

As much as I want to take her up on her offer, I can't. "Lark, I don't know what's wrong between you and Craig, but if you don't want to talk about it to the Pinkies, I feel sure you don't want all of Shady Grove to know." I grab my keys and cell phone from the counter. "Blair has a radar for trouble. She'd rip you apart."

Lark's eyes fill with tears. "I'm such a weenie these days. But you're right."

I give her a quick hug. "I'll call you after she leaves. Maybe you can come over and help for a while then."

"Okay." She clings to me for a sec. "You're the best, Allie."

I feel like a worm as I drive to the park. The best what? I'm quickly becoming a champion at feeling sorry for myself. By the time I pull into my parking place, I'm convinced that I don't care what Blair does. "Bring it on," I mutter.

Tansy shows up for her morning walk, and *tut-tuts* about me working by myself. I brush her off and she leaves. Thirty minutes later, Blair arrives with a cameraman I've never seen before. I don't give her the satisfaction of asking about Daniel. I tell myself if he had another wreck, I don't even want to know.

With the camera off, we don't bother with pleasantries.

I'm furious. "Blair, what you did to Adam this morning was wrong. You should be ashamed. And why are you here again so soon? You were just here day before yesterday. Did your spy call and tell you I was working by myself?"

"I'm sure I don't need to remind you that you signed a contract agreeing to this publicity. Lack of cooperation is a reason for disqualification."

234

"Wouldn't you just love that?"

"What I want has nothing to do with it." She motions to the cameraman. "Roll camera."

"A startling development with TLC Landscaping. Apparently when you count on friends and family to work, their personal problems come with them. We're here at the city park with Allie Richards. . .and no one else. Allie, I understand one of your employees has a sick child. But I thought your brother would be here. Has he deserted you, as well?"

I paste on a smile. "Actually, he's gone to pick up some supplies. Thanks for your concern, though."

"What about Lark Murray?" She thrusts the microphone in my face.

My smile may be a little twisted by now, but it stays in place. "What about her?"

"Where is she?"

"Oh." I kind of laugh. "She couldn't be here today."

Apparently even Blair recognizes a brick wall when she sees it. She moves on. "Monday you were sure you'd have no problem getting done in time. Now, with all of these employee problems, are you nervous about finishing this job before the judging?"

I take a deep breath. "I'm confident we'll finish in time." If I have to work by myself around the clock.

"Do you think your friends have let you down?"

I think of Lark and her problems with Craig. And Dylan having the flu. Then I remember what Adam said about me having to be in control. I look straight at the camera. "No, definitely not. My friends are incredibly supportive, and I'll never be able to repay them."

At noon I sit down against the oak tree and scarf down a sandwich. I wad up the wrapper in my hand and rest my head against the rough bark. My eyes are closed when I hear a rustle beside me.

"I was hoping I'd find you here."

# thirty-one

I open my eyes to find Daniel looking down at me. How can one man's smile make the whole world seem brighter?

"Here I am."

He sinks down beside me. "How's it going?"

I shake my head. "Don't ask."

"Too late. I already did." He reaches over and takes my hand in his.

I jump slightly but don't jerk away. Instead I watch in fascination as he intertwines our fingers.

I've made it clear that we're just friends. Today, we're friends who hold hands. So what?

We stare at our hands in silence for a few seconds. I'd love to know what he's thinking. Then he says, "Blair make it over here?"

"Oh yeah." Still resting against the tree, I turn my head to look at him. "Don't worry. I held my own with her."

His dimple flashes and he squeezes my hand. "I knew you could."

I know I should pull away, but it's amazing how much strength I'm drawing from the contact. "Where were you?"

He shrugs. "I had to go back to the doctor for my follow-up. I got the all-clear."

"Good. Did you see this morning's show?"

"Yeah. Have you talked to Adam?"

Why hadn't I? I should have called him as soon as I saw the segment. Some sister I am. I was so worried about getting to work. "No, but he should be here any time. He's gone to Memphis to pick up a part."

"I'm sorry about the clip. I don't even remember seeing that."

"Oh, I know. That's skillful editing on Blair's part. You couldn't help it."

"We missed you at the soccer game last night."

"Yeah, me, too. I forgot about it."

"Ouch. I bet you were disappointed to miss it." He looks at me and the sadness in his eyes makes my stomach hurt. "Allie, I think you'll win this contest, but if you don't, it's not the end of the world."

I slip my hand from his. "Not to you. But I have to win."

"Because of the girls?"

He reaches for my hand again, but I cross my arms in front of me and nod. "And that's why you're going to continue to date Trevor Wright, even though you don't care a thing about him, isn't it? Because of the girls?"

I stand and throw my sandwich wrapper in the trash can. How dare he bring that up? "Who I date is my business. Just because I don't want to cast my lot with someone who, by his own admission, has no idea what his future holds, is no reason for you to criticize my choices."

He pushes to his feet, and when he speaks I have to strain to hear him. "When are you going to understand that none of us know what the future holds?"

"Unlike you, I have two children who count on me knowing."

"Then they're in for a disappointment." He puts his hand on my arm. "Wake up, Allie. This isn't you. You're letting fear push you into blind ambition. And I'm here to tell you from experience, nothing ruins a life faster. Look at Blair. Is that what you want to be like?"

I jerk away and take off at a sprint to the other side of the park. Not very mature, I'm sure. But at least it keeps me from hitting him.

If I'd known the sandwich was going to turn into a knot in my stomach, I'd have skipped lunch. On top of my run-in with Daniel, Adam was supposed to be here with the part for the fountain an hour ago. Not long from now, Craig will stop by to install it. The glue has to dry for twenty-four hours, then this time tomorrow we can do a test run. All of that is assuming Adam shows up. I've called his cell several times since Daniel left, but no answer. Now I'm half afraid he saw "Get Real, Shady Grove" this morning and skipped the country. I'm wrestling the last of the Bradford pear trees into place when he finally appears. I stabilize the root ball of the small tree and jog over to greet him.

He climbs out of the truck, his T-shirt dirty and wrinkled, but I'm so glad to see him I don't even care. "Hey, you okay?"

He nods and runs his fingers through his hair. Uh-oh. The universal sign of men for "You won't believe what happened."

"What's wrong?"

"I'm sorry, Allie. The place closed right before I got there."

I stop where I am, the knot in my stomach exploding into an incredible tightness in my chest. Am I having a heart attack? Or just dying of disappointment? "You didn't get the part?"

He shakes his head. "Sorry. I got so flustered this morning after I saw Blair's show that I—"

"You know what? I don't even care. I'm sorry I put you through this. Just forget it." Tears are burning my eyes. I can't even look at him. I don't blame him for being upset, but sometimes being a grown-up means you have to push past that. I was counting on him.

"Wait a minute. . . ."

I spin around. "No, seriously. Consider yourself off the hook. Go home. Play a video game. I'll figure out how to handle this by myself."

"You're firing me?" His voice is incredulous.

"Whatever you want to call it."

"Fine." He whirls around and jumps in his truck. A few seconds later, he guns it and spins out of the parking lot.

I sit down right where I am, a sob catching in my throat. Who am I kidding? Winning the contest is a lost cause. And since the first-place prize is my only hope for the immediate future, I'm sunk. So now what?

In the quiet, the mockingbird starts a song. I can't identify the tune, but I'm reminded of Daniel saying how sad it would be not to sing your own song.

He's right. Win or lose, this is the song I have, so I'm going to finish the final chorus. I murmur a prayer as I manhandle the tree into its hole and tamp the dirt down around the root ball.

"Still working by yourself?"

I look up to see Tansy, walking in place, right behind me. "Yeah, you could say that."

"Everything okay?"

"Right as rain." Technically that's not lying, since rain is anything but right these days. And what am I supposed to say? I'm 99 percent sure she's the one who is passing information to Blair, so I'm not planning on giving her any more ammunition.

"Guess what?" She's still walking in place.

"What?"

"I'm late for my afternoon walk today because I went to the doctor."

"Oh? Are you all right?" That old Southern politeness. My mama ingrained it in me. What can I say?

"Yes, and thanks to you, I've lost five pounds."

I stop working and turn to face her. "Really? How?"

"I've walked here for years but never lost even an ounce. But since you started working here, I wanted to hurry and get out of your way, so I've picked up my pace considerably. Lost five pounds," she repeats proudly.

Duh, silly me, as Katie used to say when she was a toddler. How could I have suspected this sweet—if slightly eccentric—lady of being the mole? Blair must have hidden cameras or tape recorders. "That's great, Tansy."

"Well, I'll let you get back to work. I sure do like what you're doing here. I was just telling Blair the other day that your crew works so hard. And some days you have to work all by yourself."

Um. Stop. Rewind. Blair? "Oh? So you know Blair?"

"Oh yes, dear. I baby-sit for her daughter after school. I think Blair feels sorry for you since you don't really have a crew."

"What makes you think that?"

"She told me to keep an eye on you and tell her if you ran into any problems. Isn't she thoughtful?"

"More than you know." I say it through clenched teeth.

"Well, she was so sad this morning when I called and told her you didn't have a crew today. Did she stop by to check on you?"

"Yes, she did." And she should be ashamed using a sweet, innocent women like this, but I'll take that up with her.

"I'm surprised she didn't stay to help you herself. She's just that kind of person, you know." Talk about the Twilight Zone. I have a serious suspicion that Tansy and I live in alternate realities.

"Well, I need to finish up so I can get home. Congratulations on losing the five pounds."

"Thanks." She gives me a little wave and hurries away.

An hour later a truck horn makes me look up. Craig. Here to finish the fountain. I jump up and get to the parking lot before he can get out of the red truck that proclaims MURRAY PLUMBING.

I decide not to mention Adam. For one thing, he's my brother. For another, I'm far from perfect. Just look at my track record for getting along with people today. "Something came up and we didn't get the part today. I'm sorry. If I get it tomorrow, will you still put it on?"

He nods. "That won't give us much time for a test, but if everything goes perfectly, it could work."

"Thanks. It'll be here tomorrow afternoon." I take a good look at the worry lines on his face. Those weren't there a few weeks ago. "You know, you and Lark are going to have to talk."

"She knows where I am."

"Sometimes we have to just bend our pride and go to the other person, no matter who is at fault." I talk a good Dr. Phil, even if the thought of me passing out relationship advice *is* totally ridiculous.

"Allie, Lark doesn't want me to seek her out. She wants me to leave her alone."

I think that's a tear in his eye. And I'm positive I'm way out of my element. "Craig, I'm sorry."

"See you tomorrow afternoon."

"Yeah. See ya."

You would think that two big arguments in one day would be enough for anyone. But not Allie Richards. I'm going for a world record. Although, in my defense, this one isn't my idea.

When I drag in from work an hour after suppertime, Mama corners me in the kitchen. "Allie Nicole, I can't believe how ridiculous you're being. You fired your brother."

"I just let him off the hook."

"Do you know what your brother went through for you today?"

"Blair's humiliation? Yeah, I saw the show."

"I don't care about a stupid TV show." She doesn't raise her voice, but I get the point. "He left his cell phone at home and when his truck broke down, he had to walk five miles to get help.

And then he fixed the truck and went on to Memphis anyway, bound and determined to get the part for you." She storms out and lets the screen door slam behind her.

I'm lower than a worm. Suddenly Adam's wrinkled, dirty shirt—a symbol to me this afternoon of his don't-care attitude—means something completely different. I rest my head on the pantry door and give it a bump. Why hadn't I let him explain? Because I wasn't thinking about him. I was thinking about me.

Adam's right. It's all about me.

Daniel's right. I'm turning into Blair.

And Mama's right. I'm unbelievable.

# thirty-two

I breathe a sigh of relief as I see the WELCOME TO SHADY GROVE sign up ahead. It's 11:00 a.m. and by leaving well before daylight, I've already been to Memphis and back.

I've come to a decision on this six-hour round-trip journey.

Even though I still intend to give it my best, winning the contest isn't much of a possibility any longer. And like Daniel said, the outcome isn't in my control. At first I couldn't see past the disastrous ending of something I—and my friends and family—have worked so hard for. But somewhere around Trumann on the way home, I have an epiphany. Until the last couple of days, I've enjoyed this project more than I have any work I've done in my adult life. This is what I want to do, only without the camera following me around. And one thing I know—God wouldn't give me a dream so strong and so real if there wasn't a way to accomplish it. So about the time I drive through Jonesboro, I begin working out a backup plan.

Admittedly the plan is still a little rough. But the way I see it, if I start small and work part-time while I build my business, with God's help I can do this. It won't be the same as having the city contract and the new truck. Not to mention the money. But I'll pay the hospital in payments and if they turn me over to a bill collector. . .well, I'll know that I'm doing all I can. The girls and I have each other, and pot pies aren't all that bad. Hey, at least I'm not spoiling them with material wealth.

With this plan comes an added bonus. Peace. Conditional peace, I know. I have several apologies to make. But it sure beats the chaotic turmoil I've had inside me for the last few weeks.

I still don't see any hope for Daniel and me. I'm too pragmatic to allow myself to marry a man who takes risks as easily as others take vitamins. But knowing how I feel about that blue-eyed, Harley-riding rebel, I don't see much purpose in going out with Mr. Wright anymore either. It wouldn't be fair to him.

As I pass the Shady Grove population sign, it hits me. I'm coming home in more ways than one.

A few minutes later, I park in front of Mama's house and kill the motor. The hood is up on Adam's truck. Only his legs are sticking out from under the front end. I amble slowly up the walkway. You know how on sitcoms when people talk to the person under the vehicle, it's always the wrong person? Well, Adam's bright orange flip-flops are a dead giveaway. The man under the truck is none other than the brother I know and love. Even though he may not care much for me at the moment. "Adam? Got a minute?"

He scoots out and looks up at me, his face streaked with black. "Well, at least you didn't say 'Are you busy?' I'll give you that."

"Yeah, that kills me when people do that when they can see you are. . . ." My voice fades off. He's trying to give me the out of acting like nothing happened. But I owe him more than that. "I'm really sorry, bro. For what I said. For how I acted. I let you down. In a lot of ways. You've done so much for me these last few weeks, and I want to be sure you know how much I appreciate you."

"I know."

"Do you really or are you just trying to stop me before I get mushy?"

"Both." He grins. "Mama's in the house."

I nod. "That's my next stop."

He slides back under the truck. And I look up to see Mama standing at the front door, holding it open for me. I run to her and she hugs me tightly. "Glad to see you came to your senses," she murmurs against my hair.

"I'm sorry." It's easier the second time around. Of course it helps that she has to forgive me since she gave birth to me. At least that's how it works in my family. Something else to be thankful for, I suddenly realize.

"Is Lark still at my house?"

She nods. "I think so. I'll tell you right now, if her granny were still alive, she'd shake some sense into that girl. Leaving her big, strong, good-looking husband all alone."

"I know, Mama. Sometimes we have to work things out for ourselves, though." Like yours truly.

"I guess she's sitting over there trying to figure it out. I saw Rachel's car pull up earlier, but then she left by herself."

I'd called Rachel last night and told her not to worry about working today. With me gone, and Adam, Lark, and Victoria not working, there wasn't much she could do.

When I leave Mama's, I drive on over to the park. There's

nothing I can do for Lark right now. To my shock, Rachel and Victoria are finishing up the south side when I pull up. I jump out and run to them. "What are you doing here?"

Rachel grins. "We figured you could use some help."

I hug her and then Victoria. "How's Dylan?"

"He was able to go to school today. I would have called you yesterday, but I didn't know until this morning."

"I'm so glad he's better."

"Me, too."

"And we're glad you made it back to work," Rachel teases. Then her face grows solemn. "I tried to get Lark to come but couldn't budge her."

I make a snap decision. "Here's the plan. Meet at my house at nine thirty tonight. Can you?"

They both nod.

"What do you have in mind, shugah?"

"An intervention."

Rachel's brows draw together. "For Lark?"

"Yep. We've got to figure out how to help her."

"Count me in for sure," Victoria drawls.

"Me, too." Rachel motions to the south side of the park. "Can you tell we've done anything?"

"It looks fantastic."

"Thanks."

"Did either of you watch Blair's show this morning?" I left home way too early to even think about it.

Victoria raises her hand. "I did. Just a short clip of you working by yourself yesterday and then her interviewing you. But it was nothing terrible."

I nod. "It doesn't really matter." I start to fill them in on my epiphany, but my cell phone rings in the middle of it. The school. Unease niggles at my mind as I flip it open. "Hello?"

"Allie. It's Meredith. How are you today?"

The school counselor is a nice woman, but we aren't close acquaintances. Cold fear clutches my heart. "Is something wrong with one of the girls?"

"They're both fine. Physically, at least."

"What's wrong with them otherwise?"

"Possibly nothing. But Katie apparently told her teacher that she and Miranda were staying with your mom these days."

I sink down to a tree root and attempt a laugh. "Well, my mother has been helping out a lot while I'm working on this project, but their primary residence is still with me. Is Katie in your office?"

She clears her throat. "Actually she's in Principal Dickerson's office. They both are. When Miranda heard what Katie said, she said it was a lie, and I'm afraid they had an altercation."

"A fight? You mean a fuss?"

Hesitation again. "It took two teachers to separate them."

"Oh no." Could it be any worse?

"I'm sorry, Allie. I'm not sure what's going on there. Maybe it's just the pressure of the contest? But they've both been suspended until Monday."

Ask a stupid question, get a stupid answer. Things can definitely get worse.

"I'll be right there."

I can't stop the tears as I flip the phone shut.

"Trouble at school?" Victoria asks.

"Yeah, you could say that." I tell them what happened. "I've got to go get them."

"Of course you do." Rachel hugs me. "Victoria and I will take care of things here. Your place is with Katie and Miranda."

"We'll be praying for you," Victoria whispers as she hugs me. "You can count on it."

"I'm going to spend some time with them and figure all this out. Y'all don't have to stay here and work." I hate to tell them that there's no way we can get it all done anyway.

"But we want to." Rachel pushes me toward my SUV. "Now go."

Funny how even once we grow up, it's still no fun to go to the principal's office. My hands are clammy and my knees rubbery by the time I get to the door. What if this goes on their permanent records? Is this how Daniel felt that day so long ago when he got expelled?

I grimace. There's got to be a way to make everything quit coming back to Daniel. Surely there's a seminar out there somewhere for heart retraining. I'll have to look into it when this mess is over.

I shove the door open and barely glance at Betty before I see Katie and Miranda sitting side by side on the couch in the main office. Katie runs to me and buries her head in my side. I squeeze her tightly and hold out my other arm to Miranda. She stands and slowly comes toward me, head held high like Wendy in Peter Pan, forced to walk the plank but determined to do it with dignity. When I put my arm around her she collapses against me, though. "Mom, I'm sorry. We didn't mean—"

"We'll talk later," I whisper, mindful of Betty's gaze on us. "Let me take care of things here first."

I get them settled back on the couch and take a deep breath. "Is Principal Dickerson in?"

Betty nods toward his slightly open door. "Yes, he's waiting for you."

I tap on the door and it opens under my fingers.

"Allie, come in, come in." He slides his reading glasses off and holds them with both hands in front of him on his desk. His suit makes me keenly aware of my landscaping clothes. At least I got the call from Meredith before I started actually working, so I'm not dirty.

I slide into the chair across from him. I've had many friendly chats with this man since Miranda started kindergarten but never in this office. It's beyond intimidating. Katie and Miranda must have been terrified sitting here. Not that they didn't deserve a little terror, but I deserve it a lot more.

"What you're doing with the park is wonderful."

"Thank you." I fiddle with my keys. "But what I'm doing with my girls is not so wonderful."

He smiles. "I wouldn't say that at all. Up until today, Katie and Miranda have been exemplary students. And Monday I expect that to be the case again." He clears his throat. "The girls told me their version of what happened. And I'm not so sure they were actually fighting, although I can see why it looked that way to the teachers on recess duty."

"Oh?"

"I'll let Katie and Miranda tell you about it. But in light of the circumstances, I'm not going to put a suspension on their record."

I knew I liked this man. "Thank you."

"Fighting or not, they did misbehave, so how would you feel about them having an unofficial day off tomorrow to be with their mom?"

In other words, he doesn't want to tell the teachers they might have been wrong. I can certainly see that. "Sounds good." I run my hand across the edge of the desk and then meet his gaze. "What happened today was mostly my fault. I've been a little obsessed. . . okay, a *lot* obsessed with this contest."

He waves his hand toward a row of plaques on the wall. "I doubt there are many people who haven't gotten a little caught up in a competition. And since your future seems to be riding on this one. . ."

"I've figured something out about that." I jerk my head toward the outer office. "As long as God allows me to have them, they're my future. And He'll help me take care of them."

"It sounds like you've already won then." He rises and I take my cue to stand, too.

"Thank you for understanding."

The girls and I walk silently to the SUV. Once they're buckled in, I ease out of the parking lot and head toward the house. A few minutes later, the sign for the lake road changes my mind. I jerk my blinker on and swing a right at the last minute.

"Where are we going?" I hear Katie whisper.

"I don't know," Miranda whispers back.

"To a place I like to go to work things out."

"We must be in big trouble," Katie whispers.

I let them think about it until we get to the lake.

The ducks waddle out to meet us. I guide the girls through

the quacking flock of ducks to a picnic table beside the lake. The same table where I dreamed my Mr. Right dream, but we won't think about that since it leads to a subject I'm trying to forget.

"So," I say when they're both seated. "Let's figure out what happened."

Katie raises her hand, and I smother a smile. "Katie, you first."

"The teacher asked me if you'd make cupcakes for the end-of-the-year party."

"And?"

"I told her that Memaw would have to do it because we were mostly staying with her now."

Miranda jumps in. "So when Grant asked me on the playground if we were living with my grandma, I said no. He said Katie said we were, and I said Katie was lying." She frowns. "Then she tackled me."

"I wasn't lying!" Katie glares at her sister. "And I didn't tackle you."

"Yes, you did."

"I was just trying to put my hand over your mouth."

"Yeah, so hard you knocked me down."

"I fell down, too."

I try not to let my relief show. My girls weren't brawling on the playground.

I hold up my hand. "Okay, let's take this in parts. Katie, you have been staying with Memaw a lot. Did you mean to make the teacher or the class think you were living with her?"

She wrinkles her face up. "No!"

"Miranda, before you said Katie was lying, you should have made sure what she really said, right?"

Miranda puts her elbows on the table and her chin in her hands. "Right."

I look at her.

She rolls her eyes toward her sister. "Sorry I said you were lying." It's not the most enthusiastic apology in the world, but it's a start.

"Katie, when Miranda is saying something you don't want her to, does putting your hand over her mouth work?" If nothing else good comes out of today, maybe this will break her of doing that.

"No."

I wait.

"Sorry for trying to put my hand over your mouth. And for knocking you down."

If this were an episode of *The Brady Bunch*, they'd hug and make up. But in real life, this is as good as it gets. "I'm proud of you for owning up to your actions." Even if it did take a lot of prompting from me. "Now it's my turn." And we won't even talk about how much nudging from various sources it took to open my eyes.

For the next few minutes, I explain to them about my hopes and dreams for the future and how I let that turn into a master plan that I was in control of.

I'm not sure if they get it or not, but at least they act like they do.

"Are we still in trouble?" Katie sounds worried.

This is one of those times when a mom has to make the best decision she can. I want them to know they did wrong. But personally, I think they've learned a lesson and isn't that what it's all about?

"Well, you're still suspended from school for tomorrow." I look out at the lake. "I figure one day of hard labor ought to be enough punishment."

"With you?" Katie says.

Before I can answer, Miranda says, "At the park?"

"Yep."

I choose to ignore the high-five they exchange behind my back.

# thirty-three

On the way back to town, I call Rachel. She says Craig came by and installed the fountain part. She and Victoria worked the rest of the afternoon and are calling it a day.

"You and the girls okay?" she asks.

I look in my rearview mirror at the girls. Their faces are relaxed and open, a stark contrast to the pinched, worried look they've worn the last few days. "Better than."

"Good."

"I'm going to go on home and fix them some supper. I'll get them to bed early and expect y'all about nine thirty, okay?"

"Okay. Are you sure? I can't imagine you not working until dark these days. Not that I'm complaining."

I shrug even though she can't see me. "The park will still be there tomorrow. And if we're not done by Saturday. . .we tried our best."

"I'm proud of you, Allie. I wish I could help you tomorrow."

"Hey, somebody has to keep Shady Grove in line."

She laughs at our old joke. "Yeah, their spines anyway. The rest is in God's hands."

"That seems to be the theme for the week, doesn't it? Now if we can just convince Lark."

"See you then."

Lark leaves the TV long enough to eat supper with us. And even though she's still in her flannel PJs, I'll take that as a victory. The girls are still subdued from their eventful day so getting them to bed is easier than usual. By 9:25, the house is quiet.

I slip out on the porch and wait for the reinforcements. I'm not sure what to expect, but something has to give.

Victoria and Rachel arrive right on time in Victoria's Jaguar. I lead the way into the living room and they sit down without speaking. Lark finally looks up and her eyes widen. She fumbles for the remote and hits the POWER button.

"I'm glad you did that," I say dryly. "It was my job to wrestle it from you."

"What?" She clutches a pillow against her. She doesn't look glad to see Victoria and Rachel. "What are y'all doing here?"

"Bringing you to your senses, shugah."

She throws the pillow to the other end of the couch and glares up at me as if I personally delivered her to the enemy. "I told you I'd go to a hotel."

"You can't get what you need at a hotel," Rachel says softly.

"How do you know what I need?" Lark snaps.

This might be harder than we thought. No one ever snaps at Rachel. What's the point?

Since I'm still standing behind Lark, I give Rachel and Victoria the "cut" motion across my neck. "You need the same thing the rest of us do. A Pinky night out. We're long overdue. Only since we're already here and I don't have a sitter, "out" will have to be my house."

"That works," Victoria drawls. "I'll make some coffee." She disappears into the kitchen.

Lark stands and turns around to face me. "Have y'all lost your minds?"

"Girls just wanna have fun?" I say with a small smile.

"Hey, look what I found." Rachel's voice is muffled. My hall closet door is open and she emerges with a pile of board games.

"Board games." Lark sounds like she's just discovered a nest of snakes in the bathtub.

I glance over at her. "You love board games."

"At. . ." She looks up at the clock over the fireplace. ". . .nine forty at night?"

"Sure. We're all grown-ups. We don't have a bedtime." I grin. At least she's waking up a little.

Lark shoots me a glare. "I know what y'all are trying to do."

Victoria appears in the doorway with creamer, sugar, and four steaming mugs of coffee on a tray. I promise that woman was born able to hostess an impromptu party in her sleep, even at someone else's house. "Coffees all around."

"Good. We're going to need the caffeine." Rachel ignores our looks of dismay. What happened to "caffeine is a drug and sugar will kill you"? Desperate times, I guess. She has the Monopoly board almost completely set up on my old scarred coffee table. "It might take me awhile to buy everyone's property."

"Right. I'm the investment queen." Victoria bumps Rachel to

make room for her on the couch and sits down beside her. "Y'all are going down."

I pull up one of my overstuffed rockers and plop down in it. "Don't be so sure."

Lark just stands there.

"Sit down, Larkie," Rachel says. "You might as well."

She doesn't say anything, but she takes a seat in the other rocker.

"We'll even let you be the dog." Victoria pushes our favorite piece toward her and she takes it.

I sort through the remaining tokens. "I call the wheelbarrow."

"Hmm. . .fitting." Victoria looks at Rachel. "Fight you for the shoe?"

Rachel wrinkles her freckle-covered nose. "You take it. You already have so many to go with it. I'll be the car tonight. That way I can just drive right by the rest of you."

An hour later, Victoria has most of the property and I'm in jail when Rachel says, "Trust me," to Lark about the percentage of tax she needed to pay on a property.

Lark's hand freezes as she's drawing a card. "I do. But if I didn't, I wouldn't even play Monopoly with you, much less live with you."

Victoria goes ahead and rolls, but she casually says, "You don't trust him?"

"He's been doing things behind my back."

My heart flops in my chest. I'd have staked my life on Craig's fidelity. Could I have been so blind?

"Like a surprise?" Rachel's voice is soft as she counts off the spaces to move her little car around the board. I notice we're all afraid to stop playing the game, afraid Lark will stop talking.

Lark's laugh is mostly sob. I snatch a tissue from the box beside me and press it into her hand. "That's what he said. But you don't gather information about adoption, get an application, as a *surprise*." She spits the last word out like it's a profanity.

No one speaks. As Pinkies, we talk about everything. But not about Lark's infertility. It's the only taboo topic among us.

"You don't want to adopt?" I finally say.

Lark shrugs. "Craig's been after me ever since I turned thirty-five in January. 'Larkie, if we don't hurry, we'll be too old to get an infant. . . .'" She jumps up and the game pieces scatter on the board. "I told him I wasn't ready."

"Lark, sweetie. . ." Victoria stands, compassion shining in her eyes. "You always said you wanted a whole houseful of kids. What happened?"

Lark turns away from us, and for a second I'm afraid she's going to bolt. "If God wanted me to have kids, He'd have given them to me."

Rachel's freckles stand out dark against her white face. "You don't believe in adoption?"

I feel like a member of a bomb squad trying to figure out which wire to cut. My insides are quivering.

Something in Rachel's voice spins Lark around. When she sees how pale Rachel is, she sinks down beside her on the couch and puts her arm around her. "Oh, honey. That's not true."

I breathe a silent prayer thanking God for His wisdom and grace. Worrying about Rachel's feelings might be the only thing that can get Lark out of her own self-absorption.

"I believe in adoption." She takes Rachel's hand in hers. "You did a terribly brave thing giving up Jennifer to your sister and her husband. And they're a wonderful family to her." She sits back down and rests her head against the back of the couch, tears streaming down her cheeks. "This is about me, guys. Not about Craig. Not about adoption. It's me," she sobs.

I sit down on the other side of her, tears filling my own eyes. "What do you mean?"

"I figure God knows"—she has to stop and get control of the sobs—"what He's doing, not letting me have kids."

"Shugah, why in the world would you think that?" Victoria scoots the Monopoly board over and perches on the coffee table.

"My ma—" She puts her hand over her face. "My mama."

"What does your mama have to do with this?" I ask, even though I have a sinking feeling I know where this is going.

"She left me with Granny and never came back. What kind of person would do that?"

"A really mixed-up one." Rachel rubs Lark's shoulder. "But you wouldn't. Ever."

"You're my friends. You have to say that. But what if it's in my genes?"

Victoria puts her hand under Lark's chin and forces her to look at her. "Think, Lark. What about your granny? She was your mother's mom. Did you ever get the feeling she was going to cut and run?"

"No."

We sit quietly for a minute.

"Why can't I just get pregnant? Then I'd know that God trusted me to be a mother."

"Oh, Lark." The frustration in Rachel's voice echoes my own feelings.

261

"I thought I was pregnant. I was going to tell Craig Monday night. But that afternoon. . ." She swipes at her eyes with the back of her hand. "I wasn't."

"Is that why you left Craig?" I remember the wild look in her eyes when she showed up on my doorstep.

She shook her head. "I'm used to that, I guess. But that night, Craig came home with flowers. . .and a book about adoption."

Sometimes there are no easy answers. We can reassure her until the cows come home, but she's going to have to work this out for herself. I put my arm around her and Rachel does the same on the other side. Victoria completes the circle hug in the front. I'm pretty sure there's not a dry eye in the bunch.

"Thank you, guys." Lark hugs each one of us separately. "I feel better just knowing how much y'all care."

"Never doubt it," Victoria says. "Allie, do you have any ice cream?"

"Yeah. There's some Moose Tracks in the freezer."

Lark gives a shaky laugh. " 'Fraid not. Sorry."

"I have a hidden stash of Fudgsicles behind a bag of broccoli." I give Lark a questioning look. "Unless you found those, too?"

Lark ducks her head. "Actually I did. But there's still half a box."

Victoria stands again. "In that case, this meeting of the Pinkies is officially adjourned to the kitchen."

A few minutes later I bite into a frozen chocolate bar and look at my three best friends gathered around my kitchen table.

Victoria waves her fudge bar in the air. "Remember Truth or Dare?"

"Oh no," Rachel says. "I was always terrible at that game."

"Me, too, but I was trying to figure out a way to tactfully ask Allie about what's going on with Daniel Montgomery."

Lark snorts. Her face is red and splotchy, but at least she's back in the land of the living. "Vic, when did you ever worry about tact? Just ask her."

I clear my throat. "Um, excuse me. I'm sitting right here."

"So, Allie?" Victoria crosses her legs and sits back in the chair. "What's the deal with you and Daniel?"

Victoria's trying to distract Lark. I know that. But does she have to throw me to the wolves to do it?

"I told y'all from the beginning he's not the man for me."

"Not buying." Lark crosses her arms. "Your face lights up when he's around."

"Or even when somebody says his name," Rachel adds.

Does it really? How did I let this go so far? "What if he'd been killed in that motorcycle accident?"

"When are you going to stop living in What-If Land?" Victoria demands.

If I can't be honest with these women, who can I be honest with? "Well, since I'm living there anyway, let's do one more. What if I'm in love with Daniel?"

"What if you are?" Rachel reaches over and takes my hand.

I pull away. "You were with me when we found out about his accident. How will I handle it if something happens to him?"

"At some point, you have to trust God, Allie," Lark says. "You're the one who taught me that."

"Maybe you need a refresher course," Victoria mutters to Lark.

My kitchen has never been so quiet. Rachel and I are both almost afraid to breathe, I think.

Lark just stares at Victoria for a few seconds, then lowers her eyes. "Maybe I do."

I can't believe it. Lark is actually seeing the light. I guess that's worth my soul being laid bare.

# thirty-four

My flippant comment to Lark last night about grown-ups not having a bedtime has come back to haunt me this morning. We're trying to do our stretches, but all three of the Pinkies present are dragging today.

"I hope Rachel isn't snoozing on her adjusting table," Victoria murmurs to Lark and me.

"That park bench over there is looking pretty good," Lark says as she stretches her arms to the sky.

I lean against the tree and shut my eyes. "Don't even think about it."

We talked and prayed together until the wee hours, and when the alarm went off this morning, Miranda made us all get up. Even though I believe they're truly sorry for yesterday, she and Katie are excited to be part of the last day of work.

"Mom, are you sick?"

I open my eyes to see Katie, concern on her face. "No, baby, just tired."

"You stayed up too late."

"I heard y'all giggling at two thirty this morning," Miranda says, her expression stern.

Lark puts her hands on her hips. "Well, what were you doing awake at that time of the night, missy?"

Miranda opens her mouth.

Then Lark grins. "Gotcha."

Lark is actually perkier than the rest of us. I heard her talking in low tones on her cell before we left home this morning, and now she keeps looking toward the entryway of the park in a way that strongly reminds me of all the days I've watched for Daniel to show up.

Sure enough, when Craig drives in she makes a beeline for him. A few minutes later, they appear hand in hand.

Miranda leans over to me and whispers, "Looks like I can have my place back in front of the TV."

I give her ponytail a gentle tug. "Let's hope so, kiddo."

Lark's face is shining. Is that really what I look like when Daniel's around? Or at least what I did look like, back when we were still speaking to each other? I don't know much about anything these days, but I do know I owe him an apology. I'm hoping I can catch him this morning when no one else is around and tell him I'm sorry.

Hard to apologize to someone when he's not there. Lunch comes and goes with no sign of Daniel. I can't imagine that Blair would have him skip the last day of filming. My imagination starts to go wild, but I send up a silent prayer and get busy.

By midafternoon, I can see the end in sight. I never thought I'd say it, but I think we're actually going to finish. We may or may not win, but we'll be done. Just as I think this, the station van pulls up and Blair and Daniel get out. I should have known. Miss I'm-Rooting-for-You-Allie with the knife behind her back. No way she could resist being in on the last day of action. Especially if it meant we might end up embarrassed by not being done. Maybe it's time for a little table-turning.

As soon as Blair and Daniel are within ten feet of us, Craig turns the water on to the fountain. You'd think someone just made a hole-in-one by our collective "Ahh." Judging by Blair's gaping mouth, maybe we did. I wish Daniel would get her slack-jawed look on camera. But I'm sure she'd just edit it out. Making things appear how she wants them to is her specialty.

I position myself in front of the fountain when she approaches me with the microphone so that our centerpiece won't get edited out.

"Allie, we're absolutely amazed by what you've done with the place. How did you get the fountain going?"

"A lot of hard work and ingenuity, I guess." I have a feeling she's more used to getting ahead by smooth talking and trickery, so I can understand her need to ask.

"Is that a plumber I see?"

Wow, all this and a brain, too? I smile. "Yes, it is, Blair. This is Craig Murray of Murray Plumbing. He's been a wonderful help." I motion Craig over. He won't let me pay him, but maybe some free publicity will help.

"I can see that," she coos and bats her eyelashes at the camera. Behind her, Victoria rolls her eyes and Lark pretends to be gagging. "But I can't help but wonder if his services were in the budget? What will the contest committee think about this?"

Craig steps up to the microphone, and I move over to give

him space. "I'm pretty sure there's nothing in the rules about a friend helping out a friend."

I do a little inward dance at Blair's blush and lean over to add my two cents. "And I'm guessing the contest committee—and Shady Grove—will be impressed by Craig's willingness to help—at no personal gain—to make our hometown even more beautiful."

I do believe for once the girl is speechless.

But my crew—my friends and family—burst into applause.

Blair finally regains her voice and makes it my turn to blush by asking about why Katie and Miranda are out of school. I mumble something about working it out with the principal and amazingly she lets it go. But then she moves on to the one question I've been dreading. "If you had it all to do over, would you enter the contest?"

I want to say, "Well, if I'm the winner, then the answer is yes. But if I lose, then the answer is no." But I just throw the camera a teasing smile. "Ask me after the winner is announced."

More applause.

Blair motions for Daniel to cut.

As they walk by Craig, Daniel says, "Good job," and he even reaches out to shake Adam's hand on the way out. But before I can work my way over to talk to him, they're gone.

In spite of my disappointment at having to delay making peace of some sort with Daniel, we all relax after Blair leaves.

Adam hollers at me. "Al, did you already change the bulbs in the lightposts?"

I shake my head and turn back to helping Victoria lay the last of the rock around the flower beds. A few minutes later, we stand up and I survey the park. A far cry from the park that we walked into four weeks ago. "Well, if it's true what they say about it all being in the details, we've got this in the bag."

"Let me tell you, shugah. You got that right. Lark even detailed the bathroom." She wrinkles her nose. "*So* not our job. But she's convinced some judge might wander in there tomorrow and mark points off if the toilet isn't clean."

I grin. "Y'all have gone above and beyond for me and this contest."

She holds up her dirty hands. "This is a sacrifice for me. I draw the line at cleaning public restrooms."

"I think we're about done. Let's take a break."

"Sounds good."

We tell the others, and while Adam and Craig play Frisbee with the girls and Dylan, I tell the Pinkies about my plan to apologize to Daniel.

"So does this mean you're changing your mind about him?" Victoria asks.

"Who knows? But I shouldn't have acted like I did, so I'm going to tell him that."

"Hmm. . .maybe I'm not the only one who did some waking up last night," Lark muses.

"I'm still praying about it, girls. Don't get carried away."

"We'll be praying about it for you," Rachel offers.

"As long as you don't pray for what *you* think is best for me," I tease.

She strikes a dramatic pose. "Oh, come on, you know I'm just dying to be a bridesmaid again."

"This time we get to pick the dresses," Victoria says with a hard look at Lark.

"Hey. There was nothing wrong with your dresses," Lark protests, but she grins.

"Oh no. . ." Victoria drawls, "as long as you like huge bows and puff skirts."

"Puff skirts were in then." Lark looks at me. "They aren't now."

I put up my hand. "Whoa. Tell me y'all aren't seriously sitting here planning my nonexistent wedding?"

"Of course not," Rachel says. "We're just talking in abstract."

"What-If Land, you know," Victoria drawls.

"Well, y'all best come back to the real world. I still have the same doubts about Daniel I always had. And from what I can see, he's not even speaking to me."

Lark nods. "And that's why we're going to be praying for you."

There's just no reasoning with some people.

As we leave the park, I'm a woman with a mission. Curiosity may have killed the cat, but I'm dying to see the work of the other finalists. Until today, I've avoided the library and the city hall because I didn't want to get intimidated. But it's all over but the crying, as Lark's granny used to say, so I make a left instead of a right out of the park entrance.

"Where are we going, Mom?" Katie asks from the backseat.

Miranda huffs. "We have to get ready for the game. Aren't we going home?"

"Yes, we are. We're just taking a little detour."

City Hall comes up first. I drive by slowly, craning my neck like a first-time tourist. Apparently they're all done. And I'm impressed. Blooming flowers in big beds on each side of the entrance, hanging pots of red geraniums on the porch, and the crepe myrtles lining the sidewalk. Well, they're professionals after all. Already had a truck with their name on it.

The library isn't quite as impressive, in my opinion. Maybe the hunky guy spent too much time posing for the camera. Not to mention flirting with Blair. It's nice, though—if you like a lot of shrubs. I do like the weeping willow they planted in the open area by the bench. Even though it isn't fully grown, it's beautiful. These guys did a great job, but it doesn't appeal to me as much as the city hall does. And truthfully, I like what we did at the park just as well or better than either of these. But it's not up to me, is it?

"Now are we going home?" Katie's voice jars me. I'd been so immersed in checking out the competition that I'd almost forgotten they were with me.

"Right this very second." I pull into the nearest driveway and turn around, relieved to know we have a chance of winning and suddenly anxious to get to the soccer game and apologize to Daniel.

As I drive home, I wish I could say that I feel an incredible peace and I'm no longer worried about how the judging will go tomorrow. But that would be a lie. I'm nervous. I dread waiting a week to find out the results. And I still desperately want to win.

But, I'm satisfied. Satisfied that we've done our best. Satisfied that I didn't let fear keep me from taking a chance to better our lives. And satisfied that I'm going to trust God to make this work out for everyone involved. And for now, that satisfaction is enough.

When I read through the e-mail one more time, I can't help but think of what I'd like to say.

*Daniel,*

>*I was hoping to get a chance to talk to you at the game tonight, but it didn't seem to work out.* (Thanks to Blair and Candice being on either side of you the whole night like Secret Service men protecting the commander-in-chief.) *Give me a call tomorrow if you have a chance.* (If you still care anything at all about me.)

*Until then,*
(Love? Your friend? Who knows?)
*Allie*

The real e-mail without my extraneous thoughts is short and sweet. Perfect.

I hit the SEND button and sit back in my chair. Time to go to bed and forget about tomorrow.

Yeah, right. In my dreams.

# thirty-five

The mayor's about to make the big announcement. I'm standing on the front steps of the courthouse beside the other two finalists with a huge crowd gathered around. "And the winner is. . ." *Bam!*

I jerk straight up in the bed as another clap of thunder sounds outside. Bummer. I was just getting to the good part of the dream. I squint at the clock. 5:02 a.m. The sky outside the window lights up briefly and there's another distant boom. Wonder if I can get any weather on the radio? I hit the POWER button and turn the volume down.

Perfect timing. "Severe thunderstorm warning in effect until 6:00 a.m. This storm contains damaging wind and golf-ball- to softball-sized hail."

I'm wide awake now. With the judges coming around noon, what will all my flowers and shrubs look like after hail falls on them? Softball-sized? Might as well be dinosaur size.

I push the cover away and bring my attention back to the radio announcer just as he says, "The storm is expected to reach Shady Grove, Arkansas, at approximately 5:40 a.m."

Thirty-five minutes. Thankfully, Mama's an early riser. She answers on the second ring.

"Mama, it's me." Your needy daughter. I've called on her more in the last month than I have in the whole last five years. She's going to deserve a Mexican vacation when this is all over. Not that I can afford it. But it's the thought that counts. "Any chance you could come over and stay with the kids?"

"Allie, what's wrong?"

I can hear the concern in her voice. I don't usually get up this early, even on my best days. "There's a storm coming. I need to go see if I can cover the flowers. I hate to ask you, but would you mind sitting with the girls until I get back?"

"I'll be right there."

"Thanks."

Five minutes later, she lets herself in. I'm already in the foyer, slipping into the only rain slicker I can find, a thin plastic one I picked up for eighty-eight cents at Wal-Mart. A Girl Scout I'm not. "One way or the other, I should be back by breakfast."

"Be careful, honey." She hugs me.

I drop a peck on her cheek. "I will."

The door shuts behind me. Thirty minutes until the predicted time of arrival for the storm.

My plastic jacket flaps behind me as I run to the storage shed and grab three old tarps and some tent stakes right inside the door. I snatch a hammer off the workbench, secure the door, and take off to my SUV.

"Gotta hurry," I mutter to no one as I climb into the driver's seat, flinching as a lightning bolt streaks the sky in front of me.

The drive seems like it takes forever, partly because I have to hold the steering wheel so tightly against the wind. I pull into the park and kill the motor. I pray as I run, asking for everything from grace, mercy, and peace, to letting me get the flowers covered. The air seems calmer, but constant thunder rumbles in the distance.

As soon as I get the tarp spread out and stick a tent stake through a corner grommet, the wind comes back with renewed vigor. "No!" I try again, holding the stake with one hand and the hammer with the other. A noise behind me pulls my attention away. I turn to see the other two tarps tumbling across the park. Frustration pounds in my head like the beat of an angry tom-tom drum. I can't let go of the one I'm securing or it will blow away, too. If I could just cover the flowers, they'd have a chance to survive the hail. Otherwise. . . I push to my feet, the tarp dangling from my hand, and stand there with the wind blowing through my hair. It hits me like the answer to a math equation that a solution has been just out of grasp until now. Otherwise. . .it's out of my hands.

I roll up the tarp the best I can and take off to catch the two renegades where they've blown against the fountain. When I get there, I gather them up and watch as the first drops of rain strike the surface of the pool of water. The future is out of my hands.

It always has been really. Yeah, I needed to do my best in the contest and I needed to choose wisely when considering a husband. But. I. Am. Not. In. Control.

As if to prove my point, the rain starts pounding down, stinging my face.

"Allie?"

I spin around at the sound of Daniel's voice.

He lifts the bundle from my hands. "I take it you gave up on covering the whole park in tarps," he yells over the rushing sound of wind and rain.

I nod. "I'm not in control," I holler back.

A grin splits his face. "I see that." He puts his arm around my shoulder and guides me to the natural shelter formed by the thick limbs of the old oak tree.

"You're not supposed to get under a tree when it's lightning." Maybe I am a Girl Scout, after all. The man of my dreams is rescuing me and I'm giving him safety tips.

He shakes his head. "I just heard on the radio. The storm has gone south. We're just going to get some rain off of it."

I nod again. The wind shifts, and the rain starts blowing against us sideways.

So much for shelter. Rain, rain, go away.

He puts his arms around me. "I'll try to keep you from getting too wet," he says in my ear.

I grin. Rain, rain, come on down.

"What are you doing here?" Not to look a gift horse in the mouth, but how weird that he'd show up right now, unless my mother called him and that's really not her style.

"Couldn't sleep after I got your e-mail," he says in a husky voice.

"Why?"

He draws back and raises an eyebrow.

Okay, silly question.

He pulls me against him and speaks into my ear again. "Anyway, then I heard the storm warning and had a feeling you'd be here." Even with water running down my neck, I could get used to this way of communicating.

I laugh. "Great. I'm not just crazy. I'm predictably crazy."

"I have to admit most people wouldn't think about taking on a hailstorm."

I mock-pout, drawing courage from his nearness. "Hey, you were supposed to deny my insanity, not point it out."

"I call it like I see it."

Might as well get it over with. I keep my gaze on the stubble on his cheek, resisting the urge to trace his scar with my finger. "Daniel, I'm sorry for how I acted."

"I know."

This time I'm the one who pulls back to see his face. "You do?"

"Yeah."

Even in the grayness of dawn, with rain sluicing down on us, his eyes are so blue I could get lost in them.

"And I figured out just now—"

"I know."

Okay, this is not fair. It's my epiphany. "How?"

"I've been through the same kind of thing. It's hard to give up control. Until you realize you never actually had it to begin with."

"Exactly!" I'm amazed.

"It seems like we've been here before."

His strong arms are cradling me, protecting me from the torrents of rain. I'm pretty sure if I'd been here before I'd remember. "Oh. You mean under this tree."

He chuckles against my ear and leans back slightly, locking me in his gaze. I shiver. Water runs in tiny rivulets down his face. I give in this time and reach out and trace his scar with my finger. "Where'd you get that?"

"Don't try to change the subject, Allie." His deep voice gives me chills that have nothing to do with the rain.

"I wouldn't dream of it."

"Would you dream of this?" He touches his lips lightly to mine.

I might.

"I love you." He says it so simply. And my heart thuds in my chest so hard I feel like I'm going to keel over.

I stare up at my motorcycle-driving, novel-writing man and feel a smile tilt my trembling lips. "I love you, too." My tears mix with the water pouring down on us.

He pushes my hair back and kisses the tears from my cheeks, then covers my mouth with his. It may be raining in Shady Grove, but, for the first time in a long time, the sun is shining in my heart.

# thirty-six

Never in the history of mankind—or womankind—has a week gone by so slowly. I've baked cupcakes for both of the girls' end-of-the-school-year parties, cleaned my house from top to bottom, helped Mama clean her house, and worked in my yard. And spent most every evening with my favorite cameraman and the best two daughters in the world. But it still felt like today would never come. And now that it's here, I'm wishing for time to go backward. How fickle am I? When it comes to time, anyway.

"Mom, are you ready yet?"

I really should just record Miranda saying that to save wear and tear on her voice. She could just push a button when she's feeling impatient.

I slide into my jeans and snatch my red blouse off the hanger. I'd been tempted to try to blend in but, win or lose, at some point today all eyes will be on me anyway. Might as well look as good as possible. "In a minute."

Who would have dreamed when I wore this outfit for my surprise birthday party that my life would change so much in such a short time? I slip into my matching eBay-deal-of-the-century sandals and check my makeup, just as Katie calls, "Mom, they're here!" As if to back up her claim, the doorbell rings and Buddy barks madly.

"Be right there! Let them in and put Buddy outside." I hurry down the hall in time to greet Daniel, Candice, and Elijah. Candice is beaming, so I'm pretty sure she forgives me for mistreating her brother. If I had any lingering doubt, it's dispelled when she hugs me.

Daniel winks at me over her shoulder. "I'm next," he mouths.

I grin and give him a fast hug. He pulls me back and drops a quick kiss on my mouth. I feel my cheeks grow hot, but no one else is paying the least bit of attention. *Lighten up, Allie.*

It's going to take awhile for me to get used to having a man in my life again, but I'm looking forward to the learning experience.

We get to the courthouse in plenty of time, in spite of having to park several blocks away and walk. I'm pretty sure all of Shady Grove has come out for the kickoff of the centennial celebration.

"Looks like the whole town is here," Daniel murmurs, as he gets the lawn chairs out of the back of the truck.

"You took the words right out of my mind." I drop back to wait on him as Candice and the kids walk on down the sidewalk. "I guess I really am predictable. You might get bored."

He laughs and hits the LOCK button on the key fob. "I'd say that's one thing I'll *never* have to worry about with you around."

"Oh look, there's Victoria and Dylan. And Adam and Mama and Rachel. And Lark and Craig." I wave broadly.

He just smiles at my obvious change of subject. "Yep. The gang's all here."

A few minutes later we're all gathered together up by the steps, where Blair insisted we sit. The other landscaping teams are up here, too, but I'd still be worried about her determination to get us up in the spotlight if Daniel hadn't assured me that no one knows the winner except the city council members. And they've been sworn to secrecy.

The grand-prize truck is right beside us, and when I see it I swoon like a teenage girl at a concert. It's the perfect truck. Brilliant blue, crew cab, with a landscaping bed. And a heavy drape over each door where the personalized company sign must be.

Victoria taps me on the shoulder. "Stop salivating, shugah. They're getting ready to start."

Everyone in our group laughs, and we turn our attention to the mayor, who makes a grand speech about Shady Grove and how blessed we all are to live here. "And now for the moment you've all been waiting for. . ."

Daniel slides his hand around mine.

"The kickoff of the Shady Grove Centennial Celebration."

Oh, yeah. That. I smile at myself.

Blair is standing on stage beside him, and she whispers to him, keeping her camera smile in place. Channel Six brought out the whole shebang for this event. There are cameras and lights everywhere.

The mayor listens to her and clears his throat. "But before we kick off this grand, historical, year-long event with some music from our own Shady Grove barbershop quartet, it's my pleasure to announce to you the winner of the Beautiful Town Landscaping Contest. . . ."

You know how in movies sometimes they freeze time for

everyone but the hero? And he moves normally but everything else is in slow motion? This moment is like that. Calm descends on me. I can see the anticipation on the faces of not just my crew, but the other crews, as well. And suddenly I know I really am okay with whatever happens. Because what happens will be God's will. Not mine. And I'm good with that.

"Allie Richards and TLC Landscaping."

Now I know what Miss America feels like when they call the first runner-up and she realizes she's won. I'm frozen. My friends and family erupt from their chairs. And suddenly everyone is hugging me and patting me on the back, but it doesn't sink in until I see Blair's face. She's not a happy camper.

"Speech, speech," the crowd is chanting.

The mayor looks down at me. "Allie, it looks like they want to hear from you."

I shake my head, but Daniel puts his hand to my waist and says, "Knock 'em dead, honey."

My legs tremble as I walk up the courthouse steps. When I reach the podium, I grip it like a lifeline. The crowd grows quiet. What am I supposed to say?

I clear my throat. "Nobody told me I needed a speech."

They laugh. And I relax a little. There's Brother Jamison from church. And Meredith, the school counselor. Principal Dickerson. My in-laws, with what might be proud smiles. I even see Bob, my old boss from Coble's. These are just people I know. And a few hundred I don't, but I'm not going to think about them.

I lean toward the mike. "I've learned a lot during this contest. Like not to plant spreading petunias with marigolds." I wink at Tansy, who is waving at me. "Because. . .well, they spread."

They laugh again. I loosen my death grip on the podium. "And I also figured out that life would be pretty sad without friends and family." I give our group a little wave, then look back at the crowd. "But I learned my biggest lesson last Saturday morning." I take a deep breath. "Even though it turned out sunny, some of you may know that we had a storm warning early that day." I see several people nod, while others—late sleepers, apparently, or maybe just forgetful—look puzzled. "And I headed over to the park while it was still dark, determined to cover my flowers to protect them from the predicted hail."

I take another deep breath. Nothing like airing your faults in front of the whole town. "The wind whipped that tarp right out of my puny little hands every time I tried to hammer a tent stake through it. Thinking about it now I feel pretty silly." I glance at the TLC group and see tears streaming down Lark's face. "It didn't take me long to realize something." I grin, through my own tears. "Well, maybe it took me longer than it would have most of y'all. I'm a little hardheaded."

The whole crowd chuckles, and I can tell they relate. Either that or they know me.

"I realized that some storms can be prepared for. . . ." Daniel's watching me intently, his expression serious. "But most can't. And in those particular storms, God is our tarp and faith is the tent stake that keeps the wind from blowing it away."

They're all watching me intently. "And that's all we have, but it's enough."

To my amazement, the crowd—even the other landscaping teams—rise to their feet as one body in thunderous applause. I must look as shaky as I feel because Daniel meets me at the bottom of the steps and puts his arm around me to guide me back to our seats. "Way to go," he says against my ear.

"Is this the same woman who used to fake a stomachache right before speech class every day?" Lark asks as she wipes her tears away and hugs me.

I give her a weak grin. "You should feel my stomach right now. I wasn't faking."

Thankfully the barbershop quartet takes the stage and everyone forgets about me. Well, almost everyone. Later, when the drapes are taken off the truck doors to reveal beautiful, professional-looking signs that say TLC LANDSCAPING, ALLIE RICHARDS, OWNER and my phone number, Blair approaches me. I brace myself. But all she says is, "Congratulations."

"Thanks."

She walks away, and next time I see her she's consoling the hunky guy from the other crew.

Victoria sticks a cold Dr. Pepper in my hand and nods toward Blair. "She seems to be taking it pretty well."

"She's probably picking out her next victims," Lark says. "I hear the 'Get Real, Shady Grove' segment was such a hit, she's going to keep it going during the whole centennial celebration featuring different aspects."

"Humph," Rachel eyes Blair and takes a swig of her spring water. "Remind me to stay as far away from this celebration as possible from now on."

"Me, too," Victoria says.

"Oh, yeah. Like y'all did me." I smile. "In case I haven't already told y'all, thank you from the bottom of my heart."

"Yeah, you told us, but we're figuring on hearing it again."

Lark grins. "Eternal gratitude, you know."

Daniel walks up just as we burst out laughing and shakes his head.

"Sorry, Daniel. Our Pinky friendship comes as part of the package deal. You want Allie, then you have to tolerate us," Victoria drawls.

"Why do I feel like I may be getting more than I bargained for?"

I give him a hug and whisper in his ear. "Because you're a smart man."

Dear Readers,

Allie Richards has been living in my head for years. Before I ever wrote the first word, I cheered for her to follow her dream, in spite of the hard times and setbacks. As a writer who didn't sell my first book until I was almost forty, this theme appealed to me on a deep level. No matter what your walk in life, I hope this book makes you stop and think that you can follow your dream, too. As Allie learns (and as I've learned over and over as I waited for a story to sell), sometimes it takes baby steps, but the journey can be made, with God in control. Go for it!

On a personal note, you may not realize this, but you are a huge blessing in my life. A writer without a reader is like a computer without a keyboard or monitor. Unusable.

Thanks for making me usable.

Christine Lynxwiler

## DISCUSSION QUESTIONS:

1. Rachel encourages the Pinkies to find the good in every situation. Is this possible? Even if it's not possible in every situation, is it worth trying?

2. After she's turned down for a bank loan, Allie indulges in a short pity party. She snaps out of it by thinking of her daughters. How do you bring yourself out of a pity party?

3. Daniel spent his childhood trying to protect his mother and sister from his dad's alcoholism-induced temper. In order to escape, he wrote stories of how life would be if he were in charge. Then later he got kicked out of school for fighting and left town. Did this change of locale provide the escape he was looking for? Are there problems that we can't escape simply by changing our zip code?

4. When Adam was betrayed by his friend, he chose a different way of escape. What was it? Did it work?

5. During their discussion about hiring Adam, Allie's mom says that Allie is almost as bad as he is, only in a different way. What does she mean by that?

6. Victoria is from a wealthy family, but she's trying to teach her son responsibility by having him mow the lawn. Why would she do this? Would you have your children do chores if you were wealthy enough to pay someone to do them? Why?

7. All four of the Pinkies still count on Lark's granny's wisdom, even though she died awhile ago. Has there been someone in your life whose wisdom lives on even though they're already gone? Do you find yourself thinking about what they would do or say in a situation?

8. Lark doesn't want to adopt because she's afraid she'll turn out like her own mother. Is this a valid concern? How might she find peace in this situation?

9. Allie needs to be in control. To what extent do we have the option to be in control? How do you cope when life spins out of your control?

10. Allie wants a man who can promise her "always." Is this a valid expectation? Is there any human being who can promise you always? How does Allie discover the answer to this question?